Forbidden Fantasies

By Lynn LaFleur

Forbidden Fantasies

LYNN LaFLEUR

Kate,
Such a fun
book to write!
I hope you enjoy
it.

Lynn
LaFleur

red
AVON

An Imprint of HarperCollinsPublishers

This is a work of fiction. Names, characters, places, and incidents are products of the author's imagination or are used fictitiously and are not to be construed as real. Any resemblance to actual events, locales, organizations, or persons, living or dead, is entirely coincidental.

HarperCollins books may be purchased for educational, business, or sales promotional use. For information please write: Special Markets Department, HarperCollins Publishers, 10 East 53rd Street, New York, NY 10022.

FIRST AVON PAPERBACK EDITION PUBLISHED 2009.

Interior text designed by Diahann Sturge

Library of Congress Cataloging-in-Publication Data
LaFleur, Lynn.
    Forbidden fantasies / Lynn LaFleur. — 1st ed.
        p. cm.
    ISBN 978-0-06-163272-3
    I. Title.
    PS3612.A376F67   2010
    813'.6—dc 22   2009006091

09 10 11 12 13   WBC/RRD   10 9 8 7 6 5 4 3 2 1

Celina

One

Join me to remember our good friend,
Carol St. Claire.
Carol died while celebrating life.
She would not want us to grieve, but to celebrate life also.
Meet me on the S. S. Fantasy *on Thursday, April 10,*
Port of The Everglades, Fort Lauderdale.
Jasmine Britt

Celina Tate read the invitation once again. She blinked back the tears that sprang to her eyes as she touched the raised letters on the sheet of cream linen. She couldn't believe Carol was gone. Vibrant, outgoing Carol should not have died so young.

"Celina!"

She turned at the sound of her name to see Elayne Wyatt quickly walking toward her, tugging two suitcases behind her. Tucking the invitation back into her tote, she hurried across the parking lot to meet her friend.

Elayne grabbed her in a fierce hug. "Oh, it's so good to see you!" Holding Celina's arms out to the side, Elayne looked her over from head to feet. "You look amazing. Did you have a boob job?"

Laughter sputtered from Celina's mouth. "No! I promise, everything is real."

"Lucky you. You're more gorgeous than you were the last time I saw you. How's that possible?"

"Good vitamins."

"What's the brand? I'll start taking them today."

Celina gazed at Elayne's short cap of black curls, deep brown eyes, olive skin, and voluptuous figure. She and Carol had always drawn the most attention from men back in college because of their exotic looks. "You don't need vitamins. You're perfect."

Elayne snorted. "Yeah, right. I'd be perfect if I lost forty pounds."

"Will you stop that? You don't need to lose an ounce. Besides, you wouldn't be able to hold up those double Ds if you lost any weight."

"True." She grinned. "I've never had a man complain about my girls." Grabbing the handles of her suitcases, she led the way toward the terminal. "Have you seen Jasmine yet?"

Celina shook her head. "I talked to her this morning before I left my house. She said she'd meet us on the ship."

"Do you know what's going on? I grilled Jasmine, but she wouldn't tell me anything about this trip."

"Me either. All she told me is that she'd arranged everything, and we'd love it."

"Well, she has the bucks to do it right, that's for sure."

Money had never been in short supply in Jasmine's family.

Celina knew that Jasmine had inherited a fortune when her paternal grandfather died. As an investment broker, she'd known where to put her inheritance to avoid unnecessary taxes or penalties.

That didn't mean she didn't like to throw money around sometimes . . . like for this trip.

Elayne gripped the handle of the door leading into the terminal. "Are you ready for this?"

"Absolutely," Celina said with a grin.

Rand Paxson watched the two women walk up the gangplank and onto his yacht. The brunette was gorgeous, no doubt about that. He loved a woman with generous curves, and she definitely had those. Her breasts would more than fill his hands. He'd enjoy exploring them, along with the rest of her body.

His cock twitched when he looked at the blonde.

Running a singles cruise meant plenty of opportunities for sex. Rand enjoyed the freedom, the chance to taste a different woman on each trip.

Sometimes two.

An image flashed through his mind of the two friends who took the cruise last month. They'd both been eager to sample whatever the captain had to offer. He'd offered them plenty . . . one riding his tongue while the other rode his cock. He'd lain on the bed to recuperate from an intense orgasm as they kissed and caressed. Watching them lick each other's pussies had led to the fastest recuperation he'd ever experienced. The second round had been even hotter than the first.

Damn, it had been fun.

His first officer, Jonathan Hurn, leaned on the railing next to Rand. "Enjoying the view?"

"Immensely."

"Nice tits on the brunette."

"I noticed."

Jon chuckled. "Yeah, I'll bet you did."

"The blonde isn't flat."

"Yeah, but I like 'em bigger than her. You take the blonde. I'll take the brunette."

"Deal."

Jon turned and propped his elbows on the railing behind him. "You know, there's always the chance the blonde won't want to be next in your line of conquests."

"That's true. Nothing in life is a guarantee."

"She'll fall all over you, and you know it. The women stumble over their feet to get in bed with you."

"It's a power thing. They all want to fuck the captain." Rand straightened and faced Jon. "And don't give me your 'poor mistreated me' look. You don't spend many nights alone either."

"I'm alone four nights a week. I see no reason to be alone the three nights we sail."

Rand had always felt the same. Jon hadn't been exaggerating when he said most of the women on the cruises tried to bed the captain. Finding a willing partner had never been a problem for Rand.

He loved kissing a woman, touching her, sliding his shaft into her sheath. He liked those little sounds she made in her throat when she was about to come. The feel of her fingernails digging into his buttocks, her sweat-slick skin, the musky scent of her pussy . . . Rand loved it all and craved it as often as physically possible.

Life was definitely sweet.

Jon glanced at his watch. "I'm gonna check to see if my friend has boarded yet." He clapped Rand on the shoulder. "Catch you later."

Rand looked over the railing again. He didn't see the two women, so they must have boarded. He would meet all twelve passengers tonight at dinner. Until then, he had plenty to do to keep busy.

His schedule didn't include dropping by the blonde's cabin to make sure she was comfortable. However, as captain, it would be a nice thing to do.

Celina sat on the edge of the queen-size bed and smiled. What an amazing room. She hadn't known what to expect when the purser, Andrew, had shown her to her cabin. She'd thought it would be cramped, with barely enough space to turn around. Instead, the room also included a sitting area complete with an overstuffed sofa and a small desk. The attached bathroom contained a glass shower large enough to easily hold two people.

Several brochures and papers lay on the nightstand. Celina picked up a glossy brochure with the picture of the two-hundred-foot yacht and S. S. *Fantasy* in bold script on the front. Opening it, she scanned the list of amenities and activities. For a small ship, it didn't lack for things to do. First-run movies in the main salon every night, a game room including several computers, swimming pool and hot tub on the upper deck, a library, dining rooms on two levels, bars on all three. It seemed whoever designed the ship did so for the guests' complete comfort.

Celina reclined on her side, leaning on one elbow. She turned the page of the brochure and continued to read.

★ ★ ★

The crew of the S. S. *Fantasy* is here
for your pleasure and comfort.
We will fulfill your every need, yet discreetly vanish
when you do not need us.
Every passenger is single. There are no rules.
There is nothing you cannot do while on board.
Enjoy each other . . . in every way.
Your most erotic fantasy can come true.

She reread the last line—"Your most erotic fantasy can come true." She wondered exactly what the crew did to make a passenger's fantasy come true.

How intriguing.

Fantasies were all she'd had lately. Work had taken her out of town so much, she'd barely unpacked before she had to leave again. Dates had been almost nonexistent for several months. The few times she'd gone out with a man, their dates had ended quickly without any desire for her to see him again, much less have sex with him.

She silently blessed whoever invented vibrators and dildos.

Celina turned to the next page. She gasped softly when she saw the picture of the captain. There was also a picture of the entire crew, but she barely noticed it. She couldn't tear her gaze away from the captain. He leaned on a metal railing, the ocean at his back. A breeze ruffled his shoulder-length dark brown hair. Brown eyes crinkled at the corner from his smile. His tan skin looked dark against his white uniform. Broad shoulders, a wide chest that tapered down into a trim waist. She could see a sprinkling of dark hair in the opening of his shirt.

She wondered if the hair flowed down his stomach all the way to his cock.

Now that *is fantasy material.*

Celina could easily imagine him standing by the bed, slowly unbuttoning that white uniform shirt. He'd peel it off his shoulders and let it fall to the floor. With his gaze locked to hers, he'd unbuckle his belt and pull it from the loops. Before the belt hit the top of his shirt, he'd have his pants unfastened. He'd tug them past his hips, freeing his hard shaft . . .

A gentle knock on her door shook her free of her fantasy. Laying the brochure back on the nightstand, she rose and went to the door.

She blinked when she saw the captain on the other side. Warmth filled her cheeks. She'd just imagined him without a shirt—or any other piece of clothing—and now he stood outside her door.

He smiled and tipped his head. "Ms. Tate. I'm Rand Paxson, your captain."

"Yes, I know. I mean, I was reading the brochures about the ship when you knocked."

"That's why I'm here. May I come in?"

"Yes, of course." Celina opened the door wider and stood aside so he could enter. Her heart beat heavier with him so close in the room. She imagined that most female passengers reacted the same way. The good looks, the crisp uniform, the air of power . . . they all combined to make him an incredibly sexy man.

He stood with his legs slightly parted, his hands behind his back. "I wanted to personally welcome you aboard the S. S. *Fantasy.* Do you have any questions about the yacht?"

"I haven't seen much of it yet. I'm waiting for my friend to arrive."

"That would be Ms. Britt."

"Do you know Jasmine?"

"Not personally. But I do know all my passengers' names and whether they've boarded yet. She and Mr. Cummings are due to arrive within the hour." He took a step toward her. "Do you have any other questions that I might answer for you?"

Celina caught the faintest whiff of an outdoorsy scent. She didn't know if it came from a bottle or simply from him. The clean smell made her toes curl into the carpet.

She wondered what he'd say if she asked him the question she wanted to ask—whether or not he fucked any of his passengers.

Of course he does. He's looking at me right now as if he'd love to start nibbling on my neck and work his way down.

Which wouldn't be a bad thing.

Celina picked up the brochure from the nightstand and turned to the part she'd read. She pointed to the line about the erotic fantasy coming true. "What does this mean?"

He moved beside her, close enough for their arms to touch, and glanced at the spot where she pointed before looking into her eyes. "Just what it says. This is the S. S. *Fantasy.* We're here to make sure your most erotic fantasies come true."

Up close, his eyes were mesmerizing, enticing. She could see her reflection in the pupils. "How do you know about the fantasies? Do your passengers tell you?"

He stared into her eyes another moment before walking to the door. "Our course takes us into the Bermuda Triangle. A person never knows what might happen there." He opened the door. "We'll be leaving soon. You should come up on deck and enjoy the view." A gentle smile touched his lips. "Until later, Ms. Tate."

He closed the door behind him, leaving Celina to wonder exactly what would happen once they set sail.

Two

Celina breathed deeply of the warm, salty air. Holding her hand up to shield her eyes from the sun, she gazed out over the blue water. They hadn't left the dock yet, and she already felt calmer, more at peace. She desperately needed this time away from her job and all the headaches it caused.

"Ms. Tate?"

Celina turned to see a lovely young woman with short blond hair, wearing a crisp white uniform similar to the captain's. A gold name tag on the flap of her breast pocket read *Anna*. "Yes?"

"Ms. Britt has arrived. She asked that you join her and Ms. Wyatt in the upper-deck salon."

"Thank you."

Anna turned as if to walk away. Now would be the perfect time for Celina to find out more about what she'd read in the yacht's brochure. "Anna?"

The stewardess faced her again. "Do you need me to direct you to the salon?"

11

"No, that's fine. I'm sure I'll find it. I read one of the brochures about the ship. I don't understand the part about the passengers' fantasies coming true. I asked the captain, but he didn't tell me anything. That's just some marketing gimmick, right? A person's erotic fantasies don't actually come true on this yacht. I mean, that isn't even possible."

A faint smile turned up Anna's lips, and her eyes sparkled with mischief. "The captain will explain everything about the ship tonight at dinner."

"You won't tell me anything now?"

"I prefer to heed my captain's wishes, Ms. Tate."

Celina understood that. Still . . . "Not even a hint?"

Anna smiled. "The captain will tell you tonight. Have a nice time with your friends, Ms. Tate."

It would be difficult for her to have a good time with her friends with curiosity eating away at her. She was tempted to find the captain and make him explain exactly what the brochure meant.

Nice, slow torture would work.

Celina sighed. Too bad fantasies couldn't actually come true on this ship. She could easily imagine all kinds of scenarios where torture would soon turn to pleasure.

An active imagination could be a fun thing.

Celina found the winding staircase that led to the top deck. The sound of Jasmine's tinkling laughter directed her. She would know that sound anywhere.

She found Jasmine and Elayne sitting on tall, deep blue chairs, flirting shamelessly with the crew member behind the bar. The gold tag on his pocket read *Samir*. Dark hair, dark eyes, and a killer smile meant he had to be very popular with the female passengers.

Celina walked up behind her friends and tugged on their hair. "He can't handle both of you at once."

Jasmine grinned over her shoulder. "He'd have a lot of fun with both of us at once." She slid from her chair and grabbed Celina in a fierce hug. "Hi, Cee."

"Hi back." Celina tightened her arms around her friend. "It's so good to see you."

"You too." Jasmine released her but kept a firm grip on Celina's hands. Tears glimmered in her eyes. "You look wonderful."

"If I look so wonderful, why are you crying?"

Jasmine waved away Celina's question. "Silly sentimentality." She wiped a tear from her cheek. "Okay, enough of that. We're here to party and have a good time. No crying allowed."

"Right. No crying allowed."

Celina looked at Jasmine from head to toe. Her dark brown hair flowed like a waterfall past her generous breasts. She wore tight jeans that showed off her long legs to perfection. A patterned scooped-neck T-shirt in shades of green and brown made her hazel eyes shine. "You're gorgeous."

"I know," Jasmine said with a grin.

Celina laughed with her friend, then looked at Elayne. "So what's the plan?"

"The plan right now is for this hunk to make us something wicked to drink." Elayne turned her hundred-watt smile on Samir. "Isn't that right?"

He returned her smile. "Absolutely. Anything you want, I'll make," he said in a lilting Middle Eastern accent. "What's your pleasure?"

"Surprise us."

"I'll make you ladies something very special. Why don't you relax in one of the sitting areas?"

"Good idea." Elayne slid off her chair. "Let's get comfy so we can talk."

Celina led the way to a grouping of two armchairs and a love seat. She chose one of the chairs, curling her legs beneath her. She studied her two friends as they sat on the love seat. Celina hadn't seen Elayne for two years, Jasmine three. They kept in touch via telephone and e-mail, but getting together hadn't been a priority for any of them. That bothered her. Good friends should never go so long without seeing each other. A person never knew when something bad would happen.

Like with Carol.

"I'm already loving this," Jasmine said with a contented sigh. "Four days of pampering. I won't want to leave the ship."

"How did you find out about this yacht?" Celina asked.

"One of my clients told me about it. She took the cruise when her divorce was final. When I heard about Carol . . ." She stopped, blinked several times, then continued. "Hearing about Carol's death made me realize how short life truly is." She looked from Celina to Elayne and back again. "We're best friends. No matter how busy our lives are, we should never go so long without getting together."

"Amen to that," Elayne said.

"And I figured we three single women would have a blast on a sex cruise."

Celina didn't have the chance to ask her friend exactly what that meant, for Samir arrived with their drinks. He'd topped off the pink and frothy beverages with a skewer of tropical fruit. He placed the tray on the low table in front of the love seat. "Here you are, ladies. Enjoy."

"What did you make for us?" Elayne asked.

"Something special." He tipped his head and smiled. "Call me when you're ready for a refill."

Elayne picked up one of the drinks as Samir walked away. "Damn, he has a fine ass."

Jasmine picked up her own drink. "Don't you think he's a little young for you?"

"Hey, we're only thirty-one. That's hardly over the hill. He's probably . . ." She tilted her head and wiggled her mouth back and forth. "Twenty-three, twenty-four, with all the stamina of youth." She shivered playfully. "Mmm, don't you just *love* stamina?" Picking the skewer out of her glass, she bit off a fat cherry. "I wouldn't mind using some of that youth for a few hours."

"I'd rather have someone with more experience. A man who knows how to touch a woman to give her the most pleasure." Jasmine swirled her straw through her drink before taking a sip. "Wow, this is good. I wonder what he put in it?"

"You mentioned this being a sex cruise," Celina said, trying to get Jasmine back on the subject. "What are you talking about?"

"My client—Rose—said it's known as the sex cruise. All the passengers are single. There are no limits or rules. If you want to fuck a guy out on deck in front of everyone, no one will say a word about it."

Elayne's eyes widened. "Are you serious?"

"Absolutely. Rose said one night she was in a four-couple orgy in the salon on the main deck. Said it was H-O-T."

Celina slowly swished her straw through her drink. "That's what the brochure meant."

"What brochure?" Jasmine asked.

"The one in the cabin. Didn't you read it?"

She shook her head. "I haven't been to my cabin yet."

"There were several brochures in my cabin. One of them described the ship, showed a map, pictures of the crew. It said the crew is here for our comfort, but will disappear when we don't need them. It also said that the passengers are supposed to enjoy each other."

Elayne grinned wickedly. "Sounds like fun."

"I'm all for fun." Jasmine shifted on the love seat and crossed her legs. "That's the whole point of this trip—to have fun and celebrate Carol's life. That's what she would've wanted."

Yes, that's exactly what Carol would've wanted, but Celina couldn't help but wonder if Carol would've wanted Jasmine to spend so much money. She looked around the spacious salon. Her job as the manager of an upscale department store in Miami had taught her to recognize quality at a glance. Everything on this ship was top-of-the-line. That had to mean the cruises weren't cheap. "What does one of these cruises cost, Jasmine?"

"It doesn't matter. I can afford it."

"It *does* matter. It's wonderful of you to think of honoring Carol's memory this way, but Elayne and I should help with the expenses."

Jasmine waved her hand, as if shooing away a pesky fly. "Look, I make a ton of money at my job. My grandfather left me his entire estate. I have to spend the money *somewhere*. What better way to spend it than on my two best friends?" A gleam of mischief lit up her eyes. "Besides, I can call it entertaining clients and write it off my taxes."

Elayne laughed. "Honey, if you can write a sex cruise off your taxes, I want to meet your accountant."

16

Celina laughed along with her two friends. She'd missed this . . . the special camaraderie the three of them shared. Carol had been a good friend too, but not like Elayne and Jasmine. Although she'd made many friends since college, none of them made her feel as happy, as contented, as loved, as these two.

She raised her glass. "A toast, ladies." She waited until they'd lifted their glasses also before speaking again. "To Carol. Wherever she may be now, I know she's skydiving or scuba diving or racing a motorcycle."

Her voice caught on the last word. Carol had died while racing a motorcycle. Celina cleared her throat and swallowed the lump of emotion. "And to friendship, the special kind that lasts forever."

Jasmine touched her glass to the other two. "And to the sex cruise!"

"Yeah, baby!" Elayne said with a grin. "I am ready for some fun." She emptied her glass with one gulp. "Where's that hunky Samir? I need another one of these."

Her eyes widened and her lips parted in a silent "O." Celina glanced over her shoulder to see what had captured her friend's attention. A man strode toward them, wearing the same white uniform as the rest of the crew. At least six feet tall with a swimmer's lean build, he walked with an air of confidence.

"Damn," Elayne whispered.

He stopped by their seating area and smiled at each of them. "Ladies. I see Samir has been taking care of you."

His name badge read *Jonathan.* Celina doubted if he was a steward. He must be an officer. "Yes, he has."

"Good. We want our passengers to be happy. I'm Jonathan Hurn, the first officer, at your service." He looked directly at

Elayne. "Don't hesitate to ask if there's anything I can do for you."

Elayne's gaze traveled over his body, stopping at his groin. "I'm sure there are *lots* of things you can do for me."

One corner of his mouth tilted up in a rakish grin. "That's why I'm here . . . to see to your comfort and pleasure."

Elayne licked her bottom lip as she peeked at his groin again. "Exactly how . . . involved do you get in your passengers' pleasure, Jonathan?"

"As involved as you might want."

Celina watched Jonathan's gaze dip to Elayne's breasts and linger for several seconds. Sparks flew between them, so obvious that Celina could almost see them. She had no doubt her friend would soon be rolling around on Jonathan's bed.

Lucky girl.

"Would you like a tour of the ship?" he asked Elayne.

"I'd love it." She set her empty glass on the table and stood. "See you later, girls," she said without one glance at them.

"Well," Jasmine said, once Elayne and Jonathan had left, "I think we've been abandoned."

"I think you're right."

"He could've offered to give *all* of us a tour of the ship."

"I'm pretty sure you and I disappeared the moment he saw Elayne."

"Especially her boobs."

Celina chuckled. "True."

"So, since we've been totally ignored, I vote for a swim. Let's change and meet at the pool."

"Deal."

Three

Celina donned a tiny lavender bikini barely big enough to cover her nipples and mound. She looked at herself in the full-length mirror, turning one way, then the other. She smiled. Splurging on herself had been worth it. After she'd talked to Jasmine about the trip, she'd gone on a shopping spree . . . something she hadn't done in months. It felt wonderful to wear all new clothes, right down to her underwear.

Slinky, lacy underwear that covered even less than the bikini.

An image of the captain flashed through her mind. She wondered if he would approve of the way she looked in the bikini, or the underwear.

Or in nothing at all.

She'd had lovers, even though her love life had been non-existent for several months. Work had consumed her, leaving her little time for breathing, must less dating. One-night stands had never been her style. She liked to talk to a man, get to know him, before she made love with him.

A woman could always change her mind.

The sex cruise. That's what Jasmine had called this trip. Why not? Elayne had already hooked up with the first officer. Celina had no doubt Jasmine wouldn't be alone for long. She knew of no reason why she shouldn't indulge in some of her wildest fantasies with a willing man, especially since she'd never see him again once she left the yacht. One about six-one with shoulder-length dark brown hair and deep brown eyes would do nicely.

She ran one fingertip over the top of her breast and down to her nipple. It puckered beneath the thin bikini fabric. She imagined Rand's finger touching her, Rand's lips closing over her nipple to suckle. Good looks didn't mean a good lover. Celina knew that. But deep inside, she suspected that Rand would be an incredible lover . . . skilled, attentive, lusty.

The lusty part sounded really good.

Celina doubted if she'd ever be free enough to have sex with a man out on deck for everyone to see. Spending time alone with him was entirely different. She'd always believed that two people could do whatever they wanted to please each other. Some of her most enjoyable sexual experiences had been when she'd simply *let go* and done what felt good.

Letting go with Rand wouldn't be a problem at all.

The yacht sailed every weekend. She wouldn't be surprised if the captain had sex with a different woman on each cruise. This time, Celina was determined she would be the woman in his bed.

She smiled. Oh, yes. She liked that idea a lot.

Picking up her tote from the bed, she threw it over her shoulder and left her cabin.

★ ★ ★

Celina spotted Jasmine lying on her stomach by the pool, talking to a man reclining on a chaise lounge. A *naked* man. Celina's footsteps faltered. The man was in his mid-twenties, with pale blond hair, a deep tan, and an obvious lack of modesty. With his broad chest, flat stomach, and impressive cock, she could easily understand why he wouldn't hesitate to show off his body.

She dropped her tote on the chair next to the man. "Hey, Jaz."

"Cee, hi. This is Barret. We've been getting to know each other. Barret, my good friend, Celina."

Barret smiled, showing straight white teeth. "Hi, Celina." His gaze quickly passed over her body. "It's a pleasure."

A shiver ran through Celina at the wolfish look in his eyes. A hunk he might be, but he made her uncomfortable. Still, manners ingrained in her by her grandmother insisted she be polite. "For me too, Barret."

He gestured toward the lounge next to him. "Sit, please. Would you ladies like a drink?"

"I'd love one," Jasmine said. "Samir made something for us earlier that was to die for."

"Then I'll have Samir make you another one." He flashed his blinding smile again as he walked away.

Jasmine rolled to her side and watched Barret walk away. She sighed heavily. "What a body. Did you see the size of his cock?"

"Everyone on the ship saw the size of his cock." She tugged a lounge closer to Jasmine. "That's what he wants."

"Yeah, probably." Jasmine returned to her stomach and propped up on her elbows. "He told me this is his fourth cruise. He loves everything about it . . . the route, the food, the freedom. His clothes come off as soon as he boards, and he doesn't get dressed again until the ship returns to the dock. Well, except for dinner. How hot is that?"

"You did say this is a sex cruise. Sex is easier without clothes."

"That's true. And naked is always nice." She pushed her sunglasses to the top of her head. "Barret said something I don't understand."

Celina stretched out on the lounge and crossed her ankles. "What's that?"

"Right before you got here, he said he especially liked the fantasy part of the cruises. I didn't get the chance to ask him what that means."

"It's in the brochure I told you and Elayne about when we were in the salon. It said something about the passengers' most erotic fantasies coming true. I asked one of the stewardesses about it, but she wouldn't tell me anything. She said the captain would explain everything at dinner."

Jasmine frowned. "How are our fantasies supposed to come true?"

"I don't know. Anna wouldn't tell me anything. She said she preferred to honor her captain's wishes."

"Well, now I'm curious. I think we should find the captain and ask him."

"I already did."

Jasmine's eyebrows shot up. "And when did you talk to the captain?"

"He came to my cabin before we set sail."

"Oh, really?" Smiling wickedly, she sat up and scooted closer to Celina's lounge. "Tell me everything."

Celina laughed. Her friend was always ready to hear something juicy. "There's nothing to tell. He came to my cabin and

welcomed me aboard. I assumed he did that with all the passengers."

"Not me. I haven't even seen him yet. What does he look
like?"

"Dark hair, brown eyes, deep tan. Tall, great body. *Very*
handsome."

Jasmine sighed dramatically. "I think I'm in love."

Jealousy stabbed Celina in the middle of her chest. She
didn't want Jasmine anywhere near Rand. His tongue would
hang out after one look at that lush body and long waterfall
of hair. "We probably shouldn't bother him now. I mean, he's
busy with sailing the yacht."

"I guess. Well, there's always dinner, right? He's supposed
to explain everyth—"

She stopped. Her eyes widened. Celina was about to ask
what had happened when Jasmine uttered a soft, "Damn."

Curious what had captured Jasmine's attention so thoroughly, Celina glanced over her shoulder. A man stood at the
rail, gazing out over the water. The wind tousled his shaggy
brown hair. He wore a simple white T-shirt, faded jeans, and
deck shoes. She saw his face only in profile, but it was enough
for her to admire his good looks. He was tall and slim with
broad shoulders. Any woman would give him a second look.

She turned back to face her friend. Jasmine was still staring
at him. "Lots of hunks on this ship, aren't there?"

When Jasmine didn't answer, Celina waved her hand in
front of her friend's face. "Yo, Jaz!"

Jasmine jerked and swiveled her head back to Celina. "Huh?"

Celina chuckled to herself. The man by the railing had certainly captured Jasmine's attention. "I said, there are a lot of
hunks on this ship."

"There certainly are." Jasmine's attention swung back to the dark-haired man. "He looks like he could use some company."

"And you're just the person to help him out, right?"

Jasmine grinned. "You know me so well." She stood and adjusted her bikini so the top showed the greatest amount of cleavage. "I'll see you later."

Both of her friends had deserted her in favor of a man. Celina couldn't blame them for that. If she had to choose between a man and swimming with a girlfriend, she'd choose the man too.

Although the turquoise water in the pool looked inviting, swimming had lost its appeal. A nap in the warm sun seemed like a much better idea. Sighing softly, Celina tilted her head back and closed her eyes.

An image filled her mind . . . an image of Rand walking up to her chair, naked and aroused. She imagined reaching for his hard cock, wrapping her hand around it. She'd slide her hand up and down his flesh, whisk her thumb across the head to spread the drops of pre-cum. Then she'd slowly lick them off . . .

"Enjoying the sun?" Rand asked.

Celina's eyes snapped open. The captain stood next to her chair, as naked and aroused as she'd pictured in her mind.

He shifted, and the bright sun hit her directly in the eyes. Celina quickly closed them again. When she opened them once more, Rand still stood by her chair, but now he wore his white uniform.

She must've dozed off and dreamed of the captain standing there naked. That had to be the explanation of why she'd seen him without clothes one moment and with them the next.

Celina raised her hand to shield her eyes from the sun. "Yes, it's wonderful."

He smiled. "Good. Seeing to your pleasure is why we're here." He motioned to the chair next to her. "May I join you?"

"Don't you have to drive the ship?"

His lips quirked. "You steer a ship, Ms. Tate, not drive."

"Oh." Her cheeks filled with warmth, and it had nothing to do with the sun beating down on her. "Sorry."

"No apologies necessary. My first officer is taking care of the ship now."

"Is that Jonathan?"

"Yes. Have you met him?"

"Long enough for him to whisk Elayne off for a tour of the yacht."

Rand chuckled. The husky sound made her belly quiver. "I'm sure Jonathan made sure Ms. Wyatt enjoyed her tour."

Yeah, I'll bet he did.

Celina realized she'd never given the captain permission to join her. He still stood, looking down at her, apparently willing to stand until she told him he could sit next to her. She wondered if that came from good manners, or part of his seduction technique. Charm a woman and she'd fall into his bed quicker.

"Please, join me, Captain."

"Thank you. And it's Rand. 'Captain' is much too formal."

"Then please call me Celina."

He tipped his head. "Celina it is."

Oh, yeah, the man could charm a frightened fawn to eat right out of his hand. She watched him sit down, his legs spread so she could see the enticing bulge at his crotch. It would definitely be fun to explore that bulge . . . and every other part of him.

Celina enjoyed sex, but she'd never been one to fantasize

25

about it so much. She couldn't seem to stop the fantasies about Rand . . . the touches, the kisses, the deep strokes inside her body. She pictured his tongue swiping across her nipples, turning them into hard peaks before he began to suckle.

Her clit started to throb.

His gaze dipped to her breasts. "Would you like a tour of the ship also?"

"I would."

He looked back at her face. "A private tour?"

Without saying the words, he was asking her if she wanted to have sex with him. Celina nodded.

Rand's brown eyes smoldered with heat. "I'd like that." As quickly as the heat filled his eyes, it disappeared. "Unfortunately, my duties don't allow for that now. Perhaps after dinner?"

"After dinner would be nice."

He ran one finger over the back of her hand. She felt that caress deep inside her pussy. "Until later."

Celina watched him walk away, admiring the way his white trousers fit snugly across his ass. Tonight, she'd dig her fingernails into those delectable cheeks.

She could hardly wait.

Rand sipped the excellent Merlot while listening to Barret Ackerman drone on about his latest photo shoot in Miami. Barret's success didn't make his conversation any more interesting. He was a regular on the cruise, so Rand had to be polite and treat him as he would any other passenger. It wasn't easy. Rand would rather sit through ten hours of a soap opera than listen to Barret brag about his modeling career.

The woman sitting next to Barret didn't look bored. Mara Lindner seemed fascinated with every word that came out of his mouth. Maybe she was hoping for a repeat of what happened this afternoon. Rand had passed Mara and Barret in the main salon. She'd been bent over a chair while Barret fucked her from behind.

It was a scene Rand had seen many times. Barret prided himself on nailing all six women on every cruise. Rand had sex with his passengers too, but he picked one who nabbed his interest and enjoyed her exclusively. Well, there had been the two friends last month, but that had been something rare. Rand preferred to show one woman his attention.

Rand looked from Mara and Barret to the other passengers at the table. Glynnis Sanborne sat at Barret's left. An outgoing woman in her late forties, she looked like she'd had one too many Botox injections.

Next came Ian Cherry, CEO of a manufacturing corporation. A little loud, more than a little overweight, he had no trouble guzzling the free liquor.

The charming Jasmine Britt sat between Ian and Chase Cummings. Rand knew little about Chase, other than that he was Jonathan's friend. The man seemed more interested in picking at his food than talking to the lovely brunette sitting next to him. Too bad, because Jasmine seemed very interested in Chase.

Seated directly across from him at the foot of the table, Jonathan had eyes only for Elayne Wyatt on his left. Rand couldn't blame him for that. Elayne was a voluptuous beauty who openly flirted with the first officer. He had no doubt Jonathan's "tour" had included showing Elayne his cabin . . . and bed.

Lamar Felter sat next to Elayne. Mid-twenties and very fit, he kept sneaking looks at Tony Baldino. Rand focused on

Tony, sitting on his right. Tony snuck just as many looks at
Lamar. Rand had no doubt the two men would be together
before the night was over.

Doretta Wolford sat at Tony's right. She talked exclusively
with Ferris Grover, seated next to her. The two thirtysome-
things had met on the cruise last month. They lived at opposite ends of the country, but must have connected so well that
they decided to meet again on the yacht. That pleased him.
Rand liked when two people fell for each other on his ship.

Then there was Celina.

Rand sipped his wine again as he studied her. She was
lovely, no doubt about that. But it was more than looks. She
fascinated him. From the moment he saw her boarding his
ship, to their conversation in her cabin, to his gentle touch of
her hand by the pool, she fascinated him. He could hardly wait
until he could be alone with her.

But for now, he had duties as the captain. He set down his
wineglass and stood. "Ladies and gentlemen, I want to officially welcome you aboard the S. S. *Fantasy*. The evening is
yours to do anything you wish. A movie will start in the main
salon at ten. The pool and hot tub are especially pleasant at
night beneath the stars. A dessert bar is available on the upper
deck. My crew and I will do everything in our power to make
sure your cruise is enjoyable. Please don't hesitate to call on
any of us at any time if you need something.

"Please excuse me as I have to return to work. You are welcome to stay here as long as you wish."

He looked directly at Celina. "Until later."

Four

Celina watched Rand walk away. He'd been polite and attentive to all his passengers at dinner. But his last two words had been directed at her. He'd told her without informing any of the other passengers that he still intended to be with her tonight. What he hadn't done was tell them about the fantasies coming true.

Jonathan stood and offered his hand to Elayne. Before he whisked her friend off again for another "tour," Celina rose and stepped in front of the first officer. "Excuse me, Jonathan."

He faced Celina and smiled. "Yes, Ms. Tate. What can I do for you?"

"The captain didn't explain about the fantasies. He was supposed to do that at dinner."

"What fantasies?" Elayne asked.

"The ship's brochure said the passengers' most erotic fantasies can come true," Celina told her friend before turning to the first officer again. "What does that mean?"

Elayne looked at Jonathan. "I wouldn't mind knowing that too."

"Are you sure you wouldn't rather ask the captain?" Jonathan said.

"I'm asking *you*."

Jonathan released a deep breath. "The thing is, Ms. Tate, I can't explain the fantasies. I don't know how they come true. They simply do."

"That isn't possible."

"No, you wouldn't think so, but it is. Think of anything you want sexually. The most outrageous, wildest fantasy you could possibly imagine. It will happen to you."

Elayne crossed her arms beneath her breasts. "Sounds intriguing. And fun."

Jonathan winked at her. "Do you have wild sexual fantasies, Elayne?"

"I might."

He cradled her neck in one hand and slid his thumb over her jaw. "Now *that* sounds intriguing."

Apparently, Celina had lost Jonathan's attention . . . not that she could blame him for preferring to be with Elayne than answering a bunch of questions. "Where can I find the captain?"

"He'll be at the wheel, but he doesn't allow guests there."

"He's about to make an exception."

Celina turned, determined to find Rand, but stopped when Jonathan took her elbow. "Ms. Tate, the captain doesn't allow guests in the pilothouse. It's the only place on the ship that's off-limits." He smiled. "I'm sure he'll talk to you later. Why don't you try out the dessert bar while you wait? I'll let him know you wish to speak to him."

It appeared she had no choice but to wait. Releasing a soft sigh, Celina nodded. "I'd appreciate it if you'd tell him I want to speak to him as soon as possible."

"Will do."

"So how about if we hit that dessert bar, Elayne?"

She looked from Jonathan to Celina and back to Jonathan. Celina could see the indecision in her friend's eyes. Elayne obviously wanted to be with Jonathan. Celina was about to tell Elayne to forget about the dessert bar when he spoke.

"Go with your friend, Elayne. I'll let the captain know Ms. Tate wishes to speak with him. I'll catch up with you later."

"Okay."

Not even a run-in with a naked Barret spoiled Celina's appreciation of the dessert bar. She couldn't resist the chocolate-covered strawberries. She placed four large ones on her plate and followed Elayne to a table.

Before she got the chance to take one bite of the juicy fruit, she saw Jasmine heading their way. Jasmine walked with her head down, a frown marring her forehead.

"Damn, damn, damn," she huffed as she flopped down in the chair opposite Celina.

"What's wrong?"

"Chase. I don't understand him. I practically attacked him, and he pushed me away." She blew out another deep breath. "A man has *never* ignored me like he does."

That didn't surprise Celina. Jasmine had always gotten the guy when she wanted him. To have a man turn her down had to be a blow to her ego.

"He's so . . ." Jasmine stopped. Leaning forward, she plucked one of the strawberries from Celina's saucer and popped it in her mouth. She chewed slowly before speaking again. "He's gorgeous, for sure, but he's also . . . mysterious. There's something going on with him that he won't tell me."

"Like what?" Celina asked.

"I don't know. He seems . . . sad and alone. Something happened to him, something that hurt him badly."

"Isn't he Jonathan's friend?" Elayne asked.

Jasmine nodded. "Think you can get Jonathan to spill the beans to you?"

"I can try." Her lips turned up in a wicked grin. "Of course, we haven't talked much yet."

"Bragging is so unbecoming, Elayne."

"You'd be the one bragging if Chase had fucked you."

"Yeah, I would." She tossed her long hair over one shoulder. "I don't know what it is about him that draws me, but it's definitely there. I can't stop thinking about him."

"Love at first sight?" Elayne asked, taking the last bite of her cheesecake.

"Oh, puh-*leese*. I do *not* fall in love."

"There's a first time for everything."

"Not for this gal. All love does is complicate a good time."

"You sound like Elayne." Celina looked from one friend to the other. "I didn't know you two were so cynical about men."

"You haven't been married." Elayne wiped her mouth and laid her napkin next to her empty saucer. "Love hurts. All the hearts and flowers stuff from romance novels is crap. Sure, it starts out great. Hormones are raging, and the sex is hot. Once that calms down, and you have to face real life, it isn't fun anymore. I should've learned that with my first husband. But no, I had to fall for Winston and dig myself another hole."

Celina touched Elayne's hand. "You were happy with Winston."

"Yeah, at first, until I figured out he was content to stay home and drink beer while I worked. Uh-uh. I don't mind that I earn more than a lot of men, but I won't support him. Marriage is supposed to be a partnership. Neither of mine was."

Celina hated that her friend had been hurt so badly . . . not once, but twice. No matter what had happened to Elayne, Celina believed in love and marriage and happily-ever-after. She had to believe in it because she wanted it so badly.

It wasn't any fun to wake up alone day after day.

Her heartbeat stuttered when she saw Rand walking toward their table. The breeze tickled the ends of his hair, making it dance on his shoulders. She'd always loved longer hair on a man. She liked to grab handfuls of it while she kissed him.

Rand stopped at their table. "Ladies," he said with a smile. "I see you've been enjoying the dessert bar."

"The lemon cheesecake was incredible." Leaning forward, Elayne rested her forearms on the table. "Any chance of getting the recipe?"

"You'll have to speak to the chef about that. Henri is very protective of his recipes."

"Maybe I can convince him to share with me."

Rand laughed. "I have no doubt that if anyone can get Henri to give up one of his recipes, it would be you, Ms. Wyatt."

"You are a charmer, aren't you, Captain?"

He dipped his head. "I do my best."

He turned his attention to Celina. Even in the dim lighting, she could see the heat in his eyes. "Ms. Tate."

"Captain."

"Would you like to see my ship now?"

"Yes, I would." She looked at Elayne and Jasmine. "I'll see you later."

Elayne grinned. "Have a good time."

Celina glanced at the hot tub as she and Rand walked past it. Barret and Ian had their mouths wrapped around one of Glynnis's nipples. Her head was thrown back, eyes closed, lips parted in pleasure. Celina's footsteps faltered. She'd never witnessed people having sex. Movies, yes, but not real people.

As she watched, Barret slid his hand from Glynnis's breast to beneath the water. She moaned. Celina couldn't see Barret's hand, but she had no doubt he was stroking Glynnis's pussy.

Moisture seeped from Celina's channel.

Rand's warm breath coasted over her ear. "Do you like watching?"

"I've never . . ." She had to swallow the knot in her throat before she could speak again. "I've never watched anyone make love."

"It's exciting." His arm slid around her waist, his hand splaying over her stomach. "And arousing."

Ian's hand disappeared beneath the water too. Dim lights glowed in the bottom of the hot tub. If Celina took a few steps closer, she could see *exactly* where the men were touching Glynnis. She was tempted to do exactly that.

Instead, she turned to face Rand again. "You promised me a tour, Captain."

"Yes, I did. Where would you like to start?"

Playing games had never been Celina's style. She believed in being up-front and honest whenever possible. "We both know how the 'tour' is going to end, Rand. So the question is, where do we make love?"

Five

Rand liked Celina's directness. She didn't play games. She didn't pretend she didn't feel the attraction between them as strongly as he. He'd wanted her since the moment he'd seen her walking toward his ship. Now, in only moments, he'd have her in his arms the way he'd longed to.

He raised her hand to his mouth and lightly kissed the back. "I can give you a tour of the ship, or we can go directly to your cabin. It's your choice, Celina."

She looked into his eyes a moment before stepping closer. Lifting her lips to his, she kissed him. "My cabin," she whispered.

Her lips were soft and warm. One small taste wasn't nearly enough. Rand cradled her neck in his hand. He tickled each corner of her mouth with the tip of his tongue before taking her lips in another kiss.

Celina clutched the lapels of his shirt. Rand inhaled sharply at the sweet pleasure-pain of her fingernails in his chest. Wrapping his arms tightly around her, he slid his tongue past her lips. He tasted the tart flavor of the strawberries she'd eaten. He swept her mouth again with his tongue, then withdrew and began nibbling on her bottom lip. He nipped, licked the bite, and nipped again.

Celina whimpered.

"I want you." Rand ran his tongue down her neck and into the vee of her dress. "God, I want you."

"I want you too."

She smelled incredible . . . a light floral scent mixed with woman. Rand nuzzled between her breasts as he tugged one shoulder strap down her arm.

She wasn't wearing a bra.

Cradling her breast in his hand, he licked the nipple and pebbled areola. Her nipple responded, growing harder beneath his tongue. He laved the peak before closing his lips around it to suckle.

Celina tunneled her hands into his hair and clutched his head. "Rand."

Her breathless voice urged him to suckle harder. He slid one hand to her buttock and squeezed. Round and firm, just the way he liked it. Everything about Celina's body pleased him.

He could hardly wait to see all of it.

"Rand," Celina said louder.

The gentle tugging of his hair made Rand release her nipple. He looked into her eyes.

"You have to stop."

Stop? She couldn't be serious. His cock felt as if it could explode, and he hadn't even seen her naked yet. "What?"

"Not here, please." She glanced toward the hot tub. "I don't want anyone to see us making love."

Of course she wouldn't. Celina wasn't like her friend Jasmine. Rand had no doubt the uninhibited Ms. Britt would be willing to bare all for anyone who cared to look. He dropped a kiss of apology on her lips. "I'm sorry. I got carried away."

"Should I be flattered that you lost control?"

A hint of a smile turned up the corners of her mouth. Desire still coursed through his body, yet her teasing made him chuckle. "I don't normally attack a woman in front of other people."

"You didn't attack me, Rand." She touched his face, her fingertips grazing his cheek. "I kissed you first."

"Yes, you did. And I loved it."

She smiled. "I did too. You're an incredible kisser."

"So are you." The tip of his tongue brushed her lips before he covered her mouth with his. He tilted his head to the right, then the left, as he kissed her again and again.

"Rand," Celina whispered between kisses.

"What?"

"My cabin. Now."

He'd been raised to never argue with a lady. Rand took her hand and led her toward the stairs.

Samir was behind the bar in the upper-deck salon, preparing something green and foamy. Rand didn't know what Samir put in some of the concoctions he created, but they were all delicious and potent. Tonight, for Celina, only the best would do.

"Samir, bring a bottle of champagne and two glasses to Ms. Tate's cabin please."

"Right away, Captain."

The steward smiled at her. Celina assumed all the crew would know about her and Rand soon. On such a small ship, word would travel fast. She normally wasn't one to lay her private life open for all to see. In this case, it didn't matter to her. She wanted Rand and didn't care who knew that.

She slipped her hand in his and was rewarded with his smile.

He opened the door to her cabin. She stepped inside, her gaze immediately falling on the bed. One of the stewardesses had already turned back the covers. A long-stemmed pink rose lay on the pillows. Lamps on either side of the bed cast a soft, romantic light around the room.

The perfect place for seduction.

Celina crossed to the bed and picked up the rose. She heard the door close behind her as she lifted the flower to her nose. She sniffed deeply of the sweet scent. It made her think of long, lazy afternoons lying in a hammock with the beauty of Mother Nature all around her.

Rand's arms slipped around her waist. He rested his chin on her shoulder. "You like roses?"

"Very much."

She moved the rose beneath his nose so he could smell it. "It's nice." He nuzzled the sensitive area behind her ear. "But you smell better."

His warm breath in her ear sent goose bumps erupting across her skin. "Elayne was right. You are a charmer."

Her teasing should've made him smile. His expression remained serious, his eyes intense. "I'm not trying to charm you, Celina. I mean every word I say to you."

A man as handsome as Rand didn't have to lie to get a woman into bed. He didn't have to resort to flowery phrases or phony compliments. She'd seen the sexy looks Doretta, Mara, and Glynnis directed at him. Any of those three women would gladly invite Rand into her bed. Instead, he was here with her.

She turned in his arms and kissed him.

She caressed his shoulders, his chest. Her thumbs brushed across his small nipples. The growl deep in his throat spurred her to continue. She touched his nipples again, then ran her hands slowly down the front of his body. She paused when she reached his belt.

"Don't stop," he rasped against her mouth.

Looking into his eyes, Celina passed Rand's belt and laid her hand over the hard ridge in his trousers.

He growled again before cradling her face in his hands and kissing her thoroughly. His tongue slid into her mouth, dancing over hers. Celina moved her hand over the ridge as they kissed, learning the shape and size of his cock.

Very nice.

A knock on the door startled her. She pulled away from Rand, ending their kiss.

Rand's eyes still burned with desire. "What? Why did you stop?"

"Someone's at the door."

The knock sounded again. "Damn," Rand muttered. "It must be Samir."

"You did tell him to bring champagne."

"My crew is too efficient sometimes."

Samir's interruption didn't reduce the size of Rand's erection. She gave it another gentle squeeze before dropping her hand. "Would you like me to answer the door?"

"No, I'll get it."

Of course he would. Celina imagined Rand's crew was used to seeing him with a woman.

Samir entered the cabin, carrying a tray with a bottle of champagne and two crystal flutes, plus a plate of strawberries and bowl of whipped cream. He set the tray on the low table in the seating area.

"Anything else, sir?" he asked Rand.

"No, thank you. Have a nice evening, Samir."

"You too, sir." He nodded at Celina. "Ms. Tate."

She watched Rand open the bottle of champagne, his movements sure and steady. The cork gave a soft *pop* when he worked it from the bottle's neck. He'd obviously done this many times.

She wondered how many women had shared champagne with him.

"Samir didn't seem surprised that you're here with me."

Rand glanced at her, then picked up one of the flutes. "I asked him to bring us champagne."

"I'm sure I'm not the first female passenger you've shared champagne with."

He filled the second glass with the bubbly liquid. "Does that bother you?"

"I have no illusions about your sex life, Rand. You're an incredibly handsome man in a position of power. I'm sure many of your female passengers throw themselves at you."

A slight frown crossed his face. "You didn't throw yourself at me, Celina."

"Not exactly, but I believe I've made it clear that I want you."

He handed her one of the flutes. "The feeling is mutual."

She looked at him over the rim of her glass as she sipped her drink. It flowed over her tongue and down her throat, leaving a warm trail to her stomach. "Mmm, very good."

"Let me taste." Instead of sipping from his own flute, Rand kissed her, his tongue whisking across her lips. "You're right. Very good." He slid one arm around her waist. "But I need another taste to be sure."

His mouth covered hers. Celina moaned softly. Rand's lips slid over hers, coaxing them to part. Celina touched his tongue with the tip of hers. He accepted the love play, gently biting her tongue and drawing it farther into his mouth.

The man definitely knew how to kiss.

Rand took the flute from her hand. He set it and his own on the nightstand. When he looked back at her, Celina drew in a sharp breath at the heat in his eyes. Placing his hands on her waist, he gently squeezed before moving them up and down her torso. The heels of his hands brushed the sides of her breasts.

"You have an incredible body, Celina."

"I'm not as busty as Jasmine, or as voluptuous as Elayne."

"I don't want Jasmine or Elayne. I want you."

He cradled her breasts as he kissed her again. His thumbs flicked her nipples, and they immediately hardened. Each flick sent her desire higher. Celina loved his touch, but she needed more. She needed him naked.

She dropped kisses beneath his chin and down his neck to the opening of his shirt. "I want your clothes off."

Rand didn't want to stop touching her long enough to strip. Her breasts felt so good in his hands . . . soft, warm, the nipples hard. Celina might not be as busty as her friends, but she had sexy long nipples, perfect for sucking.

She tugged his shirt from his pants. She unbuttoned it while he lowered the straps of her dress and filled his palms with her breasts. They were tan, with no white lines from a swimsuit top.

41

"Do you sunbathe nude?"

"Sometimes." The last button of his shirt came loose, and she parted the fabric. Rand swallowed hard when she ran her fingernails from his collarbone to his belt. The light scratch of her nails sent a shiver up his spine and made his balls tighten. "I like the feel of the sun on my skin."

"I like the feel of your hands on my skin."

"It is nice, isn't it?" She kissed the middle of his chest while pushing his shirt off his shoulders. "I want to touch you everywhere."

That sounded perfect to Rand, as long as he could touch her also. Reaching behind her, he slowly lowered her zipper and slipped the shoulder straps off her arms. Her dress fell to a pool around her feet. Celina stood before him wearing a pair of tiny white panties, white sandals, and a vixen's smile.

He wanted to lick every inch of her.

Rand dropped to his knees. He lifted her left foot and slid off her shoe, then repeated the action with her right foot. Grasping the waistband of her panties, he tugged them past her hips. Blond hair covered her mound.

"Nice." He kissed each hipbone. The tip of his tongue darted into her navel as he ruffled the hair with his fingertips. "Very nice."

She arched her hips, pushing her mound closer to his mouth. "Touch me."

He nipped the curve of her belly. It quivered, earning her another nip. "Do you want my fingers or my tongue?"

"Your tongue."

He liked that she didn't hesitate with her answer. Rand had been with women who wouldn't talk to him, as if he were a mind reader and knew instinctively what they wanted sexually. Celina was different. She knew what she wanted and wasn't afraid to tell him.

He pulled off her panties and let them fall on top of her dress. Placing his hands between her thighs, he pushed outward. She spread her legs at his silent request. The scent of her musk drifted to his nose.

"Wider."

She obeyed him, spreading her legs another few inches. Rand slid his thumbs over her labia. She was so wet, her juices quickly coated his thumbs.

He looked into her eyes while he raised one digit to his mouth and sucked off her cream.

Celina tunneled her fingers into his hair and drew him back to her pussy. "Lick me."

Clutching her buttocks, Rand dipped his tongue between her thighs. He circled her clit, then darted inside her channel. He repeated the process over and over, lapping at her cream as quickly as it formed.

She tasted hot and salty-sweet. Delicious.

Celina's breathing became heavier, more labored. Rand clasped her waist and guided her to sit on the bed. As soon as she was seated, he hooked his arms beneath her knees and tugged her buttocks to the edge. Celina fell back on the bed, her arms at her sides, her eyes closed.

Rand pulled her legs apart and stared at her pussy. Wet, swollen, dark pink, her curls glistening with her juices. He licked her from anus to clit and back, moving his tongue over her slowly, gently . . . savoring her flavor. When she arched her back and dug her fingers into the bedspread, he knew she needed more than slow and gentle. He increased his movement, stroking over the feminine folds with the flat of his tongue. He wiggled the tip over her clit.

"There. Oh, Rand, there please."

Only too happy to please her, Rand focused his attention on Celina's clit. He licked her for several moments before he parted his lips over her clit to suckle. Her juices continued to seep from her channel, running down to her anus. Rand swiped his thumb through her cream and pushed it into her ass.

Celina moaned loudly. At first he thought he was hurting her, that she didn't like anal play. The next moment she lifted her hips from the bed, pressing her pussy against his face.

"Deeper. Go deeper."

Instead of doing what she requested, Rand removed his thumb. She whimpered in protest. "Shhh. Don't worry, babe. I'll take care of you."

He thoroughly wet two fingers in his mouth and pushed them inside her ass, moving them in and out as he licked her pussy again.

"Oh, *yesssss*! That feels so good." Celina grabbed his head, clutching handfuls of his hair. "Move your fingers faster."

She was so close to an orgasm. Rand pushed his fingers inside her as far as he could and suckled her clit, trying to drive her over the edge. She bucked her hips and pulled his hair. A low moan came from deep in her throat.

"God!"

Her anus squeezed his fingers. He pushed his thumb into her pussy and felt the contractions grab it, as if to pull it farther inside her. He continued to lick her clit. Instead of disappearing beneath the hood, it stayed hard and swollen, begging for his attention.

Rand kissed the inside of each thigh. "You aren't through."

Raising up to her elbows, Celina peered at him through her legs. She shook her head.

"Can you come again?"

"Definitely."

Rand smiled. "I like the sound of that." He continued to move his fingers and thumb inside her. "Like this? Or do you need something else?"

She sat up, framed his face in her hands, and kissed him deeply. "I need your cock."

Six

$\mathcal{H}$eat flared in his eyes. Celina kissed him again, stroking his lips with her tongue. She could smell herself, taste herself, on his mouth.

Celina had lost her virginity at seventeen in the backseat of her boyfriend's car. Lovers had flitted through her life since then, some good, some lousy. No man had ever affected her as deeply as Rand. One look into his deep brown eyes made her breath hitch. A single touch of his fingertip on her skin, and she shivered. Her body responded to him on the most basic level of woman to man.

She'd felt desire. This was so much more.

"I love the way you kiss," he said, his voice husky.

The compliment earned him another stroke of her tongue. "I like kissing."

"And having your pussy licked."

His lips quirked. Celina smiled to herself at his teasing. If he was trying to shock her, it wouldn't work. "Mmm, yes."

He kissed each of her knees. "I'll gladly do it again."

She gazed at the large bulge in his trousers. "I think it might be your turn for some attention." She tugged on his hands. "Stand up."

Once he was standing, Celina reached for his belt. Rand drew in a sharp breath when her fingers brushed his cock. She looked up at him and licked her lips. "Yes, it's definitely time for you to get some attention."

She unfastened and unzipped his trousers. He wore plain white briefs. His hard shaft stretched them until the cotton became almost transparent. Celina's mouth watered with the desire to taste him, to feel his firm flesh slide past her lips and into her mouth.

She pulled down his briefs until his cock was freed. It sprang up toward his stomach, thick and hard, the head dark pink. Celina palmed it in one hand, his balls in the other. "I'm going to enjoy playing with this."

"I have no complaints about that." Rand pushed his trousers and briefs past his hips. "You can play as much as you want."

Now with more room, Celina used both hands to touch him. She caressed the length of his cock again, then slid her hands up his body. She brushed over his small nipples with the pads of her thumbs, burrowed through the line of dark hair that ran across his chest and down his stomach. She'd always loved hair on a man's chest. Rand had the perfect amount—not so much he looked like an animal, but enough to tickle her fingertips.

A drop of clear liquid formed on the tip of his rod. Celina licked it off. She circled the head with her tongue before licking off another salty drop that had formed.

Rand growled.

She looked into his eyes as she licked off the third drop. "Do you like that?"

"Keep it up, and you'll soon find out exactly how much I like it."

Celina grinned at his choice of words. She squeezed the base of his cock. "Looks like it's already *up* to me."

"It's about to be buried deep inside you."

Her clit throbbed at the thought of Rand's full length inside her. She felt torn between the desire to keep pleasuring him and the desire to have his cock pounding into her pussy.

He took the decision of what to do away from her. "Lie down."

Celina scooted backward until she rested her head on the pillows. She watched Rand take off the rest of his clothes. Her breathing grew deeper with each bit of skin that he revealed. The tan covered his entire body. The dark hair that arrowed down his stomach lightly covered his legs and arms. He didn't possess the large muscles of a bodybuilder, but of a man used to physical labor. He stood by the bed, his gaze traveling from her hair to her toes and back.

"You're beautiful, Celina."

The desire in his eyes made her feel beautiful. She held out one hand to him. "Come here."

Rand gladly obeyed her. He lay beside her, drawing one of her legs over his hip. He pressed his shaft into her stomach as he caressed her back.

"Your skin is so soft." He kissed her neck, her shoulder. "I love touching you."

She lifted her leg higher up his hip. Her movement pushed his cock harder against her. Rand groaned. "Damn, you feel good."

"Inside me, Rand. Please."

Nothing would make him happier than to fuck her. He wanted to bury his rod inside her so deep, she'd feel it all the way to her soul. Not yet. First, he wanted her to come again.

Rand cradled her breast while kissing her deeply. She melted against him, opening her mouth to accept the thrust of his tongue. Rand couldn't get enough of kissing her, touching her. He gave her breast one more squeeze, then ran his hand down the front of her body to between her thighs. Her generous cream let two fingers slide easily into her sheath. She arched her hips, driving his fingers even farther inside her.

"Deeper, Rand. Go deeper."

He pressed upward into her G-spot. "There?"

"Yes. Oh, yes."

"Do you want me to lick your clit while I do this?" He moved his fingers, massaging the sensitive area. "Or your ass?"

Her keening moan signaled the start of her orgasm. The walls of her pussy clamped onto his fingers. Her body trembled, her pussy leaked more cream. Rand continued to caress her G-spot as Celina closed her eyes and threw back her head. Her mouth fell open, her breath escaping in a ragged sigh.

He'd never seen a woman so beautiful while having a climax.

She lowered her head. Her eyes were hooded and a tender smile crossed her lips. "Wow."

"Wow is right. I love watching you come." Rand kissed her once, twice, while continuing to caress her labia. His fingers were slick with her juices when he lifted them to her mouth. "Taste yourself."

Looking into his eyes, Celina drew his fingers into her mouth. She licked every bit of her essence from his flesh. Each time her tongue passed over one of his fingers, he felt the caress in his cock.

"Like the way you taste?" he asked.

She nodded.

He dipped his fingers between her legs again and lifted them back to her mouth. "Do you lick your fingers when you masturbate?"

She held his wrist as she cleaned his fingers again. "Yes."

His rod throbbed from the mental picture of Celina bringing herself to a climax, then licking the juices from her fingers. Groaning, he burrowed his face in her neck. "Jesus, that sounds good." He leaned down and laved both nipples. "I've got to get inside you."

Rand rose to his knees. He kissed Celina's nipples, her belly, her mound. "Roll over to your stomach."

Once she was on her stomach, Rand took one of the pillows and tugged it beneath her hips. He moved between her legs, pushing them open with his knees. Her slick pussy glistened in the lamplight.

He dragged his thumb through her silky folds. "You're so pretty here. All wet and pink and swollen." Needing to taste her again, he bent over and licked her slit. "Mmm. Delicious."

She looked at him over her shoulder. "You said you wanted to get inside me."

"I do." He spread her cheeks and licked her again. "I want to do everything to you."

"Everything?"

"Yeah." Gathering her cream on his thumb, he spread it over her anus. "You wouldn't believe the thoughts going through my head."

"Oh, I think I might."

Rand pushed his thumb into her ass. "You don't sound concerned or disgusted."

"There's nothing disgusting about two people pleasuring each other, no matter how it's done."

"So you're willing to try something . . . different?"

She smiled, slow and wicked. "How do you know it would be . . . different?"

Desire coursed through his body at her words. His cock swelled, his balls tightened. He stretched out on top of her, nestling his shaft between her buttocks. "My God, you are so hot." He nipped the back of her neck, circled her earlobe with his tongue. "I've never met a woman as free as you."

She arched her hips. Rand groaned when his balls slid along her velvety folds. His control snapped. He couldn't wait any longer to be inside her.

He moved away long enough to open the nightstand and remove a condom and bottle of lube. Once he'd sheathed his hard flesh, he returned to his spot on top of her. Slipping his hands beneath her breasts, Rand entered her with one long glide.

"Yeah," he rasped. "Oh, yeah. Damn, your pussy is dripping."

He lay still, not wanting to move yet for fear he'd come too soon. When she arched her hips again, he couldn't help thrusting forward. He pinched her nipples between his thumbs and forefingers. She gasped. Rand immediately released her. "Did I hurt you?"

"No. Not at all. More."

He alternated between kneading her breasts and pinching her nipples as he quickened his thrusts. "Like this?"

"Yes." She raised up to her elbows, giving him more room

to touch her. "Pinch them harder." She groaned when he did what she requested. "Mmm, yes. Like that. Just like that."

Rand gave her nipples one more tug before releasing them. He straightened and reached for the bottle of lube he'd placed on the bed. Flipping up the top, he squeezed a generous glob onto his fingers. He began fucking her again as he spread the thick gel over her anus.

Tight. Wet. Silky. Closing his eyes, Rand savored the feel of Celina's soft pussy surrounding his cock. He didn't want to move. He wanted to stay here, buried inside her, for the rest of the cruise.

The fierce desire clawing at him made remaining still impossible. Rand drove two fingers into Celina's ass as he pumped into her sheath. She pushed back at him, meeting every one of his thrusts.

She released a sound between a gasp and a scream before the walls of her pussy clamped onto his cock. Rand thrust once, twice, as the pleasure flowed through his body.

Celina sighed when she felt Rand's lips touch her shoulder. He gently tugged on her knees until she straightened them and lay on the bed. His body surrounded her, making her feel safe as well as thoroughly satisfied.

"You okay?" he whispered in her ear.

"Mmm, I'm great."

"Now that is an understatement." He kissed the back of her neck. "I'd describe you as amazing."

"You're pretty amazing too."

"And this was only round one."

"Is there going to be a round two?"

"I guarantee it."

Goose bumps scattered across her skin when he nipped

her earlobe. Celina shifted to her side so she could accept his kiss. Rand cradled her breast, his thumb stroking her nipple while he kissed her. Heat began to build low in her belly again.

A gentle beep came from Rand's trousers pocket. Ending their kiss, he blew out a deep breath. "Damn."

"What's wrong?"

"I'm needed in the pilothouse. Jonathan wouldn't page me if it wasn't important." He brushed his thumb across her nipple again. "I'm sorry. I really wanted that round two."

"Don't be sorry. I know you have a job to do." She touched his face, her fingertips gliding over his cheek. "Will you come back later?"

Taking her hand, he kissed her palm. "If I can."

She watched him rise and head for the bathroom. Rolling to her back, she hugged one of the pillows to her stomach. She smiled. What an incredible lover. Rand knew how to touch a woman to drive her desire to the top of the scale. It would be very easy to become addicted to his lovemaking.

She hoped he finished his job soon so he could come back for round two.

He came out of the bathroom. Celina gazed at his body, admiring the broad shoulders, hair-dusted chest, flat stomach, strong thighs. Even flaccid, his cock was impressive. She longed to taste him again.

He leaned over the bed, caging her between his arms. "You're burning me with your eyes."

"Am I?"

"You keep looking at me like that, I'll ignore Jonathan's page."

Celina grinned. "Promise?"

Rand chuckled. "I'd love to, but I can't." He dropped a soft kiss on her lips. "Hold that thought, okay?"

"Okay."

He dressed quickly and gave her one more kiss before he left. Once he was gone, Celina sipped her champagne while thinking about her time with Rand. Scorching sex with a handsome hunk. What more could a woman want on her vacation? No worries, no embarrassing "morning after" moments. They were both willing and knew whatever happened between them would only last for three days.

And two more nights.

She set her glass on the nightstand and lay down. She thought of the way Rand looked when he'd undressed. He had an incredible body. With his dark hair and skin, he reminded her of a pirate. Tall, strong, confident. Wearing tall boots and wielding a whip, he'd be in complete command of his ship.

And her.

She snuggled into the soft pillow and closed her eyes. Yes, she could definitely imagine Rand as a pirate . . .

Seven

$\mathcal{A}$ gentle breeze brushed Celina's face, cooling her heated skin. She smiled, enjoying the warmth and the salty scent of the ocean. She could hear the waves lapping against the side of the ship. The sound made her feel peaceful.

The sun beat down on her, hot and relentless. It soon became too warm instead of soothing. She shifted, trying to get away from the sun's rays.

She couldn't move. Frowning, Celina slowly opened her eyes. She didn't recognize anything in front of her. Instead of gleaming white, she saw old, grayed wood. Tall masts held billowing sails. There were no salons, no bars. She no longer stood on the deck of the S. S. *Fantasy*, but on the deck of a . . .

Pirate ship?

Celina looked down at her chest. She'd never seen the blouse she wore. Pale yellow in color, four ties held it closed across her breasts. A thick rope wrapped across her stomach. Her arms were stretched behind her, her hands bound. She tugged, but her efforts made the rope cut into her wrists instead of freeing her.

Frantically, Celina turned her head as far as she could and looked around. She saw no one else. She was alone on the deck, tied to a wooden post.

But how? This didn't make any sense.

"I see you're awake."

Celina whipped her head toward the sound of the voice. She blinked, certain she couldn't really be seeing the vision in front of her. Rand stood six feet away. At least, the man looked like Rand. Instead of the crisp white uniform he should be wearing, he wore dark brown pants, brown boots, and a loose white shirt that was open to his waist. The breeze teased the material, giving her glimpses of his bare chest. His hair was pulled back and tied in a queue, a day's worth of whiskers covered his cheeks and jaw.

"Rand?"

He frowned. "That's 'Captain' to you." He removed a coiled whip that hung from the post next to him. "I thought time alone would teach you who is in command. I see you will need further lessons."

Celina's eyes widened as she watched him slowly uncoil the whip. Surely he didn't intend to use that on her! "What are you doing?"

"Showing you who is in command." A flick of his wrist and the whip smacked against the deck. Celina flinched. "My only problem is deciding where to start. Those lovely breasts need my attention." He flicked the whip again. "But the thought of turning you over a cannon and applying my whip to your ass is very tempting."

Celina's heart began to pound. Surely this wasn't real. She

had to be dreaming. Rand wasn't standing there, dressed like a pirate and holding a whip. If she closed her eyes for a moment, she'd wake up and be back in her bed on the yacht. Yes, that's exactly what would happen. Taking a deep, even breath, she closed her eyes.

They popped back open when the tip of Rand's whip whooshed by her ear. His lips curved up in a wicked grin as he pulled the whip back to his side.

"Sleeping is not allowed, Celina. You must be awake for your lesson."

"I don't understand this," she whispered.

"You don't have to understand. All you have to do is accept whatever I decide to do to you."

He drew back his arm. Celina closed her eyes tightly and braced herself for the strike. She felt the air on her chest from the whip's movement, but no pain. She looked down. The top tie of her blouse had snapped in two. "How did you . . ."

"I'm very good with my whip."

Another flick of his wrist, and the second tie was broken. The breeze picked up the edges of her blouse, exposing the inside slopes of her breasts.

"The view is getting better, but I want more."

So did Celina. She should be scared out of her mind. Instead, her body heated with each flick of his whip. Her nipples beaded, pressing against her blouse.

Rand's gaze snapped to her breasts. He smirked. "Why, Celina. Are you getting excited?"

She refused to answer him. His whip snapped again, breaking the third tie. "I suggest you answer my question before I use the whip on your skin."

"I don't get excited by barbarians."

"No? Your body says otherwise."

One more flick, and the last tie was broken. A sudden gust of wind blew Celina's blouse completely open. Rand stared at her breasts as he stalked toward her. He ran the handle of his whip over one hard nipple. "I think your body is very excited." Switching to the other nipple, he caressed it with the whip's handle until it hardened too. "I think it wants whatever I do to it." He looked into her eyes. "Does it?"

Celina swallowed when he ran the handle over her nipples again. Back and forth, stroking one nipple, then the other. Moisture formed between her thighs. Her clit throbbed. "Please," she rasped.

"Please what?" He let the whip fall to the deck. "Please fuck you?"

Rand dropped to his knees before her. Celina's breath hitched when he drew a large knife from the sheath on his thigh. He grabbed the waistband of her pants. She sucked in her stomach and held her breath. With one long cut, he split her pants from waist to crotch.

He spread her labia with his thumbs. "If you don't get excited by barbarians, why are you so wet?"

A long swipe of his tongue stole her voice so she couldn't answer his question. He licked her again, then darted his tongue inside her channel. "Oh, yes. Nice and wet." He touched her clit with his thumb, softly rubbing it. "You want my cock, don't you? You want me to fuck you long and hard until you scream out your climax."

He kept rubbing her clit, using the barest of touches. Tormenting her. Celina tried to arch her hips, tried to get closer to that wicked thumb. The ropes wouldn't let her move more than a fraction of an inch. "Rand, please!"

He looked up at her, that wicked grin back on his lips. "Please what? Tell me. I can't read your mind."

"I want to come."

"How? With my thumb?" He replaced his thumb with his lips and gently suckled her clit. "Or maybe my tongue. Would that do it for you?"

He suckled her clit again. Celina mewled deep in her throat. The pleasure grew inside her with each pass of his tongue over her sensitive flesh. Her orgasm began to build low in her belly.

It died when he pulled his mouth away from her. Celina cried out in frustration. "No, don't stop!"

"I have no intention of stopping."

Standing before her again, he pulled the tie at his waist and opened his pants. His cock sprang up, full and hard. He slid his arms behind her knees, spread her legs wide, and entered her. Celina gasped at his initial thrust, then moaned from pleasure. Her eyes drifted closed, her mouth dropped open. He buried his face in her neck as he drove into her. The ropes holding her to the post and binding her wrists meant she couldn't move. All she could do was accept Rand's deep thrusts.

"God, you're sweet," he growled next to her ear. "I love how tight and wet your pussy is. I'm going to come so deep inside you."

He shifted his hips from side to side, brushing the base of his cock against her clit. The orgasm built again, even quicker than the first time. It enveloped her body when Rand bit her neck. Celina squeezed her eyes shut as the pleasure flowed through her. She barely had time to take a breath when Rand groaned and trembled.

Soft kisses fell on her lips, her cheek, her eyelids. "That's it," he whispered. "Keep your eyes closed. Rest now."

That sounded like a wonderful idea. Celina sighed and rested her head on Rand's shoulder.

The insistent ringing of the telephone seeped into Celina's consciousness. She pried her eyes open and frowned at the noisy instrument. Whoever was on the other end better have a damned good reason for calling so early.

She pushed her hair out of her face as she reached for the receiver. "What?" she said sharply.

"Well, don't snap my head off," Elayne said. "It's not my fault you're lazy."

"Hey, Elayne. Sorry. I'm not a morning person."

"Are you still in bed? Did I interrupt something?"

"Just my sleep." She yawned and her jaw popped. "What's up?"

"Jasmine and I were getting worried about you. It's almost ten."

"It can't be." A quick glance at the clock on the nightstand proved Elayne told the truth. "I can't believe I slept so late."

"Did Rand wear you out?"

Celina could hear the smug tone in her friend's voice. She decided to ignore it.

"No comment?" Elayne asked.

"None."

"Fine. Be that way. See if I give you any details about Jonathan and me."

Celina chuckled. She knew her friend couldn't wait to give out all the details of her and Jonathan's time together.

"Jasmine and I had coffee," Elayne said, "but wanted to wait for you to eat. Get your buns up here."

"Give me fifteen minutes."

"Twelve. I'm hungry."

Celina hung up the receiver and threw back the covers. She yawned again, then inched toward the edge of the bed. She moaned when muscles she hadn't used in several months protested the movement. Then she smiled. What a wonderful way to earn sore muscles.

She thought about the handsome captain as she stepped beneath the warm shower. She'd taken lovers and hated herself the next morning for giving in to her hormones. That wasn't the case with Rand. She didn't regret one moment with him. He'd been amazing. Three orgasms. That didn't happen to her. She occasionally had two with a man, but never three. And she'd never had an erotic dream after making love.

An erotic dream that seemed so real, she could still feel the wisp of air from the whip as it broke the ties on her blouse.

Celina finished her shower quickly for she didn't want to make Elayne and Jasmine wait for her. She stepped into panties and pulled on her bra. She winced when her bra strap touched a tender spot on her back. Ignoring the tender spot, she finished dressing and left her cabin.

She found her friends on the upper deck where brunch was served, sitting at a table with Mara and Doretta. Elayne stood as soon as Celina walked up to the table.

"It's about time! I'm ready to pass out from hunger."

"What about the bagel and cream cheese you ate a few minutes ago?" Jasmine asked.

Elayne slapped Jasmine's shoulder. "Shh! You weren't supposed to tell her that."

"I didn't realize your food was a government secret."

Celina chuckled. "I'm sorry I made you wait a whole two minutes, Elayne."

"You're forgiven. This time." She looked at Mara and Doretta. "Would you ladies like to join us?"

"Thanks," Doretta said with a smile, "but we've already eaten. We're going to get ready for our trip to the island. See you later."

"The infamous island," Jasmine said, once the two ladies had left. "Rose told me about that."

Elayne led the way to the brunch buffet. "So you can tell us. What island?"

"The company that owns the yacht also owns a small private island." She picked up a plate and began to fill it with fresh fruit. "We'll dock there this afternoon. There's volleyball, swimming in the ocean, and a big cookout on the beach tonight."

"Sounds nice." Elayne bypassed the fruit and heaped her plate with scrambled eggs and ham. "So why did you call it infamous?"

"Everyone is nude."

Celina paused while reaching for the pitcher of orange juice. "Everyone?"

Jasmine nodded. "Rose said most of the passengers didn't even bother to be dressed when they left the ship."

Elayne accepted the glass of orange juice Celina handed her. "Well, this is one gal who won't be playing volleyball in the nude. My girls would give me two black eyes."

"I'm not ashamed of my body." Celina picked up silverware and a napkin. "But I don't know if I can walk around nude in front of strangers."

"Sounds like fun," Jasmine said with a grin.

"It would to you." Elayne added a slice of toast to her plate. "You and Carol were always ready to try something new and daring back in college."

62

"Yeah, we were. I'll admit that. Carol is the perfect example of how short life can be. I want to experience everything I can. If that includes walking around nude in front of a bunch of strangers, I'll do it. We're on this cruise to have fun."

Celina exchanged a look with Elayne before following her friends back to their table. "You're really going to bare all in front of everyone?"

Jasmine shrugged. "Why not? When in Rome, yadda yadda."

"You have more courage than I do." Elayne spread her napkin over her lap. "I'd rather stay on the ship and attack Jonathan."

"Maybe if I walk around naked, Chase will notice me."

Celina watched her friend push a piece of sausage around her plate. So that was it. Jasmine couldn't get the man she wanted to notice her. That must be a first for her. Men had always fallen at Jasmine's feet. That was the way she liked it. She had enough money to buy half of Chicago, yet preferred to be spoiled by men. She'd always said she wouldn't spend her money as long as men were willing to spend theirs on her. "Chase isn't the only single man on the ship, Jasmine."

"But he's the only one I want." Sighing heavily, she laid her fork on her plate. "There's something about him that . . . calls to me. I don't know how else to say it. He seems so sad. I want to make him feel better."

"Sex isn't the only way to make him feel better."

"Maybe not, but it's a great way to start." Picking up her fork again, Jasmine speared the piece of sausage and popped it into her mouth. "I love sex. It won't be any hardship on me to get Chase into bed."

"Speaking of bed," Elayne said, wiping her mouth with her napkin, "how was Rand?"

Celina smiled. "Incredible."

"I knew he would be." She propped her elbow on the table and rested her chin on her fist. "Is he huge?"

"Oh, yeah."

She laughed along with Elayne and Jasmine. Her laughter died when she leaned back in her chair. A slat in the chair pressed the sore spot on her back.

"What's wrong?" Jasmine asked.

"I don't remember bumping into anything, but I must have. I have a bruise on my back."

"Let me see."

Celina leaned forward. Jasmine tugged down the back of her tank top and pulled her bra strap away from her back. "That isn't a bruise, Cee. You have a huge splinter in your back."

"I can understand rug burns," Elayne said, "but how did you get a splinter in your back?"

Celina's dream flashed through her mind. Rand had taken her against a wooden post. But it had been a *dream*. It hadn't really happened.

"All the color drained out of your face." Elayne reached over and squeezed Celina's hand. "Are you okay?"

"Yes, I'm fine. I just . . . ." She forced a chuckle. "It's silly."

"What's silly?"

"I had an erotic dream about Rand. He was a pirate. I was tied to a wooden post on the deck. He took me against that post. But it was only a dream, so I don't know how the splinter got in my back."

Celina glanced from Elayne to Jasmine. Both of them wore concerned looks. "What? It was only a dream."

"Was it? I'm not sure." Jasmine blew out a breath. "I was fantasizing about Chase last night. I imagined him chasing me through a forest. When he caught me, he fell on top of me and started touching me. I woke up before he fucked me."

"So we both had erotic dreams. That isn't so unusual."

"Celina, I had leaves in my hair when I woke up this morning."

Goose bumps erupted over Celina's skin. "Leaves?"

Jasmine nodded. "I can't explain that any more than you can explain the splinter in your back."

Elayne pushed her plate to the center of the table. "You gals are freaking me out here."

"Did you have a dream too?" Jasmine asked.

"Jonathan and I were on the bridge of a spaceship, flying through some unknown solar system. It had to be a dream. There's no way that could be real."

"Did you notice anything unusual when you woke up?"

Elayne drew her bottom lip between her teeth. "I always sleep in a huge T-shirt and panties. When I woke up this morning, I was wearing this one-piece silky thing. It was the same piece of lingerie I'd worn on the spaceship in my dream."

Your most erotic fantasy can come true.

Celina remembered the words from the ship's brochure. "It's the yacht. The yacht is making our fantasies come true."

"That's impossible," Elayne said, frowning.

"So how else do you explain what happened to us? To *all* of us?"

"I can't, but there has to be an explanation. A ship can't have any kind of power."

"We're in the Bermuda Triangle," Jasmine said. "Maybe that has something to do with it."

Celina remembered the captain saying the same thing.

"Rand told me a person never knew what might happen once the ship entered the Bermuda Triangle."

"So what are we supposed to do?" Elayne asked.

"I know what *I'm* going to do." Jasmine wiped her hands and laid her napkin beside her plate. "I'm going to the island and try my best to get Chase naked. That is my number one priority."

Celina couldn't believe Jasmine was taking all this so casually. "What about the fantasies?"

"If they have to do with me fucking Chase, I'm all for them." She stood. "Later, ladies."

Once Jasmine had left, Elayne looked at Celina. "What are *you* going to do?"

"I'm going to find Rand and get more information about these fantasies. I want to know what to expect on the rest of this cruise."

Eight

Celina searched the entire yacht but couldn't find Rand any-where. She checked with all four stewardesses and stewards. None of them had seen Rand since early that morning.

It was as if he'd disappeared.

Celina wandered back into the main salon in time to see most of the passengers heading toward the exit. It appeared everyone planned to go to the island and plant their feet on solid ground for a few hours. Or make out among the palm trees.

While making out in front of everyone on the ship held no appeal, taking a stroll along the beach sounded good. She still wanted to talk to Rand about the huge splinter in her back, but had no choice except to wait until she found him.

The volleyball game had already begun by the time Celina made it to the beach. Most of the passengers and crew had opted to go nude while some wore swimsuits. It didn't surprise her to see a nude Barret. She stopped and watched him for a moment. How interesting, the way everything . . . bounced when he spiked the volleyball.

Chuckling, she turned away from the game and continued down the beach. She spotted Elayne sitting on a blanket beneath a palm tree with Jonathan. She watched Jonathan lower Elayne to the blanket as he kissed her. They weren't nude, but Celina had no doubt they soon would be.

She thought about joining them. When Jonathan slid one leg between Elayne's, Celina decided she shouldn't intrude on their privacy.

Instead of walking toward her friend, Celina turned and strolled into the grove of palm trees. Alone time would be good. She could lie in the sun without worrying about anyone bothering her. Especially Barret. He'd hit on her twice. Apparently, the man didn't like the word "no."

Barret was very handsome, but Celina wanted more from a man than good looks to have sex with him. She could have sex with any number of men she knew. Satisfying her hormones' call wouldn't be a problem. Finding a man she wanted to spend more than a few hours with . . . that was the problem.

The image of Rand popped into her head. It wouldn't be a hardship at all to spend several hours with the captain.

Celina found a secluded spot in the middle of several ferns. Palm trees surrounded her, but an opening through the fronds allowed the sunlight to peek through. She spread her blanket out on the soft sand. After a quick look around to be sure she was alone, she removed her bikini and stretched out on her stomach.

She hoped her place stayed secluded. But it wouldn't surprise her to have a couple wander nearby, looking for a quiet spot to make love.

The sun beating down on her back and buttocks made her

warm and sleepy. She'd have to make her presence known if a couple did come by. Or maybe not. Maybe she could peek. She'd watched Barret, Glynnis, and Ian in the hot tub last night for a few moments. She'd been tempted to step closer to the tub and watch everything they did to each other. Instead, she'd turned away to be with Rand.

Rand wasn't here now. If a couple decided to enjoy each other, she could look.

Celina, don't be silly. You can't watch two people having sex.

The idea was tempting. Sighing softly, she closed her eyes.

She stirred when a muffled groan filled the air. Not sure if she'd actually heard something, she lifted her head and listened. She waited a moment, but heard nothing else. Deciding she must have been dreaming, she laid her head on her folded arms and closed her eyes again.

The groan reached her once more, followed by a guttural, "Oh, yeah."

A couple was having sex a short distance from her hiding place. Celina had to decide if she should remain still and try to ignore them or quietly get up and leave.

Or take a peek.

Her face burned at that last thought. She'd thought about watching a couple having sex before she drifted off to sleep, but she couldn't actually do that. It would be an invasion of their privacy.

Why not?

Watching herself and a partner in a mirror didn't count as seeing two live people making love. She could crawl over to the ferns and peek. No one would know.

"Suck it," the man growled. "Take it all the way down your throat."

Curiosity battled discretion inside Celina. Curiosity won. Moving as quietly as possible, she crawled over to a small opening in the ferns. She pulled back a thick leaf and peered through the hole.

A naked Lamar sat on a blanket, leaning back against a palm tree. His legs were splayed open, giving her a clear view of his impressive cock. His eyes were closed, his expression one of pure ecstasy, while Tony licked his balls.

Tony?

Celina never expected it would be two men on the other side of the ferns. She quickly dropped the leaf so she couldn't see them. Biting her lower lip, Celina debated about what to do. She could hear the sounds of oral sex . . . the moans, the slurping, the low growling.

She wanted to see everything.

Parting the ferns again, Celina gazed at the two men. Tony slid his lips down Lamar's cock until it completely disappeared inside his mouth.

"God, that's good," Lamar breathed. He ran his fingers into the other man's hair. Holding Tony's head still, Lamar began driving his rod into Tony's mouth. "Yeah. Oh, yeah. Love fucking your mouth."

Warmth flowed through Celina's body. Her clit began to gently throb. Still watching the men, she spread her legs and slid her hand between her thighs. Her feminine lips were swollen and covered with her cream.

She had no idea seeing two men having sex would be so exciting.

Celina rubbed her clit as she watched the lovers. Tony released Lamar's cock long enough to thoroughly lick two fingers. He pressed those fingers against Lamar's anus. Lamar let his legs fall completely open and arched his hips. Tony pushed his fingers inside Lamar's ass as he took the man's cock into his mouth again.

"That is so hot," Celina whispered.

A warm hand covered hers. "Let me help you with that," Rand rasped into her ear.

Celina looked over her shoulder. Rand knelt next to her, as naked as she. She glanced down his body. His hard cock stood straight up, a drop of fluid leaking from the slit. She whimpered at the sight.

He kissed her, swiping his tongue across her lower lip. "Keep watching them," he said.

She did as he said, peering through the foliage at the two men while Rand caressed her clit. Tony continued to suck on Lamar's cock, his mouth moving up and down quickly, then slowing the pace. He gripped the base of Lamar's rod and circled the head with his tongue. They kissed deeply, passionately, before Tony began sucking on Lamar again.

It amazed Celina that Lamar could last so long without coming.

"It's hot watching two men, isn't it?" Rand slid his other hand between her buttocks and pushed two fingers inside her channel. "Do you like it?"

"Yes."

"I can tell. Your pussy is dripping."

He rubbed her clit in small circles, adding to the sensation of his fingers inside her. Celina mewled with pleasure. Her climax was so close. Just a little more . . .

Rand nipped her earlobe. "I'll bet you'd like to watch them fuck."

The orgasm galloped through her body. Her legs grew

weak. She barely had the chance to gasp before Rand entered her with one thrust. He gripped her hips, holding her on her knees, as he pounded his cock into her pussy.

"Damn, I love how wet you are."

Celina rested her forehead on her folded arms. Rand's thrusts increased, going a bit farther inside her each time. He'd stop, circle his hips, then begin thrusting again. Each movement brushed her clit. Each movement drove up her desire once more.

It crested when Rand slid his hand between her legs and pinched her clit.

Celina was still trying to recover from two intense orgasms when Rand groaned loudly. He gripped her hips, his fingers digging into her skin, while his body trembled.

Certain her legs would give out at any moment, Celina slowly reclined on the blanket. Rand followed her down, his softening cock still nestled inside her warmth. He pushed aside her hair and nibbled her earlobe. Celina hunched her shoulder and giggled.

"That tickles."

"You didn't think it tickled a few minutes ago."

"That's when I was turned on."

Rand pressed his groin against her buttocks. "I like it when you're turned on."

Celina could feel him getting hard again. "You recuperate quickly."

"I do with the right woman."

She knew Rand only spoke the truth, yet his words reinforced the knowledge that she was nothing more than his current voyage's fling. Women wanted to fuck the captain, the quarterback, the lead singer in a rock band. It was human nature. It didn't make him a bad person. He had no reason to give up all those women simply because her feelings for him ran deeper than a shipboard romance.

Keep it light, Celina. You went into this knowing it would be a one-time fling. That's all you wanted from Rand. You can't change those rules now.

She moaned in pleasure when Rand withdrew from her body. She rolled to her back as he stretched out on his side next to her. He touched her stomach, his fingertips lightly caressing her skin.

"Wow," Celina said. "That last orgasm almost blew off the top of my head."

Rand grinned. "I do aim to please."

"Your aim is excellent." She inhaled sharply when he lifted her hand to his mouth and licked her palm. "You are an incredible lover."

"I try to be. It's important to me to please my partner."

"You've definitely pleased this partner."

"I'm glad," he whispered, before his lips covered hers.

It was a gentle kiss, a loving kiss. Celina sighed to herself. She could fall in love with him if she wasn't careful.

Rand ended the kiss with a soft nip of her lower lip. He slid his hand down her stomach to her mound. "I can't be close to you without wanting to make love to you."

"And this is bad . . . why?"

He chuckled. "I have work to do."

"Work later. Play now." She rolled to her side, trapping his hand between her thighs. His fingers brushed her clit. "It's been seven months since I've been with a man. I'm going to attack you every chance I get."

His eyebrows rose as if her statement shocked him, but she could see the laughter shining in his eyes. "Attack?"

"Mmm-hmm. Did I happen to mention that I love sex?"

"You didn't say the words, but I got that impression."

"You're so clever." She gripped his cock and smiled when it hardened in her hand. "I got that impression about you too."

Rand's eyes rolled back. He arched his hips, driving his shaft over her palm. "I do," he said, his voice a low growl.

"Then there's no reason for either of us to deprive ourselves."

She pushed Rand to his back, straddled his hips, and impaled herself on his cock. She braced her hands on his chest as she lifted herself until he almost slipped from her body. She held her position a moment, then lowered herself until his rod filled her channel again.

"That's the way." Rand palmed her breasts, his thumbs circling her firm nipples. "Ride me."

She was so wet, both from her juices and his cum, his shaft slid easily inside her. Celina soon developed a rhythm with Rand . . . in, out, up, down. He massaged her breasts as she rode him. Celina closed her eyes to savor the sensation of him filling her so completely. She moved faster, taking him deeper.

Rand pinched her nipples. Pleasure shot straight to her core. "Harder. Pinch them harder."

He did as she commanded, twisting her nipples as he pinched them. The extra stimulation sent Celina over the top. She keened as her climax flowed through her body.

Rand groaned and trembled beneath her.

It took several moments for Celina to remember how to breathe. She opened her eyes to see Lamar and Tony standing six feet away, watching them. Lamar gave her a thumbs-up sign and grinned before leading Tony away.

Nine

Celina found Elayne curled up on one of the love seats in the main salon. "Hi."

"Hi." Elayne held up her glass of red wine. "Want some? I can call Samir back."

Celina shook her head. "I'm fine." She joined her friend on the love seat. "Where's Jasmine?"

"I haven't seen her since breakfast. If she went to the island, I never saw her there." She sipped her wine. "Did you go to the island?"

Celina nodded. "I found a private place to sunbathe. I'm not quite ready to walk around the other passengers in my birthday suit."

"I'll second that." She drained her glass and set it on the low table in front of her. "I didn't see you."

"You were too wrapped up in Jonathan."

"Yeah, that's probably true."

The flatness in Elayne's tone surprised Celina. She thought her friend was happy with Jonathan's attention. "What's wrong?"

Before Elayne could answer Celina's question, Jasmine came bouncing into the room, a huge smile on her face. She flopped down in the chair opposite the love seat. "Oh my *God*. I just had the most intense orgasm I've ever had in my *life*."

Elayne looked at Celina, her eyes twinkling with laughter. "Do we dare ask her?"

Celina would rather ask Elayne why she'd been sad a moment ago. The amusement in her eyes now didn't fool Celina. She knew her friend too well.

For now, she'd take the cue from Elayne and switch her attention to Jasmine. "I doubt if we'll have to ask her. She'll tell us anyway."

"You're damn right I will." She looked over her shoulder at the bar. "Where's that hunky Samir? I need a drink."

As if he'd read Jasmine's mind, Samir walked through a door behind the bar. "Ladies, would you care for a drink?"

"You bet. I want one of those pink things you made yesterday." Jasmine glanced at Celina and Elayne. "How about it?"

"I'll take another glass of wine," Elayne said.

"I can't be a party pooper if you two are drinking. I'll have one of the pink things too, Samir."

He smiled. "Coming right up."

Once he had turned to prepare the drinks, Jasmine leaned forward in her chair. "You will not believe what Chase did to me."

"Chase?" Elayne's eyebrows disappeared into her curly bangs. "You mean you finally got him into bed?"

"Well, yes and no. We were on my bed, but we didn't exactly have sex."

"How can you not exactly have sex?" Celina asked.

Jasmine's wicked smile made Celina think of a woman

who'd just polished off a box of truffles. "He blindfolded me and—"

She stopped and her gaze darted to her left. "Nicola's coming."

Celina watched the stewardess approach. A lovely redhead in her early twenties, she'd been courteous and helpful every time Celina spoke to her.

"Excuse me, Ms. Britt," Nicola said. "I apologize for interrupting."

"No problem. What can we do for you?"

She faced Celina. "The captain asked me to give this to you, Ms. Tate."

The redhead held out a small envelope to Celina. She frowned, unsure why Rand would have the stewardess deliver a note instead of doing it himself. "It's from the captain?"

Nicola nodded. "Yes, ma'am. He asked me to wait for a reply."

Celina withdrew a single sheet of paper from the envelope. A bold scrawl in thick blue ink slashed across the page.

Please dine with me in my suite tonight. Eight o'clock.
Rand

"What does it say?" Elayne asked, peeking over Celina's shoulder.

Samir approached with the drinks. He began setting them on the table as Celina answered Elayne's question. "Rand invited me to dinner tonight in his suite."

She raised her head in time to see the surprised expression cross both Nicola's and Samir's faces. "What? You look shocked at Rand's invitation."

The stewardess and steward glanced at each other. "It is none of our business, Ms. Tate," Samir said. "Enjoy your drinks."

"Wait."

Celina's command stopped Samir before he turned to walk away. "I'd like to know why you and Nicola seem surprised that Rand would invite me to have dinner with him."

"It's just that . . ." Nicola clasped her hands together in front of her. "The captain has never done that, Ms. Tate. He's dined with several passengers, but he's never invited one to his suite."

Her explanation stunned Celina. It didn't make sense that Rand had never invited a woman to his suite. She assumed he'd invited *several* women to his suite for sex. "Are you sure?"

"Oh, yes, ma'am. I've worked for the captain for two years."

"And I for three," Samir said. "Nicola speaks the truth."

Celina reread the message. A tiny flutter of happiness took flight in her stomach. Perhaps this special invitation meant he cared more for her than she'd dared to hope.

Don't go there, Celina. If you wish for something that can't happen, you'll have your heart broken.

"Ms. Tate?" Nicola said. "What shall I tell the captain?"

"I'm supposed to eat with my friends at the cookout."

"Oh, pish." Elayne waved one hand as if that would erase Celina's comment. "You don't give another thought to Jaz and me. We'll be fine."

"Besides," Jasmine said, "maybe Elayne and I will have dinner with a couple of hunky guys."

"Damn straight. You should enjoy Rand while you can. You'll only have him for a couple more days."

Two days . . . and nights. She could enjoy his company and his lovemaking for two more days and nights.

Celina stuck the note back in the envelope and smiled at Nicola. "Please tell the captain I would be pleased to have dinner with him."

Rand twisted the bottle of champagne in the silver bucket so the wine would chill evenly. He looked at the table, examining it for anything out of place. Anna and Nicola had set it for him with a navy tablecloth and cream napkins. Fresh flowers in yellow, white, and palest pink filled the crystal vase in the center of the table. Henri's mouthwatering masterpieces waited on a warming tray on the bar.

I've forgotten something. I know I have.

"Music. Shit!" Grabbing the remote control from the bar, he pointed it toward the CD player. Soft instrumental notes filled the air. Rand smiled. *Perfect.*

He straightened the collar of his shirt and made sure the tail was tucked into his jeans. It felt different to wear clothes other than his uniform. He lived in the white outfits while on board. Tonight was special, and he chose to wear something that didn't scream out "captain" to Celina. Tonight, he wanted simply to be a man.

One who fiercely desired a woman.

A gentle knock on the door kicked his heartbeat into overdrive. Quickly picking up the candlelighter, he touched the flame to the two white tapers on the table. He tossed the lighter into a drawer and walked to the door. A flick of his wrist at the switch by the door dimmed the overhead lights to a faint glow.

He opened the door, and his heart dropped to his feet.

Celina stood there, a vision in the same striking blue as her eyes. Tiny shoulder straps held up her dress. It flowed over her curves and stopped at her knees. The bodice dipped between

79

her breasts, giving him a tantalizing view of the firm mounds. He could clearly see her nipples through the slinky material.

His mouth went dry with the desire to lick each hard bud.

"Good evening," she said softly.

Rand had to clear his throat. He would have sworn that he swallowed his tongue when he got his first glimpse of her. "Good evening." He stood aside. "Please come in."

The barest hint of flowers followed her when she walked past him. He bit his tongue to keep from groaning.

She stopped in the middle of his living room and turned in a circle. "It's lovely. And bigger than I expected."

"One of the perks of being the captain."

She tilted her head. A tiny smile touched her lips. "Are there a lot of perks?"

"A few. I enjoy some more than others."

"I'm sure."

She continued to smile, so Rand knew she was teasing him. He returned her smile. "How about some champagne?"

"I'd love it."

He motioned toward the couch. "Sit down, and I'll get it."

Rand watched her sink into a corner of his couch, her legs folded beneath her. Everything about her made him think of grace and femininity . . . except when they were making love. She turned into a wildcat in his arms, one who knew exactly what she wanted from a man sexually. He liked that.

Rand poured the chilled wine into two tall flutes and carried them to the couch. He handed Celina one of the glasses, then sat beside her. He held up his glass toward her.

"Here's to the evening and wherever it may lead."

Celina touched her flute to his. She looked into his eyes as she sipped. "Ooh, very good."

"Henri will be pleased to hear you like it. He's in charge of ordering the wine."

"Henri knows what he's doing. He's an excellent chef."

"He's worth every cent of the outrageous salary I pay him."

Her eyebrows drew together in a slight frown. "*You* pay him? Do you own the yacht, Rand?"

Rand sipped his drink while trying to decide how much to tell Celina. His crew knew the truth, but he'd never told any of the passengers that he was not only the captain of the ship, but the owner. The cost of a ticket was more than some people earned in an entire year. The high price didn't stop the gold diggers from taking his cruises. Rand had always been careful to only refer to himself as the captain. His crew did the same.

He didn't believe Celina fell in the gold digger department.

"Yes, I own the yacht."

"I gather you don't normally tell your passengers that."

He shook his head. "No. Too many women looking to snag a rich husband."

"So why tell me? Maybe I'm looking to snag a rich husband."

He loved the teasing light in her eyes. "Are you?"

"No. My job pays very well. I don't need a husband to support me."

"So you have no interest in getting married?"

"I didn't say that."

Rand slid his arm along the back of the couch until his fingertips brushed her bare shoulder. "Do you? Have an interest in getting married?"

"Someday. If I meet the right man."

"Who do you consider the right man?"

"I don't know. I haven't met him yet."

He could still see the teasing in her eyes, yet Rand didn't

find her answer amusing. He . . . hoped she might consider him the right man.

He had no idea where the thought came from since he'd never seriously considered marriage. He'd decided a long time ago that the single life would be perfect for him. A married man wouldn't have the freedom to sample the many pleasures of his cruises.

With Celina sitting less than two feet from him, sampling any other woman held no appeal at all.

He slipped his hand behind her nape, caressing the soft skin beneath her ear with his thumb. "Are you hungry?"

She leaned closer to him. Her gaze dropped to his crotch. She ran her tongue across her upper lip before looking in his eyes again. "Definitely."

Rand chuckled. "I meant for food."

"Oh." She sighed dramatically. "You're no fun."

Squeezing her neck, he tugged her to him until their lips were within an inch of touching. "Tell me that later when I have you naked."

A slow, seductive smile turned up her lips. "I do believe you're making a pass at me, Captain."

"You're very perceptive, Ms. Tate."

Her soft pink lips were too close to resist. Rand tugged her the last inch and covered her mouth with his. Her lips were cool from the champagne, yet quickly warmed beneath his. She parted them and accepted the gentle thrust of his tongue. A low moan of surrender came from her throat.

How easy it would be to take her now, here on his couch.

This evening was about more than sex. Rand already knew Celina was an incredible lover. He wanted to get to know her as a person, not simply someone for sex.

Reluctantly, he ended their kiss. "How about if I get you some more champagne and serve the appetizer?"

She touched his lips with one fingertip. "I thought your kiss was the appetizer."

Rand nipped the end of her finger. "I asked Henri to prepare a special meal for us."

"If it's as good as the other food I've eaten on board, I'm sure I'll love it."

Celina relaxed in the corner and sipped her wine as Rand rose. Her gaze snapped to his denim-covered buttocks. She sighed. He had an amazing ass.

He had an amazing *everything*.

He glanced at her before removing the bottle from the silver bucket. "I'll admit, I don't drink champagne very often."

"Neither do I, but I'm on vacation. I'm allowed to do things I don't normally do."

"Such as watching two men having sex?"

Warmth crept into Celina's cheeks, but she refused to look away from Rand. "Definitely a first."

He picked up a small covered dish along with the bottle and returned to where she sat. After filling both glasses, he set the bottle on the narrow table behind the couch. "Any other firsts you've experienced on the cruise?"

"I think that qualifies for the number one spot." She sipped her drink, enjoying the way the cool liquid slid down her throat. "What's in the dish?"

"The appetizer."

Rand removed the cover. Large shrimp, cut in bite-size pieces, lay in a creamy sauce. Celina inhaled deeply. "It smells incredible."

"Henri's shrimp is so good, it should be illegal." He

speared one of the pieces with a fork and held it to her mouth. "Try it."

Celina opened her mouth. She bit into the succulent shellfish and drew it off the fork. She chewed slowly, holding his gaze the entire time. "Delicious."

Desire flashed in his eyes. "You keep looking at me like that, and we'll forget all about dinner."

"That would be a shame, since Henri went to so much trouble to prepare something special for us." Celina took the fork from his hand and speared a piece of shrimp. "Your turn. Open up."

Rand parted his lips and Celina slipped the shellfish into his mouth. She waited until he'd swallowed before swiping her tongue across his bottom lip. "You had a drop of sauce there."

His nostrils flared. She saw his throat work as he swallowed. "Damn it, Celina, stop teasing me. I want this evening to be special for you. You aren't making it easy for me to keep my hands off you."

She ran her hand up the inside of his thigh. "Am I making it hard?" Her fingertips brushed his erect cock. "Oh, my. I do believe it's already hard."

She pressed her hand against his shaft. Rand arched his hips and spread his legs another few inches. He groaned softly when she slid her hand beneath his balls and squeezed.

"Oh, yes," she breathed against his lips. "Definitely hard. That's just the way I like it." Taking the dish from him, she set it on the table next to the champagne bottle. "And I know exactly what to do with it."

Ten

Rand fought to keep his eyes from rolling back in his head as Celina caressed his cock through his jeans. He should tell her to stop, that he wanted to wine and dine her before they made love. Right now, he couldn't get his tongue to work.

She straddled his lap, cradled his face in her hands, and kissed him long and deep. Rand clutched her ass and returned her passionate kisses, driving his tongue into her mouth to duel with hers. She nipped his tongue, then drew it farther into her mouth and suckled it.

Rand groaned.

Needing to touch her skin, he ran his hands underneath her dress. The feel of her bare buttocks didn't surprise him for he suspected Celina had worn a thong. Not finding a strap across her hips *did* surprise him.

"You aren't wearing panties," he whispered against her lips.

She kissed him. "No."

"Bra?"

She kissed him again. "No."

"My God," he breathed.

She tunneled her fingers into his hair. "Does that excite you, knowing I'm naked beneath my dress?"

"Excited doesn't come close to describing how I feel right now."

"Good." She released the top button of his shirt. "I want you *very* excited."

She unfastened the rest of his buttons and tugged the shirt from his pants. Spreading it wide, she caressed his chest and stomach. "You have such an incredible body."

She touched him with her palms, then only her fingertips. She brushed across his nipples, down the center of his chest, circled his navel. Rand loved having her hands on his body, almost as much as he loved having his hands on her. He squeezed her buttocks as he rocked his hips. Each movement slid his fly along her sleek flesh. He could feel the heat of her pussy through the denim.

Celina backed up on his thighs. She unbuckled his belt, slipped the button on his jeans from the hole. Looking into his eyes, she pulled down the zipper tab. Rand held his breath as he waited for her next move.

He released his breath in a *whoosh* when Celina pulled his rod through the opening of his jeans.

"I see I'm not the only one who decided underwear would be in the way." Gripping him firmly, she slid her hand up and down his shaft. "Now how handy is this? I could lift up and come down on top of your cock."

"Yeah, you could," he rasped.

She circled her thumb over the head, spreading his essence across the sensitive area. "Is that what you want?"

He looked into her beautiful blue eyes. "Yeah, that's what I want."

She rose to her knees. "Lift your hips."

Rand did as she said. Grasping his waistband, she tugged his jeans past his hips. She clutched his cock at the base and raised her dress. Rand received a glimpse of wet blond curls before she impaled herself.

"Oh, *fuck!*" Rand hissed.

"Mmm, yes. That's what I intend to do."

Celina dug her fingernails into Rand's shoulders. Closing her eyes, she threw back her head and began to ride him.

The feeling of fullness. The glide of his hard flesh into her slick pussy. The slide of his rough palms across her buttocks. Each sensation heated her blood.

"God, you're incredible." Cradling her neck, he pulled her forward and kissed her. He slid his tongue across her lips, then dove inside.

His hungry kisses and raspy words spurred her to move faster. Rand arched his hips and drove his shaft farther inside her. She whimpered. She could come soon, but didn't want to. Not yet. She didn't want this to be over.

"Damn, your pussy is wet." He nipped the side of her neck, tugged on her earlobe with his teeth. "And tight. My cock fits inside you perfectly."

She couldn't stop the orgasm. It started in her toes and spread throughout her body. Celina wrapped her arms around Rand's neck and laid her head on his shoulder while she rode out the waves of pleasure.

He continued to grip her buttocks and thrust inside her. "I love to feel you come," he whispered in her ear.

His warm breath sent goose bumps scattering over her

skin. Celina bit her bottom lip to keep from crying out when a second climax raced through her, almost as powerful as the first one.

"Yeah," Rand rasped. "Oh, *yeah!*"

He released a guttural growl and held her tightly to his chest. Celina could feel the pulsations of his cock as he came. She'd never noticed that with another man.

Two orgasms left her weak. Celina sighed softly and snuggled more firmly against Rand. She knew she had to get up, but she didn't want to. She wanted to stay right here in his arms for the rest of the night.

He kissed the side of her neck. "Hey."

"Mmm."

"You're leaking."

Celina burst into laughter. She lifted her head so she could look into Rand's face. His eyes twinkled with amusement. "How romantic."

"Well, you are." The laughter faded from his eyes, and they turned tender. He touched her face, his fingertips skating over her cheek, her lips. "That was . . . I don't know what word to use."

"Amazing. Earth-shattering. Mind-boggling."

"Any of those would work."

He touched her gently, almost reverently, his fingers traveling across her jaw and down her neck. He cradled one breast through her dress and brushed his thumb across the nipple. His delicate touch brought a lump to her throat. She already felt so much more for Rand than she should.

I can't fall in love with him. It's just sex. That's all it can be.

A loud rumble came from her stomach. Rand chuckled. "Sounds like I'd better feed you."

"You did invite me here for dinner."

"*I'm* not the one who started feeling around and distracting me."

"You shouldn't be so handsome and sexy."

A cocky grin turned up his lips. "Handsome and sexy both? Damn, you're lucky."

"Yes, I am." She lifted his hand from her breast and kissed his palm. "But enough of this fooling around. I'm hungry."

"Hold on to me."

Celina wrapped her arms around his neck again and pressed her knees against his hips. Rand rose, shifted her in his arms, and started walking. She assumed he headed for the bathroom.

She gazed around the masculine bedroom as Rand carried her through it. A queen-size bed occupied one wall, a dresser and closet another. Several seascapes hung on the walls—some photographs, some paintings.

Her visual tour was cut short when he stepped into the bathroom. "Grab that towel off the hanger. I don't want you to sit on the cold counter."

"My butt appreciates that."

He set her down next to the sink, then slowly withdrew from her. Celina felt a rush of warm liquid flow from her sheath. "You weren't kidding about me leaking."

"Told you so." His jeans had slipped almost to his knees. He hitched them back up to his waist, his soft rod hanging outside the opening. Reaching into the cabinet next to the sink, he withdrew two washcloths. "I'll get cleaned up, then give you some privacy."

She watched him cleanse his cock and tuck it back into his jeans. When he started to button his shirt, she touched his hand. "Leave your shirt open."

One corner of his mouth quirked. "You like looking at a hairy chest?"

"Mmm, yes."

"Then I'll leave it open." He tilted up her chin with one finger and kissed her softly. "I'll get dinner ready for us. Take your time."

Rand sensed Celina's presence before he saw her. His heart beat faster at the thought of seeing her again. He turned. She stood in the doorway to his bedroom, the candlelight illuminating her skin and hair.

God, you're lovely.

She stepped into the room. He pulled one chair out from the table. "Sit down."

Once Celina sat, Rand leaned over and gently kissed her shoulder. She smiled at him and caressed his cheek. "You like kissing."

"I got the feeling by how many times you've kissed me that you like it too."

"I do. Very much."

Her answer earned her another kiss, this time on her lips, before he rounded the table to take his own seat. "Henri outdid himself. I told him to make something special, something he didn't normally prepare for the passengers."

"It smells wonderful." Celina picked up her fork. "Is this beef or pork?"

"Pork tenderloin. It has some kind of mushroom sauce over it. Henri told me the name, but I don't remember what he said. I'm more interested in the taste than the name."

She chewed her bite of meat and sighed with pleasure. "The taste is wonderful. I'd like to take Henri home with me."

"Sorry. He stays with me." Rand poured each of them a glass of Cabernet. "It's taken me several years, but I have the perfect crew now. I don't want to lose any of them."

"How long have you owned the ship?"

"Eight years. I bought it when I was twenty-seven."

Celina picked up her wineglass and held it in both hands. "Tell me about the fantasies."

Other women had asked him about the fantasies. He'd never admitted anything to them. He sipped his wine while deciding how much to tell Celina.

"They aren't fantasies or dreams, are they?" she asked. "Everything actually happens."

"What makes you think so?"

She set down her glass and leaned forward, resting her forearms on the table. "Because I thought I'd dreamed about you last night. We were on a pirate ship and you took me against a wooden post. I had a huge splinter in my back this morning."

He'd had no idea she'd been hurt. None of his passengers had ever been hurt in one of the fantasies. "Are you okay? Do you need someone to look at your back? I don't have a doctor on board, but my entire crew has first-aid training."

"I'm fine. Jasmine took care of me." Picking up her fork again, she speared a piece of buttered asparagus. "Both Jasmine and Elayne have had similar experiences. We all tried to pass them off as coincidences. But they aren't, are they?"

To stall before he answered her, Rand took a bite of his potatoes. He didn't know how to explain the fantasies to Celina. He couldn't explain something he didn't understand himself.

"Rand?"

He wiped his mouth with his napkin and looked at Celina.

"We've shared something very special. At least, it's been special to me."

He wouldn't lie to her, not about the way she made him feel. "To me too."

"Then tell me the truth. Please."

Rand set his wineglass back on the table. "Henri will shoot me if we don't eat his special meal."

"You're avoiding my questions."

"You got it."

Celina frowned, then picked up her fork. "I don't give up when I want something, Rand."

"Yeah, I got that impression about you. We have that in common."

She took several bites of her meal in silence. Her silence didn't fool Rand. He had no doubt Celina's questions would start up again once she'd eaten.

She made small talk with him throughout the meal, but Rand knew that didn't mean she'd given up. He braced himself when she laid her fork on her empty plate. She didn't say a word, but her intense look clearly said she wanted answers.

"How about dessert? Henri made a chocolate cake that has—"

"I don't care what it has, Rand."

"And here I thought no woman could resist chocolate."

She didn't laugh at his joke. Blowing out a breath, Rand tossed his napkin on his empty plate. "What do you want to know?"

"Were you and I actually on a pirate ship last night?"

He nodded. "We were."

"How?"

"Because it's what you wanted."

"I don't understand."

"I told you that once we passed into the Bermuda Triangle your fantasies could come true."

"But *how?*"

Picking up the bottle of Cabernet, Rand splashed more of the red wine into their glasses. "I don't know how."

"You don't know how." Her tone clearly said she didn't believe him. "Your passengers have fantasies that come true on your ship, and you don't know how that happens."

"No."

"That doesn't make any sense."

Rand picked up his wineglass and leaned back in his chair. "I bought the yacht eight years ago. I didn't notice anything on the first few voyages, but I took a different course back then. Once I changed the course to go through the Triangle, the fantasies started coming true. I know, because I was featured in several of them."

"By female passengers, of course."

"And some male ones."

Celina's eyebrows rose. "You've been with men?"

"A few."

"Did you like it?"

"It was . . . different." He swirled the wine in his glass and took a sip. "It took me several voyages to figure out exactly what was happening and how to control it. I'm no longer part of a passenger's fantasy unless I choose to be." He grinned. "I don't choose to be in male fantasies. I like women much better."

"You were in my fantasy because it's what you wanted?"

He nodded. "I wanted you as soon as I saw you on the dock. I still want you."

"But how did you know about my fantasy? How did you know I imagined you as a pirate?"

"I just *know*. The ship makes sure I know."

"The ship can't talk to you."

Rand leaned forward. He wanted to look directly into her eyes when he spoke next so she'd know he told the truth. "I can't explain it, Celina. It's . . . a feeling, an intuition. I can . . . sense the fantasies. The ship changes to accommodate the fantasies, like she did when you imagined us on a pirate ship."

"It's an object. It can't change on a whim."

"She changes to satisfy my passengers' fantasies."

Celina tilted her head and gave him a slight smile. "You called your ship a 'she.'"

"A ship is always female."

She rubbed her forehead, as if she were trying to clear her mind to be able to take in what he said. Rand understood that. It had taken him months to be able to accept the yacht's magic.

"Does your crew know about the fantasies too?"

"Yes. They're also included in the fantasies, if that's what the passengers want."

"Like Jonathan and Elayne."

"Yes."

Celina picked up her wine and took a long sip. "This is a lot to take in."

"Yeah, it is. I wouldn't blame you at all if you decided I'm a nut and left without a backward glance."

She smiled. "I don't think you're a nut, and I have no intention of leaving."

"I'm glad. I can't eat all that chocolate cake by myself."

Celina chuckled before sipping her wine again. "One more question."

"Shoot."

"What about *your* fantasies? Do they come true?"

"I don't have fantasies. Real life is enough for me."

Propping her elbows on the table, she folded her hands beneath her chin. "You've never had a sexual fantasy?"

He shrugged. "I suppose I've had one or two, in the past. I haven't had one in a long time. I've experienced just about everything a person can sexually since I've owned the yacht."

"If you had a sexual fantasy, what would it be?"

"To have you wearing nothing but one of my shirts."

"That could easily be arranged," she said with a wicked smile. "But what else would you want? If you could have anything sexual you wanted, what would it be?"

Rand considered her question while he drained his wineglass. "I'm the captain. I'm always in charge. It would be nice to let someone else take over sometimes."

"You mean like I did a little while ago on the couch?"

He grinned. "That was fun. But it would have to be more than that."

"Like what?"

Like being tied to my bed and letting a woman have complete control over me. "I don't know. Let me think about it."

"You're avoiding my questions again."

"I'm not. I'll tell you a fantasy when I think of one."

Celina picked up her wineglass. "Maybe you won't have to tell me. Maybe your ship will."

Rand laughed. "This is my ship. She wouldn't ever betray my secrets."

Eleven

Consciousness slowly seeped into Rand's brain. Not ready to wake up yet, he turned his head on the pillow, determined to go back to sleep. Instead of sleep claiming him again, memories of making love with Celina flooded his mind. He smiled. Having her on his couch last night had been hot, but nowhere near as hot as what he'd experienced after they went to bed.

In the eight years that he'd owned the ship, he'd never had a woman spend the night in his suite. Inviting Celina to spend the night with him had seemed like the most natural thing in the world.

"I hope that smile means you're thinking of me."

Rand pried his eyes open. Celina stood at the foot of his bed, one knee resting on the bedspread. He sucked in a sharp breath. She wore the tan shirt he'd worn last night.

His cock roared to life.

"Like it?" She released the top button. "I had to roll up the sleeves since they're so long on me, but I think it's a pretty good fit, don't you?"

"I think . . ." His voice sounded like a frog's. He cleared his throat and tried again. "I think you look incredible."

"Good enough to eat?"

She plucked at her nipples until he could clearly see them through his shirt. His mouth watered. He'd sucked them last night until she came. He longed to do the same thing again. "Come here, Celina."

She shook her head. "Not yet. I think I need to drive you a little bit crazy first."

"You've already driven me crazy."

"Oh, not nearly enough."

She released another button and pulled the shirt open to expose the inner curves of her breasts. "Wanna see more?"

"You know I do."

"How much more?"

"I want you naked."

"You said last night you wanted to see me in your shirt."

"I've seen you. You're gorgeous in it. Now I want you *out* of it."

When she made no move to obey him, simply stood there with a siren's smile on her lips, Rand reached for her. Or he tried to reach for her. He silently told his arm to move, but it remained next to his head on the pillow. Frowning, Rand turned his head and looked at his right hand. He wiggled his fingers, but couldn't lift his hand.

"What the hell?"

He turned his head and looked at his left hand. The same thing happened with it. He freely wiggled his fingers, but couldn't lift his arm. He tried to sit up. That didn't work either.

He could lift his hips, but his back and shoulders stayed on the bed.

"Celina, what the hell is happening?"

"What's wrong?"

"I can't move my arms. I can't sit up." He tried again, straining with all his might to move his arms. They remained next to his head. "Shit!"

Instead of being concerned, as Rand was sure she would be, Celina continued to beam that siren's smile at him. "How convenient for me. If you can't move, then I can do whatever I want to you."

Rand tried to lift his legs. They didn't cooperate either. He could lift his hips and head, but that was all. Sweat broke out over his skin as a cold fear replaced the desire he'd felt moments ago. "Celina, *do* something!"

"I plan to." Grabbing the covers, she whipped them off his body to the end of the bed. She sighed heavily when she looked at his soft cock. "And here I thought you'd be ready for me."

"Celina, I can't *move*! Don't you understand that? Call Jonathan, or Andrew, or Sergey. Call *someone*!"

"I have no intention of calling anyone. I have you right where I want you."

He couldn't believe she was so calm about this. "Celina—"

"Do you know what I did last night before I fell asleep?"

Rand closed his eyes tightly. Maybe he was still asleep and dreaming this whole thing. He didn't understand how she could ask him about last night when he couldn't move *now*. "Celina, please call one of my crew."

"I had a little talk with *Fantasy,*" she said, as if she hadn't heard his plea.

He opened his eyes again and stared at her. "You did what?"

She crawled up on the bed next to his feet. "After we made love, I lay in your arms until you fell asleep. Then I got up and went in the living room. I felt silly at first and wasn't sure what to do, but decided to go for it. I said out loud that if you had any kind of sexual fantasy that your ship knew about, I wanted her to make it come true."

"I've never had a fantasy about being helpless!"

She tilted her head and that siren's smile touched her lips again. "Haven't you?"

Rand opened his mouth to deny her question, but stopped before uttering a word. He flashed back to last night at dinner when he'd thought about his own sexual fantasies.

Like being tied to my bed and letting a woman have complete control over me.

Surely his own ship wouldn't turn against him.

She moved between his legs, pushing them farther apart with her knees. He couldn't move, but she apparently had no problem arranging him however she wanted him. Still on her knees, she slowly ran her hands up and down his legs. "Since you're on your bed and can't move, I have to assume this is what you want. Am I right?"

Each pass of her hands brought them closer to his groin. His shaft responded to her touch, growing firmer every time she got near it.

"I love to watch your cock get hard."

Despite his helpless situation, her words and the hot look in her eyes made his rod come to full attention. Celina smiled. "Very nice. That's what I like to see."

She continued to caress his legs from knees to groin, coming within an inch but not touching him intimately. Rand arched his hips, trying to get closer to her hands.

"I think the male body is beautiful." Her gaze followed her hands . . . up, down, up, down. "The wide shoulders, broad chest, narrow waist. Seeing a man's butt in a tight pair of jeans . . . It's delicious."

Her fingertips passed close enough to ruffle the hair at the base of his shaft. "Even when your cock is soft, it's beautiful. But when it's hard, like this . . ." She inhaled deeply, her nipples pressing against his shirt, and looked into his eyes. "You're magnificent."

Rand groaned. "Celina, touch me."

"Do you have any idea how much I want you? How much I've wanted you since you came to my cabin and introduced yourself? I've never felt this way about a man. I've never felt so . . . hot."

Sweat beaded his forehead, but not from fear this time. "You're killing me."

"I've had more orgasms with you than probably all my other lovers put together. Not that there have been that many before you. I can count them on two hands and have fingers left over."

Her palms brushed up and down his thighs again. "I like touching you like this."

"I like it too, but you could move your hands in a few inches."

"I could, but I'm not ready to." She ran her hands past his groin and over his stomach. "You feel so good."

Rand sucked in his stomach and closed his eyes. He felt like he could come simply from listening to her talk.

He released a guttural cry when she licked him from his balls to the head.

"You smell good too." She nuzzled his balls before licking him again. "Like you and me and sex."

Rand clenched his fists and arched his hips when she took him in her warm mouth. Her lips slowly sank down his length, then traveled back to the head. Her tongue circled the tip, tickled the slit.

"You know what?" she asked.

He opened his eyes. "What?"

"You taste as good as you smell."

She took him deep in her mouth once more. Rand sank back into the pillow and closed his eyes again. The pleasure from her mouth on him traveled through his entire body. He grew warmer. His heart beat heavily. His breathing deepened. The orgasm built slowly, steadily. A little longer. He only needed a little longer . . .

Rand's eyes popped open when he lost the warmth of her mouth on his flesh. "Wha—" Lifting his head, he frowned when he saw the smirk on her lips. "You *are* trying to kill me."

"Not at all. I'm trying to make you as hot as possible."

"As hot as possible." A strangled laugh bubbled from his throat. "I don't know whether to spank you or kiss you."

"In your current position, you can't do either."

"I won't be stuck here forever."

"But you are now." She leaned forward, resting her hands on the bed next to his chest. "You're completely at my mercy."

Rand hissed in a sharp breath when Celina brushed his cock with her bare pussy. "You're cruel, Celina."

"No, I'm not. I'm going to make you feel really, really good."

She kissed him softly, sweetly. Her tongue swiped across his mouth, retreated, then licked him again.

She kissed like a temptress.

He drove his tongue into her mouth and returned her kisses. She touched his face, shoulders, chest. Rand tried to lift his arms so he could touch her too. They still wouldn't budge. He growled in frustration.

"Damn it, I want to hold you."

"Isn't it enough that I can hold you?"

"You know it isn't." He looked from her eyes, to her lips, to her hair, and back to her eyes. "I want to touch you."

She caressed his cheek with her fingertips. "Okay."

Rand took a breath before trying to lift his arms. He was able to move with no problem, as if Celina's simple "okay" had released him. A moment later, he pressed Celina to her back and leaned over her, holding her hands next to her head.

"You didn't play fair at all."

She ran her tongue across her bottom lip. "I know."

"You do realize I can do the same thing to you."

"You could." She lifted her chin and grinned impishly. "But you won't."

"And how do you know that?"

"Because I know you wouldn't hurt me."

"Hurt you, no. Tease you the same way you did me? You bet."

"Rand—"

He cut off her words with a kiss. Celina relaxed into the pillow and sighed into his mouth. She parted her lips and accepted the play of his tongue. Rand's kisses were the most passionate she'd ever experienced. One touch of his lips against hers, and her pussy wept.

She arched into his touch when he cradled her breast. His thumb circled her nipple over and over. Each pass sent a zing of sensation directly to her clit. "Rand," she whispered.

"Like this?"

"You know I do."

He kissed her on the sensitive spot beneath her ear. "Want more?"

A shiver raced down Celina's spine. "Yes."

He stretched her arms over her head and clasped her wrists in one hand. He brushed her nipples with the pads of his fingers before reaching for her shirt buttons. He released them one by one, alternating between watching his fingers and looking into her eyes. After he released the last button, he spread the shirt wide and gazed at her body.

"God, you're gorgeous."

He caressed both bare breasts, then slid his hand down her stomach to between her thighs. Celina's breath hitched when he touched her clit. He circled it the way he had her nipples.

"Isn't it better when I can touch you too?"

"Yes." She spread her legs wide to give him more room to touch her. "Oh, yes."

He rubbed her clit harder, faster. "Are you close?"

"I'm . . . Oh! There, Rand. Yes, right there."

She pumped her hips in time to his stroking. He still held her hands so she couldn't move. All she could do was feel . . . his touch, his kisses, his hard cock against her hip.

"That's the way," he growled. "Move for me. Come for me."

Her building orgasm fizzled when Rand took his hand away from her. Celina blinked, unsure what had just happened. "Why did you stop?"

"I have to get to work. I should've been on duty half an hour ago."

She watched, disbelieving, as Rand rolled away from

her. She waited three seconds before she grabbed his arm and pulled him back on the bed. He was laughing when she pounced on him.

"Oh, you are in so much trouble."

"Hey, you left me hanging too."

"So you decided revenge was necessary?"

"Do you have any idea how hard it was for me to move away from you when you were so close to coming?"

"I know the feeling." She tunneled her fingers into his hair. "Playtime is over. Don't you agree?"

All traces of laughter disappeared from his eyes. He wrapped his arms around her and pulled her closer to him. "Yeah. I agree."

One kiss led to two, then three. Celina went willingly when Rand lowered her to her back. He slid his legs between hers, his hands beneath her buttocks. He entered her with one long glide.

Rand kissed Celina over and over as he moved inside her. She took him so perfectly, lifting her hips to meet each thrust. He tried to be slow, tried to draw out their lovemaking to satisfy her. Their earlier love play made that impossible. Clutching her ass, he thrust deeper, faster. She wrapped her legs around his waist, her heels pressing into his buttocks.

"Faster, Rand. Faster."

He obeyed her, pounding his cock into her pussy. Celina threw back her head and squeezed her eyes shut. He could feel the contractions deep inside her milking his cock. Her release triggered his own. Burying his face against her neck, he held her tightly while his orgasm raced through his body.

Rand lost all track of time. He didn't know if he lay on top of Celina for mere moments or long minutes. When she took a deep breath, he reluctantly lifted his head. Her slumberous eyes and soft smile clearly showed her satisfaction. Unable to resist those luscious pink lips, he kissed her deeply before rolling to his back, bringing her with him to lie by his side.

Entwining their fingers, he lifted her hand to his mouth and kissed the back. "That was the most intense sex I've ever had."

"For me too."

"I'd love to stay right here with you all day."

"Sounds perfect." She tilted her head on his shoulder and smiled at him. "Shall I call for room service? I'm hungry."

Rand chuckled. "Worked up an appetite, did you?"

"Mmm-hmm."

"As tempting as the thought is to squeeze orange juice on your body and lick it off, I need to get to work. I have a ship to run."

"You have a wonderful crew. You told me it's the best one you've ever had. They can run it."

"Yes, they can, but I want to be fair. I need to relieve the night crew."

She sighed heavily. "I suppose."

Rand tilted up her chin and kissed her. "Have dinner with me again tonight. I'll have Henri prepare something even better than the pork."

"I don't think that's possible."

"He likes a challenge."

Celina ran her hand over his chest and stomach. "I should have dinner with Jasmine and Elayne. I haven't spent very much time with them. Jasmine paid for this cruise so the three of us could honor our friend."

"Your friend?"

She nodded. "Carol St. Claire. We went to college with her. The four of us were inseparable. Carol . . ." Her voice caught and tears filled her eyes. "Carol was killed last month."

Sympathy welled up in Rand's heart. He tightened his arms around Celina. "I'm sorry," he whispered.

"She died doing what she loved. I'm glad about that."

He touched her hair, caressing the soft strands. "I'll miss you at dinner, but I understand you wanting to be with your friends."

"I could come back here after dinner."

He kissed her once more. "It's a date."

Twelve

Celina turned from the magnificent view of the sea when she saw movement out of the corner of her eye. Elayne walked toward her, looking very sexy in a clingy dark green dress that flowed over her curves. With Elayne's voluptuous body and beautiful face, Celina knew why men's tongues hung out when Elayne walked by.

She smiled when her friend joined her at the railing. "Hi."

"Hi." Elayne gave Celina a quick hug. "Sorry I wasn't here sooner. I was with Jonathan."

"I figured that." She gestured toward a shaded table. Three glasses of iced tea and a plate of petit fours sat in the middle beneath the umbrella. "So everything with him is still good?"

Elayne sat in one of the chairs at the table. She took a long sip from her glass of tea before answering. "Everything sucks."

Her friend's comment surprised Celina. She'd thought Elayne and Jonathan were getting along great. "Why? You two have been practically inseparable since we've been on board."

"I know. That's the problem."

"In English, Elayne."

"I need chocolate first." She peeled back the plastic wrap on the petit fours and picked up one with dark and white chocolate drizzled over the top. She popped the treat in her mouth and chewed slowly. Celina sipped her own tea while waiting for her friend to speak.

"He said he wants to see me after the cruise."

Celina chose a small cake for herself. "You must have made quite an impression on him."

"I guess." She picked up another treat but laid it back on the plate before eating it. "He's a great guy. I've had an incredible time with him. The sex has been the hottest I've ever had."

"I hear a 'but' after that sentence."

"I live in St. Louis, Cee. That isn't exactly next door to Florida."

"Did you tell him where you live?"

Elayne nodded. "He said we'd work it out. You can't work out a thousand miles." She drew a circle with her glass in the condensation on the table. "I don't even know if I *want* to work it out."

"You just said he's a great guy. Why wouldn't you want to keep seeing him?"

"Celina, you know how awful my two marriages were. I don't want to go through that again."

"Not every man is a jerk."

"You couldn't prove that by me."

Celina hated for Elayne to give up on Jonathan without allowing him the chance to prove he wasn't a jerk. "How do you feel about him? And be honest."

Elayne looked away while she sipped her tea. Celina picked

up a second small cake and nibbled it. She didn't want to push her friend to talk, but she wanted to help if she could.

"I like him. He's not only an amazing lover, but he has a great sense of humor. He's fun and charming and handsome."

"You haven't said one negative thing about him."

"I haven't *found* one negative thing about him. But I will. Give me enough time, and I'll *always* find something negative about a guy."

"That's because you look for the negatives, Elayne. Men aren't perfect. None of us is perfect. If you care about Jonathan, don't you think it's worth the chance to find out if you two can have a future together?"

Elayne looked out over the water. "He doesn't know everything about me."

"Of course he doesn't. You haven't had the chance to learn about each other yet. You haven't had enough time."

"No, I mean . . ." She blew out a heavy breath. "I didn't tell him about . . . them."

"Oh." Celina didn't have to ask the identity of "them." She knew exactly who Elayne meant. "Don't you think you should?"

"There's no reason to if I'm never going to see him again."

"You should be honest with him, Elayne."

"I suppose."

"What if—"

Celina stopped when she saw Jasmine walking toward them. She immediately knew something was wrong. Jasmine usually moved with her head up, her hips swaying, breasts thrust out so men would notice them. Now, her friend walked with her head lowered, her shoulders slumped. She wore dark sunglasses, as if she were trying to hide from someone.

Or cover up any evidence of crying.

"Hey," Jasmine said, sliding into the third chair at the table.

Her lower lip trembled. She quickly picked up her glass of tea and sipped it, but that didn't hide her obvious distress from Celina. "You okay, Jaz?"

"Oh, I'm just peachy."

"What's wrong?" Elayne asked.

"I did something incredibly stupid."

Celina and Elayne looked at each other. Celina knew of several stupid things Jasmine had done in her life. Elayne's raised eyebrow proved she was thinking along similar lines about their friend. That hadn't stopped Jasmine from continuing to repeat her mistakes. "What did you do?"

Her lip trembled again, and tears seeped from beneath her sunglasses. "I fell in love."

Celina exchanged another look with Elayne. She never thought she'd hear those words come from Jasmine's lips. Her friend had sworn men were for a good time, that she had too much fun being single to ever tie herself to one guy. "I assume you're talking about Chase."

Jasmine nodded. "He's such a great guy. Life has kicked him in the teeth way too many times. I want to help him. I could give him so much if he'd just let me."

Elayne pressed a paper napkin into Jasmine's hand. "Are you sure he won't let you?"

Jasmine pushed up her sunglasses and wiped the tears from her cheeks. Sympathy tugged at Celina's heart when she saw her friend's red eyes. Jasmine had obviously been crying for quite a while. "I told him how I feel about him. He said I couldn't love him, that I only felt sorry for him."

"Why would he say that?" Celina asked.

"Because he's had a lot of medical problems. Some of them almost killed him." Fresh tears filled Jasmine's eyes. "He pushed me away. He literally pushed me away from him."

Elayne reached over and squeezed Jasmine's hand. "I'm sorry, Jaz."

"Yeah, me too." She blew her nose and wadded her napkin into a ball. "But you know what? I'm not going to think about Chase anymore. If he doesn't want me, it's his loss. It's our last night on the ship. I'm going to have dinner with my two best friends, then find me a hunk to spend the night with. Barret has been after me since I first met him."

"Not Barret, Jaz." Celina couldn't stand the thought of her friend being with that slime. "He's a user."

"He's hot, and that's what I need tonight. You have Rand. Elayne has Jonathan. Ian has been drooling on Glynnis the last two days. Lamar and Tony are gay. Ferris is with Doretta. Unless I hit on one of the crew, Barret is it."

"Then hit on one of the crew. I'd rather see you with Samir or Sergey than Barret."

"We don't always get what we want, do we, Cee?" Jasmine pushed back her chair and rose. "I'm going to take a hot shower and put on my sexiest dress. I'll see you two at dinner."

Celina sighed as she watched Jasmine walk away. "I'm worried about her."

"Yeah, me too, but Jasmine has always been able to take care of herself."

"I'm afraid she won't this time. She's hurting. Getting involved with Barret won't help."

Elayne chuckled. "Ironic, isn't it? Men have always chased Jasmine. Now that she's found one she cares about, he wants nothing to do with her."

"No, I don't think it's ironic." Celina looked back at Elayne. "I think it's very sad."

Rand's gaze strayed to Celina's empty chair. He didn't know how many times he'd looked at that chair during dinner, but each time he wished she were sitting in it instead of having dinner with her friends in Jasmine's cabin.

Picking up his wineglass, he leaned back in his chair and thought of the time he'd spent with Celina. He hadn't known she existed three days ago. Ever since he'd seen her walking up the gangplank, she'd fascinated him. He wasn't sure why. He'd met hundreds of women since he'd owned the yacht. He'd fucked dozens of them. The life he lived included exactly what he wanted . . . freedom, travel, great food, lots of sex. Most men would kill to have the position he held.

The empty feeling in his gut gnawed at him. He didn't understand why he suddenly felt as if something was missing in his life.

Or about to be missing.

He thought of Celina again . . . her smile, her laugh, the way she tilted her head when she listened to him. He thought of the way her hair had looked this morning, spread over his pillow. No woman had ever slept in his bed. He could easily imagine having her there every night, falling asleep with his arms wrapped around her.

He liked the way Celina made him feel. He'd never cared about spending more than a night or two with one woman. Happily-ever-after hadn't entered his mind.

He thought about it now.

He found himself wanting to be with Celina all the time. He knew little about her, yet he liked everything he did know.

She cared deeply about her friends. She was independent and successful at her job. She made him laugh. She was incredibly sexy. Whenever she left his side, a piece of his heart went with her.

He didn't want to say good-bye to her tomorrow.

"Yeah, with Jasmine," Barret said.

The mention of Celina's friend drew Rand's attention. Barret sat to his left, Ferris next to him. The passengers were assigned places at the first meal, but Rand relaxed the rules on the last night. With three women missing, he'd told his passengers to sit wherever they chose.

"I've wanted to sink into that pussy ever since I saw her," Barret said with a wicked grin.

Rand glanced at Chase, sitting next to Jonathan at the foot of the table. He wondered if Chase had heard Barret's boasting. Chase sat with his head lowered, his jaw clenched. Rand could almost feel the rage pouring off Chase. Rand wanted to feel sorry for Jonathan's friend but couldn't. If Chase wanted to be with Jasmine, he should tell her instead of letting her fall into another man's arms.

"She agreed to meet me at the hot tub at eleven," Barret told Ferris. "I can hardly wait to get my hands on those tits."

Rand blew out a disgusted breath. The man had absolutely no class. Rand tossed around words like "pussy" and "tits" in front of other men, but not in front of his female passengers. He strongly believed in courtesy to women. He believed in courtesy to every passenger, even the ones he'd like to throw overboard.

Rand looked back at Chase in time to see him roughly push back his chair and stand. He threw a look at Barret that could have knocked him through the wall before Chase turned and left the table.

"Chase!" Jonathan called out. Chase didn't stop. Throwing his napkin on the table, Jonathan hurried after his friend.

Rand made the decision in that moment that he would never allow Barret Ackerman on his ship again. He was about to call Barret aside and tell him that when Celina walked into the room.

The sight of her chased all other thoughts from his head. He stood. His gaze slowly traveled over her body as she walked toward him. Her nipples clearly showed through the white tank top she wore. He planned to spend the rest of the night licking and sucking those beautiful buds.

She smiled when she stepped up to him, but the smile didn't reach her eyes. Rand took her hand. "What's wrong?"

She glanced at Barret and gave a small shake of her head. He understood that she didn't want to talk in front of the other man. "Would you like to go somewhere private?"

"Please."

Slipping his arm around her waist, he led Celina away from the dining area and out on deck. He waited until they were completely alone before speaking. "Is this all right?"

She nodded. "It's fine."

Rand leaned against the railing and looped his arms loosely around her waist. "Talk to me."

"I'm worried about Jasmine. She made a date to see Barret later."

"Yeah, I know."

Her eyebrows furrowed. "You do?"

"He was bragging about it at dinner. He said he couldn't wait to get his hands on her tits."

"The jerk."

"I wanted to knock him through the wall. Uncouth bastard.

Why would Jasmine agree to see him? It's obvious he's nothing but an ass."

Celina laid her hands on his chest. "Because it's our last night out and she doesn't want to be alone."

"What about Chase?"

"He doesn't want her."

That statement was so ridiculous, Rand couldn't help laughing. "You can't believe that."

"That's what Jasmine told Elayne and me. She said he literally pushed her away from him."

"Celina, I watched Chase at dinner when Ackerman was shooting off his mouth. The man wanted to punch Barret into the middle of next week. Believe me, he cares."

"Then why doesn't he *tell* her? Words aren't that difficult. He only has to open his mouth and start talking."

"Talking about their feelings isn't easy for most men."

She toyed with the top button of his shirt, her gaze focused on her fingers. "Is it easy for you?"

"To talk about my feelings? I just told you how I feel about Barret."

She huffed out a breath and looked into his eyes. "That's not what I meant."

He liked teasing her, but he sensed she wanted honesty from him. He had a problem with that since he wasn't sure what to say to her. "I've enjoyed my time with you very much, Celina," he said, his voice gentle. "I'll be sorry to see it end."

"So will I." She released the button she'd been playing with. "We still have tonight."

"Do we, or do you need to see about Jasmine?"

"Elayne and I talked to her until we almost lost our voices. She's a big girl. She has to make her own mistakes. I can't stop that." Another button came loose. Rand swallowed when she slid her hand inside his shirt and thumbed his nipple. "I want to be with you tonight."

"I want that too." He cradled her buttocks and tugged her closer to his pelvis. "I had Henri prepare some chocolate-covered strawberries for you. They're in my suite."

Wrapping one hand around his neck, she drew him down for a deep kiss. "Then let's go to your suite."

Thirteen

Celina took one more look around the bathroom to make sure she hadn't forgotten anything. Satisfied that she hadn't left a bottle of shampoo in the shower, she returned to the bedroom to finish packing. She managed to fold one more blouse before she sighed heavily and sat on the bed. She wasn't ready to leave Rand.

He'd had several things to do to get the yacht ready for docking at noon. He'd walked her to her cabin this morning, kissed her sweetly, and said he'd see her before she left the ship.

Tears pricked her eyes. She had no right to expect anything more than what Rand had given her. She knew right from the start she'd have a limited amount of time with him. He hadn't promised her any more than great sex for the length of the cruise.

He'd certainly kept his word about that.

"Yoohoo," Elayne said, pushing the door open.

Celina quickly blinked back the tears. "Hey."

"Are you packed?"

"Just about." She stood and reached for the last blouse on her bed. "I brought way too many clothes."

"I did too, but I always pack too much when I go on a trip." She sat on the bed next to Celina's suitcase. "Need some help?"

"No, I'm good." She placed the blouse in the suitcase and closed the lid. "Where's Jasmine?"

"I stopped by her cabin, but she wasn't there. I don't know where she is."

"She knows we're about to dock, doesn't she?"

"I assume she does." Elayne reclined on the bed, resting on one elbow. "So, now what?"

Celina didn't understand what Elayne wanted to know. "Now what, what?"

"Rand."

"Oh." Pushing aside her suitcase, Celina sat on the bed next to Elayne. "We had a good time. Now it's over. I go back to Miami, and he chooses another woman on the next cruise to have sex with."

Elayne winced. "Sounds cold."

"But the truth. I slept with him knowing exactly where I stood. I was his current fling." She shrugged. "That's all I am to him."

"How do you feel about him?"

"It doesn't matter how I feel. He doesn't return my feelings." Celina chuckled without a trace of humor. "Pretty pathetic, huh? Talk about a cliché, falling for the captain."

"Have you told him?"

"No, and I don't plan to. We had a good time. That's all it was to him. I won't embarrass Rand by telling him I love him when I know he doesn't return my love."

"How do you know he doesn't?" Elayne reached over and squeezed Celina's hand. "You're a fantastic person. There's not one reason why he shouldn't love you."

"Except that he enjoys his bachelor life. Why shouldn't he? Beautiful women travel on his ship every week. He can have his pick of any of them."

"Did you ever consider maybe he's tired of that life? Maybe he's ready to settle down with one woman."

No, she'd never considered that. She couldn't picture Rand settling down with one woman . . . not as long as he sailed this yacht. "He has all my contact information. If he wants to find me, he can."

Jasmine came barreling into the room, putting an end to the conversation. Celina was glad about that. Any more talk of Rand, and she'd probably burst into tears.

"Sorry." Jasmine gave each of them a quick hug. "I wanted to say good-bye to Chase, but I couldn't find him."

"Are you okay with that?" Elayne asked.

"No, but I don't have any choice. He made it very clear that I don't fit in his world." Her eyes grew misty, and she cleared her throat. "Enough of that. No mushy stuff allowed. Carol would've wanted us to have a good time on this trip. We did that. We ate, drank, and fucked until we could barely walk."

"Carol would've been proud of us," Elayne said with a grin.

"Excuse me, ladies," Andrew said, knocking on the door. "We dock in ten minutes."

"Thank you, Andrew," Celina said. After he left, she looked at her friends again. "So, do we say good-bye now, or in the parking lot?"

"Here," Elayne said. "I don't want to blubber in front of a bunch of strangers."

Jasmine nodded. "Yeah. Here."

"Group hug." Celina drew both of her friends close to her. She couldn't stop the tears now since she had no idea how long it would be before she saw either friend again. With her in Florida, Elayne in Missouri, and Jasmine in Illinois, it wasn't possible to get together on Sunday for coffee.

Jasmine was the first to release the other two. "We all have great jobs that pay very well. There's no reason why we can't get together at least once a year, is there?"

Elayne wiped the tears from her cheeks. "No, there's no reason, as long as we plan ahead."

"Exactly. So let's make a pact right now." Jasmine held out her hand, palm down. "We'll get together every April from now on. It can be at one of our houses, another cruise, or a ski lodge in Switzerland. I don't care where, as long as we're together."

"Deal," Elayne said, laying her hand on top of Jasmine's.

"Deal." Celina added her hand to the stack. "Every April, no matter what."

Celina gave each friend one more hug before they left her room. She glanced around the cabin once more. Her gaze settled on the bed. She remembered Rand there with her, holding her, kissing her, sliding into her body. The sex had been incredible, yet she'd also enjoyed simply talking to him. She'd love to have more time with him to get to know the man instead of the sea captain.

Blinking back fresh tears, Celina picked up her suitcase and purse, and left the cabin.

Jonathan crossed his arms over his chest and leaned back against the counter. "You're hiding," he said to Rand.

That was true, but Rand wouldn't admit it to his friend. "I'm docking the ship."

"The ship is docked. Now you're hiding."

"Isn't that what we're all doing?" Chase asked from his stool in the corner.

Rand pretended he was engrossed with his checkoff list, even though he'd had it memorized for years. "I said good-bye to Celina this morning. I have no reason to talk to her again."

Jonathan grabbed the clipboard from Rand's hand and slammed it down on the counter. "Don't be an idiot. Go after her. Don't let her get away from you."

"You're a fine one to talk! You're crazy about Elayne. I don't see you running after her."

"She doesn't want me, man. Trust me, I'd be with her if she'd have me." He glanced from Rand to Chase. "Both of you are nuts to let your ladies get away."

"I have my reasons," Chase said, lifting his chin.

"And they're stupid. You don't throw away love, Chase. You may never meet another woman who cares about you as much as Jasmine." He faced Rand and pointed one finger in his face. "And *you*. You told me yourself you have stronger feelings for Celina than you've ever had for a woman. Do you think that'll get dropped in your lap again? Go after her."

"Jon, she never said anything to me about our affair being anything more than that. If she cared about me as more than a bed partner, wouldn't she have told me?"

"Why should she? *You* didn't tell *her*."

No, he hadn't told Celina how he felt about her. He hadn't told her he'd imagined her in his bed every night, and of building a life with her. Settling down with one woman had never been on his to-do list. She'd put it at the top.

"Go," Jonathan said. "Now. Before she gets off the yacht."

Fear kept him rooted to the spot. She might laugh in his face, or tell him they'd had great sex, but that was all. She might tell him she didn't love him. "I don't know what to say to her."

Jonathan clapped Rand on the shoulder. "The truth, Rand. Just tell her the truth."

The truth. Rand thought about that as he headed for Celina's cabin. His heart pounded harder with each step he took. He didn't know what to say to her. He'd never been in love, so couldn't say for sure the feelings blossoming inside could be called love.

He wanted the chance to find out.

Celina's cabin door was open. He stepped inside the room, and immediately knew she wasn't there. The room felt cold, without the life and warmth it contained when Celina was near.

No problem. He'd catch her before she left the ship.

He ran into Boyd in the main salon. "Have you seen Ms. Tate?"

"Yes, sir. She left the ship about ten minutes ago."

Rand's positive attitude deflated. Ten minutes gave her a healthy head start. "Okay, thanks."

He hurried toward the exit and down the gangplank. He glanced at every person he passed while jogging across the dock and through the terminal, looking for Celina's beautiful blond hair.

Nothing.

Refusing to give up, Rand dashed out the terminal exit doors toward the parking lot. Maybe she stopped to talk to one of her friends. That would give him more time to find her. If he didn't . . .

If he didn't find her here, he'd head for Miami, where she lived. He refused to give up until he talked to her.

A flash of sunlight shining on blond hair caught his attention. Celina walked through rows of cars in the parking lot, less than two hundred feet away from him. "Celina," he whispered. Then, breaking into a run, he called out to her. "Celina!"

Whirling around, she lifted her hand to shade her eyes. Rand slowed to a jog, then a fast walk as he drew nearer to her. His heart thumped heavily in his chest . . . not from his run, but from the sight of her.

In that moment, he knew without a doubt that he loved her.

He stopped inches from her and stared into her face. Not sure what to say, he decided the direct approach would be best. He cradled her face in his hands and kissed her.

She melted into his kiss, parting her lips for the thrust of his tongue. He felt her hands at his waist, clutching his shirt. She kissed him so passionately, it surprised him when she pulled away.

"Don't."

She buried her face against his shoulder. Rand slipped his hand beneath her chin and lifted so he could look at her. Tears glistened in her eyes. "Why are you crying?"

"Don't do this to me. I've already said good-bye to you. Don't make me go through that again."

He hadn't known what to say to her, how to express the way he felt about her. Now, standing here with Celina in his arms, the words came easily. "I'm not here to say good-bye. I'm here to tell you I love you."

She blinked. Her mouth dropped open. "What?"

"I love you. I'd like to spend the next forty to fifty years proving it to you."

"But-but I thought I was just your cruise fling."

"You were, at first. I'll admit that. I saw you walking up the gangplank and thought of how to seduce you. I didn't care who you were or anything about you. All I saw was my next lay. Pretty shallow, huh?" He ran his thumbs over her cheeks, wiping away her tears. "You fascinate me, Celina. I want to spend time with you, get to know you better. I'm hoping, someday, you'll learn to love me too."

Fresh tears pooled in her eyes as she touched his lips. "I don't have to learn to love you. I already do."

He kissed her again, softly. Only the sound of voices nearby made him end the kiss long before he wanted to. "Come back to the ship with me. I have some things I have to finish up, then we can go to my house."

"Rand, I don't . . ." She sighed softly. "You told me you've never been in love. Are you sure of your feelings?"

He looked into her eyes, those beautiful blue eyes that stole his breath each time she gazed at him. He'd never been so sure of anything in his life. "Oh, yeah," he whispered. "I know *exactly* how I feel."

He kissed her once more before taking her hands. "We have a lot to talk about . . . my job, your job, where we live. It's a long list. But we can work out everything. I know we can." Lifting her hands to his mouth, he kissed each palm. "I'm not as good a cook as Henri, but I grill a mean steak. We'll eat, share a bottle of wine, talk. Then we'll make love all night long. How does that sound?"

Celina smiled. "It sounds perfect."

One

Join me to remember our good friend,
Carol St. Claire.
Carol died while celebrating life.
She would not want us to grieve, but to celebrate life also.
Meet me on the S.S. **Fantasy** *on Thursday, April 10,*
Port of The Everglades, Fort Lauderdale.
Jasmine Britt

Elayne Wyatt stuffed the invitation back into her purse. She'd already read it half a dozen times, yet had felt the need to read it once again. Carol was dead. She'd been so full of life, so ready to take on the world. If given a few more years to live, she might have conquered it.

What a waste for someone to die so young.

Losing someone she cared about had Elayne thinking about her own life and where she wanted it to go. She had a wonderful job she loved, a house that would be all hers in only five more years, plenty of money in the bank. All she needed was a man who loved her . . .

No! she told herself sternly. *You've been down that road twice. Not again.*

A man was nothing but trouble. Elayne had learned that after her second heartbreak. Going out to dinner, to movies, having sex . . . all that was great. The happily-ever-after fairy tale didn't exist. Not in her world.

She planned to have fun on this cruise. She and Celina and Jasmine would mourn the loss of their friend, but Carol wouldn't want them to grieve. That had never been her way. "Have fun to the last second of your life" had been Carol's motto.

It sounded like a good idea to Elayne.

Gathering up her purse and car keys, she popped the trunk so she could get her suitcases. She always packed more than she needed to, and this trip was no exception. Since she hadn't been able to decide among four different dresses, she'd packed all of them, along with slacks, tops, shorts, and a sexy one-piece swimsuit. She slung her purse strap over her shoulder, grabbed the handles of the two large wheeled cases, and dragged them after her toward the terminal.

She had traveled no farther than a few yards when she spotted a woman who looked like Celina. Elayne stopped and peered at the lovely blonde ten yards in front of her. Despite not seeing her for almost two years, Elayne would recognize those blond curls anywhere.

"Celina!"

Her friend stopped and turned toward her. Elayne walked as quickly as she could while tugging two full suitcases behind her. Smiling broadly, Celina hurried across the parking lot toward Elayne.

Elayne grabbed her in a fierce hug. "Oh, it's so good to see you!" Holding Celina's arms out to the side, Elayne looked her over from head to feet. She was as beautiful as ever. "You look amazing. Did you have a boob job?"

Laughter sputtered from Celina's mouth. "No! I promise, everything is real."

"Lucky you. You're more gorgeous than you were the last time I saw you. How's that possible?"

"Good vitamins."

"What's the brand? I'll start taking them today."

Celina smiled. "You don't need vitamins. You're perfect."

Elayne snorted. She knew she was far from perfect. While her other three college friends had leaned toward the slim side, Elayne had always been plump. "Yeah, right. I'd be perfect if I lost forty pounds."

"Will you stop that? You don't need to lose an ounce. Besides, you wouldn't be able to hold up those double Ds if you lost any weight."

"True." She grinned. "I've never had a man complain about my girls." Elayne grabbed the handles of her suitcases again and began walking toward the terminal. Celina followed. "Have you seen Jasmine yet?"

Celina shook her head. "I talked to her this morning before I left my house. She said she'd meet us on the ship."

"Do you know what's going on? I grilled Jasmine, but she wouldn't tell me anything about this trip."

"Me either. All she told me is that she'd arranged everything, and we'd love it."

"Well, she has the bucks to do it right, that's for sure."

Elayne couldn't fault Jasmine for throwing money around since she had so much of it. Her family had made a fortune generations ago. That money had been passed down to each child. Since Jasmine was the only child of an only child, she had inherited a shitload when her mother's father passed away.

Perhaps she should feel guilty about letting Jasmine pay for this cruise. She didn't.

Elayne gripped the handle of the door leading into the terminal. "Are you ready for this?"

"Absolutely," Celina said with a grin.

Jonathan Hurn ran his finger down the checklist once more to make sure he'd done everything he should before the yacht set sail. As first officer of the ship, he often traded duties with his captain, Rand Paxson. They worked perfectly together as a team, almost to the point of reading each other's minds.

Satisfied that everything was on go, Jonathan hung the clipboard on its designated hook. He glanced at his watch. The yacht was due to set sail in an hour. Chase should be here by now.

Jonathan blew out a deep breath. He was worried about his friend. Chase had been through more in his life than any one man should have experienced. He deserved to forget all his troubles and have a good time. Jonathan planned to make sure Chase did exactly that.

Setting him up with a hot woman would be a good start.

Jonathan turned a corner and saw Rand leaning on the railing, his attention riveted to the dock. Jonathan took a peek at whatever fascinated Rand so thoroughly. Two women walked up the gangplank, a blonde and a brunette. The blonde was lovely, no doubt about it. The brunette made Jonathan's blood pump faster through his veins. Short black hair, olive skin, full lips perfect for kissing . . . or sliding down his cock.

He also appreciated her voluptuous body. Wide hips that

would cushion his pelvis. Large breasts that he could happily play with for hours. He'd bet she had nice big nipples too.

He could hardly wait to find out.

After Jonathan left Rand, he ran into Andrew, the ship's purser, in the main salon. "Hey, Andrew."

"Hey, Jon. What's up?"

"Has Chase Cummings boarded? I can't find him."

Andrew opened the small notebook he carried that listed all the information about the passengers. "I haven't checked him off my list."

"Damn it," Jonathan muttered. He hoped Chase hadn't decided to back out. Chase had said an emphatic no when Jonathan first mentioned the cruise. It had taken half an evening of cajoling and pleading to get Chase to finally say yes. "Page me as soon as he boards, okay?"

"Sure, but we're due to cast off in forty minutes."

"Yeah, I know. He'd better make it in time, or he's gonna be in big trouble."

Two

Elayne smiled as she turned in a small circle. She thought her suite would be the size of a small closet. Instead, it was spacious and airy. Various shades of blue in the color scheme made it a relaxing place where she wouldn't mind spending her time. Not that she planned to stay in the cabin for much more than sleeping . . . or sex.

Sex was at the top of her to-do list. Her job as CFO of a major cosmetics company meant long hours and a lot of travel . . . travel that rarely included any time for men. Her obligations at home didn't give her the chance to date or meet anyone new. It'd been weeks since a man had kissed her, touched her.

With six single men on the ship—not counting the male crew—it shouldn't take her long to find a bed partner.

First, she had to locate her friends. She and Celina had parted so they could find their cabins and unpack. One of those frothy drinks Celina had mentioned sounded better than unpacking. Plus, she needed to find Jasmine.

Elayne opened the cabin door to find a stewardess on the other side, her hand raised to knock. Startled, Elayne took a step back.

The stewardess smiled. "I'm sorry. I didn't mean to scare you."

"No problem." Elayne glanced at the gold name tag that said *Nicola*. "What can I do for you?"

"I'm here to unpack for you, Ms. Wyatt."

"Unpack?"

"Yes, ma'am. We want to make your cruise as pleasant as possible."

Elayne knew she was going to love this cruise. "I appreciate that." She moved aside so Nicola could enter the suite. "Would you happen to know where Jasmine Britt is?"

"Yes, ma'am. She's at the bar in the upper-deck salon."

"Which is where I'm heading. Thanks."

Elayne strolled toward the salon, admiring the yacht as she walked. Everything gleamed. Whoever did the decorating had superb taste. Working for a cosmetics company meant Elayne always noticed color. The different shades of blue—from pale to dark navy—blended perfectly with hues of gray and sparkling white.

A man whose name tag said *Sergey* was walking toward her. He tipped his head, and said a soft, "Ms. Wyatt" as he walked past her. Elayne turned and watched him until he turned the corner. Tall, broad shoulders, good-looking, in his twenties. Everyone in the crew wore white uniforms of shirts and trousers. Those trousers looked very nice stretched across his ass.

So what if he was a few years younger than she? Elayne had no intention of falling for anyone on this cruise. She wanted a good time with lots of sex and no strings. After working practically nonstop for the last six months, she figured she deserved a good time with a hot guy. Maybe even the captain.

That thought made her smile. She knew nothing about the captain, but if he looked anything like his crew, he had to be gorgeous.

She saw Jasmine's long mane of dark brown hair as soon as she entered the salon. It fell almost to her waist now. It was beautiful, but Elayne enjoyed her short curls. A quick blow-dry and fluff with her comb, and she was ready to go.

Jasmine turned her head as Elayne slid onto the tall chair next to her. A smile broke over her face. "Hi!" She gave Elayne a one-arm hug. "Oh, it's so good to see you!"

"You too, Jaz." She glanced at the man standing behind the bar. Dark hair, dark eyes, tanned skin. His name tag read *Samir*. "Have you been flirting with Samir?"

"Shamelessly."

The young man laughed. "It has been a joy talking to you, Ms. Britt."

"'Ms. Britt' is so formal." She touched the back of his hand, drawing a circle on his skin with one finger. "Call me Jasmine."

"The captain prefers we respect our passengers by using their last names."

The captain sounded intriguing. Elayne was even more determined to meet the man as soon as possible.

"May I prepare a drink for you ladies?" Samir asked.

Jasmine looked at Elayne. "Should we wait for Cee?"

"Yeah, as long as we aren't keeping Samir from his duties."

"I serve at your pleasure."

Jasmine grinned wickedly. "I like the sound of that."

Samir laughed. "You ladies will give me a swelled head."

"Sounds like an excellent idea," Elayne said.

A gentle tug on her hair made Elayne look over her shoulder. Celina stood behind their chairs, also tugging on Jasmine's hair. "He can't handle both of you at once."

Jasmine grinned at Celina. "He'd have a lot of fun with both of us at once." She slid from her chair and grabbed Celina in a fierce hug. "Hi, Cee."

"Hi back. It's so good to see you."

"You too." Jasmine released her but kept a firm grip on Celina's hands. Tears glimmered in her eyes. "You look wonderful."

"If I look so wonderful, why are you crying?"

Jasmine waved away Celina's question. "Silly sentimentality." She wiped a tear from her cheek. "Okay, enough of that. We're here to party and have a good time. No crying allowed."

"Right. No crying allowed."

Celina looked at Jasmine from head to toe. "You're gorgeous."

"I know," Jasmine said.

Celina laughed, then looked at Elayne. "So what's the plan?"

"The plan right now is for this hunk to make us something wicked to drink." Elayne turned her hundred-watt smile on Samir. "Isn't that right?"

He returned her smile. "Absolutely. Anything you want, I'll make. What's your pleasure?"

"Surprise us."

"I'll make you ladies something very special. Why don't you relax in one of the sitting areas?"

"Good idea." Elayne slid off her chair. "Let's get comfy so we can talk."

Elayne loved being with her two best friends again, talking about Carol, what they'd do on the cruise, how much fun they planned to have. She was definitely ready for some fun. Too much traveling and long hours for her job had left her emotionally and physically drained. This cruise would be the perfect cure.

She emptied her glass and decided to ask Samir for another of the pink frothy drinks. All the air rushed from her lungs in the next moment. Her eyes widened and her lips parted in a silent "O." A man strode toward them, wearing the same white uniform as the rest of the crew. He had short blond hair and intense green eyes. A deep tan seemed to be a requirement of every crew member, along with the white uniforms. At least six feet tall with a swimmer's lean build, he walked with an air of confidence.

"Damn," Elayne whispered.

He stopped by their seating area and smiled at each of them. "Ladies. I see Samir has been taking care of you."

"Yes, he has," Celina said.

"Good. We want our passengers to be happy. I'm Jonathan Hurn, the first officer, at your service." He looked directly at Elayne. "Don't hesitate to ask if there's anything I can do for you."

Elayne's gaze traveled over his body, stopping at his groin. He filled out the area behind his fly perfectly. "I'm sure there are *lots* of things you can do for me."

One corner of his mouth tilted up in a rakish grin. "That's why I'm here . . . to see to your comfort and pleasure."

Elayne licked her bottom lip as she peeked at his groin again.

Forget the captain. The first officer would do fine. "Exactly how . . . involved do you get in your passengers' pleasure, Jonathan?"

"As involved as you might want."

Jonathan's gaze dipped to Elayne's breasts and lingered for several seconds. A delicious chill raced down her spine. She could easily imagine his hands on her breasts, his mouth on her nipples, while he thrust his hard cock into her pussy.

Oh, yes. Delicious.

"Would you like a tour of the ship?" he asked Elayne.

"I'd love it." She set her empty glass on the table and stood. "See you later, girls," she said without one glance at them. She focused all her attention on Jonathan . . . and planned to do so for the rest of the afternoon.

Three

Jonathan rested his hand lightly on the small of Elayne's back as he guided her through the yacht. His heart thumped heavier, his blood pumped a bit faster, the longer he was with her. The subtle scent of her musky cologne tempted him to bury his nose in that luscious long neck while he ran his hands over her body.

The heat in her eyes when she looked at him told him she wouldn't object to his touch.

Finding a willing bed partner on a cruise had never been a problem for Jonathan. It appeared his good luck would hold out for this cruise too. Elayne wanted him as much as he wanted her.

Anticipation always made the sex sweeter. Instead of taking her straight to his cabin, as he longed to do, he took his time showing her all the amenities the ship had to offer, ending the tour in the main salon. He watched Elayne stroll around the room, dragging her fingertips across the furniture, the pictures on the walls, the tables. She was obviously a sensual person who enjoyed touching the different textures.

"It's nice." She leaned against the back of a chair. "The ship is lovely."

Jonathan tipped his head. "I'm glad you approve."

"Everything shines. The crew must clean constantly."

"The captain insists on everything being perfect for our passengers."

"He sounds like a hard taskmaster."

"Not at all. Captain Paxson is very fair to the crew. Everyone likes him."

Elayne propped her hands on the chair behind her. The new position emphasized her breasts. Jonathan's gaze wandered over her body. She wore a sleeveless, V-necked brown dress with a full skirt that swirled around her knees. The high-heeled sandals on her feet made her legs look incredible.

He wouldn't mind nibbling on her toes and working his way up her body.

"How long have you worked here?" she asked.

"Five years. I can't imagine doing anything else."

Her gaze slowly slid down to his groin. Jonathan's cock responded to the desire in her eyes, growing longer and thicker. With her gaze focused on his fly, he had no doubt she could see his shaft swelling.

"I would imagine you meet a lot of . . ." She looked into his eyes again. "Interesting people."

"I do." He stepped closer to her, until their bodies were mere inches apart. Her scent drifted to his nose. God, she smelled good. "Interesting and fascinating."

She fingered the top button on his shirt. "Jasmine said this is known as the sex cruise."

"Some call it that."

"She said one of her clients took the cruise after her divorce was final. She was in a four-couple orgy."

"That happens, yes."

Elayne released the button from its hole. "Do you participate in orgies?"

"I have, but I prefer to focus my attention on one woman at a time."

The second button came loose. Jonathan's breathing deepened when Elayne licked her lips. "Are you undressing me, Ms. Wyatt?"

A seductive smile touched her lips. "Do you object?"

"Not at all. In fact . . ." He dipped one finger into her cleavage. "I've been thinking about doing the same thing to you."

"Have you?"

"Would you object?"

"Right here? Where anyone could see me?"

He could feel her heart pounding beneath his fingertips. Jonathan slipped his hand farther inside the V of her dress. Her warm breast filled his palm.

"The passengers are reserved at first," he said. "Before the cruise is over, most of them are naked all the time."

"They just . . . walk around naked?"

Jonathan nodded. "You can't have an orgy wearing clothes."

He thumbed her nipple, and her breath hitched. He liked that little sign of her desire. "You have a choice."

He saw her throat work as she swallowed. "I do?"

Jonathan nodded. "We can stay right here and tease each other, or we can go somewhere more private and make love."

Elayne's eyes turned soft and sultry. "How about my cabin?"

Her cabin was closer than his. Jonathan nodded. He reluctantly released her breast and took her hand, entwining their fingers together.

Jonathan's cock hardened in anticipation with each step. He'd planned to wine and dine Elayne before they had sex. He enjoyed the chase, the journey to surrendering. He enjoyed the kissing, the petting, the slow removal of clothing until he and his partner were both naked and desperate for each other.

Desire wrapped around him and squeezed. There would be no buildup this first time with Elayne. It would be hot and fast and very satisfying.

Elayne opened the door to her cabin and stepped inside. Before she could turn and face Jonathan, he wrapped his arms around her waist. She drew in a sharp breath when he nipped the side of her neck.

"You're a biter."

"I'm whatever you want me to be." He slid his hands up to her breasts. "Do you want me to be a biter?" He squeezed both mounds while rubbing his cock across her ass. "Or a sucker? Or maybe . . ." He arched against her, driving his hard cock between her buttocks. "You'd prefer a licker."

Elayne reached behind her and wrapped her arms around his neck. She tilted her head, giving him plenty of room to kiss and nibble her neck. He opened his mouth over the pulse and sucked hard. Each pull of his lips made her womb clench.

"I love your breasts," he rasped in her ear. "So big. So full." He lifted and squeezed them again. Elayne arched her back, pushing them even farther into his hands. "Oh, yeah. Very nice."

His touch through her clothes set her blood on fire, but she would prefer to feel his hands on her bare skin. She was about to tell him that when he turned her in his arms and covered her lips with his.

Oh, my!

He plundered her mouth. That's the best word Elayne could think of to describe Jonathan's kiss. There was nothing gentle or tender about it. He kissed her as if he were starving for the taste of her. Cradling the back of her head with one hand, he turned his mouth one way, then the other, while his lips moved over hers.

His tongue drove deep, and she whimpered.

Elayne went willingly when Jonathan backed her up against the wall. His hands ran over her breasts, her waist, her buttocks, as he continued to kiss her. She felt surrounded by his touch, his taste. She couldn't get enough of either. Tunneling her fingers into his short hair, she parted her lips and thrust her tongue into his mouth.

"Jesus." Jonathan kissed her jaw, her neck, the sensitive spot behind her ear. "My God, you're hot."

"And getting hotter."

A rakish grin turned up one corner of his mouth. "Good. The hotter the better." He drew her dress up to her waist and pushed one hand inside the front of her panties. "You're so wet." He bit her bottom lip, soothed it with his tongue. "I've got to fuck you."

Elayne assumed Jonathan would lead her over to the bed. Instead, he pulled her panties over her hips and down her legs. He caressed the sides of her legs, beneath her dress, while standing upright again. Looking into her eyes, he finished unbuttoning his shirt. When he released the last button, Elayne jerked the shirt off his shoulders and let it fall to the floor. She feasted on the broad chest lightly covered in blond hair. She trailed her fingertips down his flat stomach and over his fly to grip his cock.

She only had a few moments to learn him through his clothes before he opened his belt and fly. Still looking in her eyes, he pushed his trousers and briefs past his hips. Elayne lowered her gaze to his cock. She whimpered again. Thick and long, it stood straight out from his body. A drop of pre-cum oozed from the slit.

"Spread your legs," he ordered.

She did as he said without hesitation. Jonathan pulled open the nightstand drawer. Elayne's eyes widened when she saw the array of sex toys, from dildos to handcuffs to butt plugs. He chose a condom and quickly slid it over his shaft. Sliding his arms under her thighs, he lifted her body as he thrust inside her.

Elayne closed her eyes and bit her bottom lip. It had been so long since she'd felt a man's hard cock in her pussy. Work and her crazy home life had interfered with her free time for much too long. She had four days on this ship and planned to spend as much time as possible fucking Jonathan.

Making up for lost time would be so much fun.

"Damn, your pussy feels good." He bit down on her earlobe, suckled it. "Tight and hot and wet. I love how wet you are."

The feel of his warm breath in her ear sent a delicious shiver down her spine. Jonathan obviously knew what to do to drive up a woman's desire until she couldn't see straight. He nipped her earlobe again, then covered her mouth in a voracious kiss.

Every bone in her body melted.

He stopped thrusting and rotated his hips. His pelvis brushed her clit. Elayne moaned in pleasure. "Do that again."

"What? This?" He rotated his hips again as he arched against her. "You like that?"

"Yesssss. It feels wonderful."

"So do you." He began pumping again . . . slowly at first, then picking up speed. "Come for me. I want to feel you come."

With her legs draped over his arms and the wall at her back, Elayne couldn't move. All she could do was hold on to him and accept his hard thrusts.

The orgasm built so quickly, Elayne barely had time to gasp before the pleasure rushed through her body. She gripped Jonathan's shoulders and bit her bottom lip. Her pussy clenched around his cock, squeezing it with each contraction.

"Yeah, just like that." He kissed her hard, deep. "Come again for me."

Laughter bubbled from her throat. "I can't come on command, Jonathan."

"Then I'll guess I'll have to do whatever I need to so you'll come again."

"Like?"

"Like . . . this."

Jonathan pulled out of her and dropped to his knees. He pushed up her dress to expose her mound. Spreading her labia with his thumbs, he stared at Elayne's wet flesh. Her hard clit peeked out from beneath the hood. This close, he could smell her musky, feminine scent. The only thing better than smelling her would be tasting her.

He swiped his tongue across her pussy. She inhaled sharply. "Jonathan," she whispered.

He lapped her clit again, then drove his tongue inside her channel. He loved licking a woman's pussy, especially when it tasted this good. He fucked her with his tongue for several moments before moving back to her clit. Her breathing became heavier the longer he lapped at her. She shifted her hips, arching her mound closer to his mouth.

"That feels so good. Don't stop."

No problem there. Jonathan had no intention of stopping. Not yet. He laved her entire slit, then drew her clit between his lips and suckled.

"Like that. Oh, yes. *Yes!*"

He pulled his mouth away from her. She released a keening groan and tightened her grip in his hair. "Please don't stop!"

"Don't worry, baby. I won't leave you hanging." Standing, he slipped his arms beneath her legs and lifted her. One thrust, and he entered her again. "I want to be inside you when you come."

He began pumping his hips, driving his cock inside her all the way to his balls. He watched Elayne's face as he fucked her. Her eyes were closed, her lips parted, her breath coming in short puffs. She was obviously lost in her own pleasure, which was exactly what he wanted. He fought back his own climax, hoping she would come again before he did.

The internal contractions from her orgasm grabbed his shaft. Jonathan couldn't hold back his climax any longer. Burying his face against Elayne's neck, he groaned loudly as the pleasure rushed down his spine and through his balls.

Jonathan locked his knees to keep from falling to the floor. If he unlocked them, he wasn't sure if his legs would work. His orgasm had drained every bit of strength out of his body.

Damn, what a ride.

He liked the feel of Elayne's soft breath on his neck. Having her in his arms for the rest of the day wouldn't bother him at all. Unfortunately, he had duties on the ship that couldn't wait.

Lifting his head from the comfortable spot on her shoulder, he kissed her gently. "You okay?"

Elayne smiled. "I'm better than okay."

"Good." He kissed her again, moaning when she pressed her tongue past his lips. "I wish I could stay here with you."

"But you have work to do."

He nodded. "I'm due in the pilothouse in about fifteen minutes. The captain takes the ship out, then I take over for him so he can make the rounds and meet all the passengers."

Jonathan slowly released Elayne's legs so she could stand. When he was sure her legs would support her, he let her go. After picking up his shirt, he headed for the bathroom.

Elayne blew out a shaky breath. Her legs felt like jelly. Her second orgasm had been even stronger than the first, and that didn't happen. For that matter, having one orgasm was usually her limit, if she had one at all. Jonathan had definitely done everything her body needed.

She located her panties on the floor and slipped them on as Jonathan came out of the bathroom. He watched her straighten her underwear and adjust her dress.

"I think you should go without panties for the entire cruise."

Elayne laughed. "And wear dresses too?"

"Absolutely." He slipped his arms around her waist and drew her body against his. "That way, I can bend you over and fuck you whenever I want to."

"You're assuming I'll want you to fuck me again."

"Yeah, I am assuming that." He slid his hands down to her buttocks and squeezed them. "Do you? Want me to fuck you again?"

"Oh, yes. Very much." She raked her fingers through his hair. "I've never had an audience for sex."

"It can be very hot."

"Do you do that a lot? Have sex in front of other people?"

He didn't say anything for a moment, as if he were trying to decide how to answer her question. "Define 'a lot.'"

"Every cruise?"

"No."

"Every other cruise?"

His eyes sparkled with devilment. "You're getting warmer."

"Are you an exhibitionist?"

"I don't look for opportunities to expose my body, but I'm not ashamed of it."

He certainly had no reason to be ashamed of his body. Elayne hadn't seen all of it, but she admired what she had seen.

Jonathan dropped a kiss on her lips. "I'm going to tell Anna to seat you next to me at dinner."

"I'd like that."

He kissed her again, longer and deeper. "Until later."

At the door, he turned and winked at her. "Wear a dress for me." He left, closing the door gently behind him.

Four

Elayne had seen the little black sheath at Macy's in Dallas on one of her business trips and couldn't resist buying it. The deep scooped neck showed off a generous amount of her breasts. The short hem displayed her legs, and the cap sleeves exposed her arms. She felt next to naked in it.

Her lack of underwear contributed to the naked feeling. Jonathan had teased her about not wearing panties for the entire cruise. He'd also asked her to wear a dress tonight. She looked forward to seeing the expression on his face when he discovered she wasn't wearing panties or a bra.

Elayne gasped softly when Jonathan strode into the room, then released her breath in a rush. He looked so handsome in his white uniform. He spotted her immediately and headed her direction. A man Elayne hadn't met yet stopped Jonathan before he reached her. Jonathan spoke to the man, but his gaze kept straying to her. She could almost feel the heat from his eyes.

Her pussy clenched in response.

More people filed in, including Celina and another handsome man in a white uniform. Elayne assumed he was the captain. She hadn't had the chance to meet him yet. She'd been with Jonathan shortly after boarding the ship, then with Celina at the pool. Celina had told her she'd just missed meeting the captain.

He was handsome and sexy, but she had no regrets about choosing Jonathan.

Elayne found her place card on the table. Jonathan was seated at the foot of the table, she on his left. He'd told her he would make sure she was seated next to him, and he had.

"You look beautiful," Jonathan said from behind her.

She turned and smiled at him. "Thank you."

"I love the dress." His gaze dipped to her breasts. "What little bit there is of it."

"Are you complaining?"

"What, you think I'm crazy?" He leaned closer and whispered in her ear. "I'd like to bend you over the table, pull down your panties, and ram my dick into your pussy."

"I'm not wearing panties," she whispered back.

He groaned. "Oh, fuck."

"Not now. I want to eat first."

Jonathan scowled at her, but she saw the playful light in his eyes. "You are a naughty lady."

"I got the impression in my cabin that you like naughty ladies."

"Not when they give me a hard-on in front of the other passengers."

Elayne giggled. "Sorry about that."

"Yeah, I'll bet you're sorry."

"I am! Honestly." She touched his chest, her fingertip gliding across his nipple. "I want your hard-on just for me."

He slipped his arm around her waist. "It will be, as soon as my shift is over. I'll be working in the pilothouse until two. Is that too late to stop by your cabin?"

"Not at all. I'll be waiting."

Elayne wiped her mouth on the linen napkin and laid it by her plate. The meal had been incredible. She'd never been a big seafood fan, but the salmon had been moist and so tender. The wild rice and vegetable medley had been a perfect complement to the fish. She couldn't remember the last time she'd dined on food that made her taste buds do a happy dance.

Picking up her wineglass, she sipped the excellent Verget Pouilly while looking at Jasmine and Chase. Jasmine had tried several times during dinner to engage Chase in a conversation. He'd given her one-word responses before turning back to his meal. The determination in Jasmine's eyes slowly turned to hurt over the course of the evening. She might say she'd never give her heart to a man, but Elayne wondered if Jasmine had done exactly that. She obviously cared about Chase, or she wouldn't be trying so hard.

Or it could be that Jasmine didn't like to lose.

Jonathan pushed his plate forward and leaned closer to her. "I have about fifteen minutes before I go on duty. Interested in a quickie?"

His boyish grin made her laugh. No one would ever be able to say Jonathan was dull. "Will there be lots of kisses during that quickie?"

"Tons."

"Then I say let's go."

Jonathan stood and offered his hand to Elayne. Before he whisked her off, Celina rose and stepped in front of the first officer. "Excuse me, Jonathan."

He faced Celina and smiled. "Yes, Ms. Tate. What can I do for you?"

"The captain didn't explain about the fantasies. He was supposed to do that at dinner."

This was the first time Elayne had heard anything about fantasies. "What fantasies?" she asked.

"The ship's brochure said the passengers' most erotic fantasies can come true," Celina told Elayne before turning to the first officer again. "What does that mean?"

Extremely curious, Elayne looked at Jonathan. "I wouldn't mind knowing that too."

"Are you sure you wouldn't rather ask the captain?" Jonathan said.

"I'm asking *you*."

Jonathan released a deep breath. "The thing is, Ms. Tate, I can't explain the fantasies. I don't know how they come true. They simply do."

"That isn't possible."

"No, you wouldn't think so, but it is. Think of anything you want sexually. The most outrageous, wildest fantasy you could possibly imagine. It will happen to you."

Elayne crossed her arms beneath her breasts. "Sounds intriguing. And fun."

Jonathan winked at her. "Do you have wild sexual fantasies, Elayne?"

"I might."

He cradled her neck in one hand and slid his thumb over her jaw. "Now *that* sounds intriguing."

His touch sent shivers dancing over Elayne's skin. She could hardly wait to feel his hands on her body again, his cock buried deep inside her . . .

"Where can I find the captain?" Celina asked.

"He'll be at the wheel, but he doesn't allow guests there."

"He's about to make an exception."

Celina turned, but stopped when Jonathan took her elbow. "Ms. Tate, the captain doesn't allow guests in the pilothouse. It's the only place on the ship that's off-limits." He smiled. "I'm sure he'll talk to you later. Why don't you try out the dessert bar while you wait? I'll let him know you wish to speak to him."

Celina sighed and nodded her head. "I'd appreciate it if you'd tell him I want to speak to him as soon as possible."

"Will do."

"So how about if we hit that dessert bar, Elayne?"

Oh, damn. Elayne looked from Jonathan to Celina and back to Jonathan. She should go with Celina, but the idea of a quickie with Jonathan sounded so tempting.

Jonathan must have sensed her hesitation. He smiled and squeezed her hand. "Go with your friend, Elayne. I'll let the captain know Ms. Tate wishes to speak with him. I'll catch up with you later."

So much for our quickie. "Okay."

Elayne watched Jonathan leave the area. His butt looked amazing in those white trousers. "Oh my God, that man is hot."

Celina chuckled. "Good in bed, huh?"

"We didn't make it to the bed. He took me against the wall in my cabin." She fanned her face and rolled her eyes. "I haven't come so hard in years." Sliding her arm through Celina's, Elayne steered her toward the stairs to the upper deck. "Have you looked in the drawers in your cabin?"

"No, not yet. I haven't even unpacked."

"You won't have to. The stewardesses do that for you. Anyway, look in the nightstands. There is every kind of sex toy you could possibly want. Handcuffs, Cee! And blindfolds, feathers, scarves, lube. I only got a glimpse of them when Jonathan opened the drawer for a condom, but I will definitely examine all those goodies."

"I suppose you plan to use some of them with Jonathan."

"As many as possible."

"So you like him?"

"What's not to like? Handsome, charming, gorgeous body. He has a big cock and knows what to do with it."

"I'm not talking about just sex, Elayne. Do you like him as a man?"

"Well, yeah. He's great to talk to and has a wonderful sense of humor." She picked up a small saucer at one end of the dessert bar. "He's fun."

Celina laid four chocolate-covered strawberries on her saucer. "Any sparks?"

"Cee, if you're asking me if I'm going to fall for Jonathan, the answer is no. After two divorces, the only thing I want from a man is a good time."

"You sound so bitter."

"I have a right to be bitter." She added a generous slice of lemon cheesecake to the white chocolate truffles on her saucer. "I got screwed over twice. I won't let it happen again."

"Not all men are jerks, Elayne."

"That's true. They don't turn into jerks until you marry them." She picked up a fork and napkin. Her eyebrows drew together in a frown as she looked over Celina's shoulder. "Speaking of jerks, look who's coming."

Barret sauntered toward them in all his naked glory. Elayne shook her head in disgust. He was a very good-looking man, but he was also a first-class jerk. It certainly hadn't taken him long to remove the clothes he'd worn to dinner.

"Hello, ladies," he said, grinning broadly. "How about joining me in the hot tub?"

"No, thank you." Elayne took a step back so she wasn't in any danger of his touching her. "We're going to enjoy our dessert."

"You can enjoy it in the tub with me."

"Maybe later," Celina said. "We need to catch up on our girl talk."

Barret's grin faded. He shrugged. "Your loss."

He swaggered toward the hot tub. His ass wasn't nearly as nice as Jonathan's.

That quickie would've been so nice.

"Let's sit over there." Elayne led the way to a small table by the pool. "I'm not quite ready to bare my bod to the other passengers. How about you?"

"My bikini is as bare as I'm ready to get."

"Jonathan said most passengers feel shy at first. Before the cruise is over, everyone is naked and not the least embarrassed."

"Gives a whole new meaning to 'let it all hang out,' doesn't it?"

Elayne giggled, and Celina soon joined her. Her laughter quickly died. Elayne turned her head to see what had sobered Celina so quickly. Jasmine headed toward their table. She walked with her head down and a frown on her face.

"Damn, damn, damn," she huffed as she flopped down in the chair opposite Celina.

"What's wrong?"

"Chase. I don't understand him. I practically attacked him, and he pushed me away. A man has *never* ignored me like he does." She blew out another deep breath. "He's so . . ." Jasmine stopped. Leaning forward, she plucked one of the strawberries from Celina's saucer and popped it in her mouth. She chewed slowly before speaking again. "He's gorgeous, for sure, but he's also . . . mysterious. There's something going on with him that he won't tell me."

"Like what?" Celina asked.

"I don't know. He seems . . . sad and alone. Something happened to him, something that hurt him badly."

"Isn't he Jonathan's friend?" Elayne asked.

Jasmine nodded. "Think you can get Jonathan to spill the beans to you?"

"I can try." Her lips turned up in a wicked grin. "Of course, we haven't talked much yet."

"Bragging is so unbecoming, Elayne."

"You'd be the one bragging if Chase had fucked you."

"Yeah, I would." She tossed her long hair over one shoulder. "I don't know what it is about him that draws me, but it's definitely there. I can't stop thinking about him."

Elayne had been right. Jasmine had fallen head over heels for Chase. "Love at first sight?" she asked, taking the last bite of her cheesecake.

"Oh, puh-*leese*. I do *not* fall in love."

"There's a first time for everything."

"Not for this gal. All love does is complicate a good time."

"You sound like Elayne." Celina looked from one friend

155

to the other. "I didn't know you two were so cynical about men."

"You haven't been married." Elayne wiped her mouth and laid her napkin next to her empty saucer. "Love hurts. All the hearts and flowers stuff from romance novels is crap. Sure, it starts out great. Hormones are raging, and the sex is hot. Once that calms down and you have to face real life, it isn't fun anymore. I should've learned that with my first husband. But no, I had to fall for Winston and dig myself another hole."

Celina touched Elayne's hand. "You were happy with Winston."

"Yeah, at first, until I figured out he was content to stay home and drink beer while I worked. Uh-uh. I don't mind that I earn more than a lot of men, but I won't support him. Marriage is supposed to be a partnership. Neither of mine was."

Talking about her ex-husbands always depressed Elayne. She didn't want to be depressed. She was supposed to be celebrating, not thinking about bad times.

She looked up to see the captain approaching their table. Seeing him in the white uniform made her think of Jonathan . . . and when he'd visit her after his shift. She was sorry she'd missed the quickie but would enjoy more time with him later.

Rand stopped at their table. "Ladies," he said with a smile. "I see you've been enjoying the dessert bar."

"The lemon cheesecake was incredible." Leaning forward, Elayne rested her forearms on the table. "Any chance of getting the recipe?"

"You'll have to speak to the chef about that. Henri is very protective of his recipes."

"Maybe I can convince him to share with me."

156

Rand laughed. "I have no doubt that if anyone can get Henri to give up one of his recipes, it would be you, Ms. Wyatt."

"You are a charmer, aren't you, Captain?"

He dipped his head. "I do my best."

He turned his attention to Celina. "Ms. Tate."

"Captain."

"Would you like to see my ship now?"

"Yes, I would." She looked at Elayne and Jasmine. "I'll see you later."

Elayne grinned. "Have a good time."

If Rand gave Celina the same kind of "tour" as Jonathan had given her, then Celina would most definitely have a good time.

"I need a drink," Jasmine said. "Wanna go to the bar with me?"

Elayne had several hours before Jonathan would be through with his shift. A drink with Jasmine would be perfect. "You're on."

Five

One drink with Jasmine turned into three. By the time Elayne made it back to her cabin, her head was spinning. She wasn't sure what Samir put in his drinks, but they were certainly potent.

The phone in her cabin rang as she opened the door. Elayne slipped out of her shoes and picked up the receiver. "Hello?"

"Hey, Elayne," Jonathan said.

She smiled at the sound of his voice. "Hi."

"I'm going to have to cancel tonight. We're having a small problem, and I'm helping Rand correct it."

"A problem with the ship?"

"Nothing serious, I promise. Rand told me to leave at the end of my shift, but I feel I should stay until everything is back to normal."

Elayne sank down on the bed. A glance at the clock next to the phone showed her it was a few minutes before one. "You still have an hour before your shift is over. Maybe you'll be done by then."

"Maybe, but I don't want you to stay up waiting for me when I may not be done for hours." His voice softened. "Go to sleep. I'll see you later today."

"Okay."

Sighing softly, she hung up the receiver. She'd been looking forward to spending the night with Jonathan. This afternoon had been incredible, but it'd only been a small taste of him. She wanted the whole meal.

She lay back on the bed. Jasmine had e-mailed her pictures of the yacht, so Elayne knew how the pilothouse looked. She could picture Jonathan at the wheel, in control of the ship. He wasn't the captain of this ship, but she had no doubt he could be. He had that air of leadership about him, the "don't fuck with me" attitude that someone in command had to have.

He'd told her he couldn't imagine working anywhere else but on this ship. Perhaps he couldn't imagine it, but *she* could. He would definitely be in command, but of another type of ship . . . one that sailed among the stars instead of across the water.

Space travel had always fascinated Elayne. With such a vast universe, Earth couldn't be the only planet where people lived. Whether they called themselves people, or aliens, or Klingons, there had to be other life-forms out there.

How fascinating it would be to look for them.

Elayne took a deep breath and closed her eyes. Captain Hurn. It sounded perfect . . .

Elayne opened her eyes when she heard the soft *ding*. She saw shiny metal doors and a lighted panel with numbered buttons to the left of the doors. An elevator? But there weren't any elevators on the S. S. *Fantasy*.

The doors slid open with barely a sound. Elayne blinked, then stepped back until she hit the wall behind her. She couldn't possibly be seeing what she thought she was seeing. She closed her eyes tightly for several seconds, then opened them again. Nothing had changed.

She stepped from the elevator and jumped when the doors closed behind her. She had a strong urge to beat on the metal doors until they opened again. Ignoring that urge, she gazed about the room. Directly in front of her, a wide screen the size of one in a movie theater showed thousands of stars whooshing by. To the sides, she saw lighted panels and counters with dozens of buttons and switches. Anna and Boyd sat to her left, Nicola and Samir to her right. Andrew and Sergey sat at a large console in the middle of the room.

She'd gone to sleep and awakened on the *Enterprise*.

Elayne shook her head. Although this looked like something from *Star Trek*, it couldn't be real. It was a dream. That had to be the answer. She'd been thinking of Jonathan as a captain on a spaceship. Her thoughts had drifted into her dreams. That made perfect sense.

A tall leather chair occupied the space in the middle of the room. Elayne slowly walked up to it and peered over the top. Jonathan sat in the chair, scribbling something on a computer tablet.

"All clear, Captain," Andrew said.

"Good. Chart our course for Sector Five."

"Aye, sir."

Elayne giggled. As dreams went, this one was pretty cool.

Jonathan must have heard her giggle for he looked at her over his shoulder. His eyes heated as they focused on her breasts. "I see the new uniform fits you perfectly."

Uniform? Elayne looked down at her body. She wore a long-sleeved, one-piece outfit that hugged every curve. The deep charcoal color was broken up by thick white stripes down her left side and above her breasts.

"Of course, I like you much better *out* of uniform."

He set the computer tablet on the stand next to his chair. Taking her hand, he tugged her onto his lap. He wrapped his arms around her waist as he kissed her.

Oh, my!

Elayne moaned and melted against him. She parted her lips when his tongue swept across them. She'd kissed many men since her first game of Spin the Bottle at her best friend's house. Jonathan's kisses made her hotter than any she'd ever received.

He cradled her breast in his hand, his thumb whisking over the nipple. She was so wrapped up in his kisses that her brain stopped working for a moment. When she could think again, she realized anyone in the room could witness his intimate caresses.

"Jonathan, we aren't alone."

"I don't care." He circled her nipple over and over with his thumb. "It doesn't bother me for anyone to see me touching you." He pinched her nipple lightly between his thumb and forefinger, and she gasped. "Here's your chance to try something you've never done. I can bend you over Andrew's station and fuck you while everyone watches."

Her clit throbbed in response to his suggestion. It excited her to think of everyone watching Jonathan fucking her. It also scared her. She didn't think she was ready for that. She shook her head.

"Your choice." He squeezed her breast before releasing it. "Everyone off the bridge," he said, his voice strong.

She saw Sergey grin before he quickly sobered. "Aye, Captain."

One by one, everyone left the bridge. As soon as the elevator closed behind the last crew member, Jonathan kissed her again. He ran his hand over both breasts, then between her legs. He pressed up with his fingertips and brushed her clit.

Oh, my.

"What are you wearing under your uniform?" he whispered in her ear.

Elayne had no idea. She thought that strange. Since this was her dream, she should know everything.

He rubbed her pussy, back and forth. Elayne parted her legs to give him more room. Each caress on her clit made her moan.

"Are you wearing one of those silky things?" He nipped her earlobe. "I love the feel of silk against your skin."

"I guess you'll have to take off my uniform to find out."

A slow, sexy smile turned up his lips. "I like the sound of that."

He squeezed her mound, then reached for the buttons on her shoulders. Elayne's breathing deepened with each button he slowly released. Looking into her eyes, he pulled down the bodice until it bunched beneath her breasts. Only then did he lower his gaze.

"Oh, yes." One fingertip slid over her silk-covered breast. "That's what I like to see." Her nipple beaded beneath his touch. "I do like you in silk."

Elayne arched her back at the delicious caress. Each circle of her nipple made her clit throb. She could feel the dampness forming between her thighs. Her body was so ready for him to take her.

She pressed his hand firmly against her breast. "I need you inside me."

"I want to enjoy the view for a bit first. Stand up."

Elayne wasn't sure if she'd be able to stand since her legs were weak. With Jonathan's help, she rose from his lap to stand before him.

"Take off your uniform. Slowly."

So he wanted a striptease. Elayne smiled to herself. She'd give him the sexiest striptease he'd ever seen.

Jonathan slouched farther down in his chair, propping his elbow on one arm and throwing one leg over the other arm. His open position let her clearly see his hard-on straining against his uniform. She licked her lips. Heat flared in his eyes.

Slowly shifting her hips from side to side, she eased her uniform over her arms and down to her waist. She paused for a moment, moving her hips and arms in a sensual dance without lowering her uniform any more. Jonathan's gaze traveled from her breasts to her hips and back again. The bulge at his crotch grew even larger.

She pushed the tight uniform past her navel. Continuing the slow, sensual dance, Elayne circled her hips while turning so her back was to Jonathan. She alternated between lowering the uniform a few inches and dancing for him. When she pushed it over her buttocks, she looked at him over her shoulder. His gaze was fastened on her ass.

"Damn," he muttered.

Elayne looked down at her body. She wore a sheer black teddy and thong made of silk. Her breasts spilled out of the top of the bra, as if begging to be touched. She bent over and braced her hands on the console. Arching her back, she lifted her ass higher and spread her legs. A low growl vibrated in Jonathan's throat.

"Off. All the way."

"I could use some help with my boots." She faced him and lifted one foot to rest on his chair between his thighs. "Will you help me, Captain?"

She played with her breasts while he removed her boots. It took him longer than it should have, for he kept looking at her touching herself. She squeezed and lifted her breasts, then plucked at her nipples. As soon as her second boot fell to the floor, Jonathan grabbed her wrists and jerked her forward. She landed on her knees on his chair with his face between her breasts.

"Mmm," he mumbled. Cradling both in his hands, he nipped first one hard bud, then the other. "God, I love your tits."

Elayne had never liked that word to describe a woman's breasts, but it sounded sexy uttered in Jonathan's deep voice.

"And your ass." He kept up the gentle bites on her nipples while he palmed her buttocks. "I want this up in the air so I can see every inch of your pussy."

"I'll have to take off the lingerie."

Jonathan shook his head. "Leave it on. I like the feel of it." He stood, took her by the shoulders, and turned her around. "Bend over."

She did as he ordered, resting on her elbows.

"Spread your legs farther apart. That's the way."

She heard the rustle of clothing behind her, along with Jonathan's heavy breathing. He dipped his finger beneath the thong and pulled it to the crease of her leg. He moaned. "I can see how wet you are."

Elayne lowered her head, resting her forehead on her arms. He slid his finger through her folds. She whimpered and arched her back, wanting more of his touch.

"I like you in this position. You're completely at my mercy. I can do whatever I want to you." He pushed one finger into her channel. "Can't I?"

"Yesssss."

"That's my girl." A second finger joined the first inside her. "I can smell your pussy. Do you know how good it smells when you're hot?"

She pushed back at him, trying to drive his fingers farther inside her. Instead, he pulled them out of her. She whimpered again.

Jonathan ran his hands up and down her back, then around to hold her breasts. He tugged down the cups so her breasts were free. Thumbs and forefingers soon turned her nipples into hard beads.

"I like you hot." He slid his cock up and down her slit as he played with her nipples. "I like it when you beg me to fuck you."

"I'm begging now."

"Are you? I didn't hear any begging."

"Please, Jonathan."

She gasped when he pinched her nipples. "Please what?"

"Fuck me."

"That didn't sound very convincing."

"Jonathan! Fuck me!"

He released a wicked chuckle. "That's better." Holding her hips, he entered her with one hard thrust.

The orgasm hit her in only moments. Elayne clenched her fists and curled her toes as the pleasure rushed through her body.

"That's the way." He picked up speed, his thrusts becoming longer, deeper. "I love how fast you come."

She didn't, not usually. But that was real life. This was a dream. She could do anything she wanted in a dream.

She spread her legs another few inches and lifted her buttocks.

"Oh, yeah. I like having this ass in the air."

His wet thumb circled her anus. The caress sent renewed desire coursing through her. "That feels good."

"Which feels good? My cock or my thumb?"

"Both."

Jonathan pulled completely out of her, then thrust back inside. He repeated the movement. On the third time, he pushed his thumb into her ass. Elayne gripped the edge of the console while he pumped into her hard and fast. She could feel the orgasm building, slower than her first one. Needing a little more stimulation, she slid her hand between her legs and touched her clit. She rubbed it in time with Jonathan's thrusts.

Elayne threw back her head and moaned when the climax grabbed her.

He gripped her hips and thrust his cock all the way inside her. She heard his loud groan before his shaft jerked, and his warmth filled her.

Elayne knew this was a dream, but everything seemed so real . . . her pounding heart, her gasping for breath, Jonathan's hands running up and down her back. She could feel the coolness of the console beneath her cheek, the damp silk against her skin.

She'd never had a more lifelike dream.

Jonathan bent over her and cradled her breasts. "Next time," he rasped in her ear, "I come in your ass."

Elayne jerked awake. She quickly looked around the room, trying to decide where she was. The ship. She was in her cabin on the ship.

She didn't remember getting into bed. She'd talked to Jonathan on the phone, and he'd told her he couldn't see her because he was working. After that, she'd lain back on the bed. She didn't remember anything after that, except . . .

The dream.

Oh, my.

What an intense dream. Jonathan had looked incredible in the captain's uniform . . . handsome, strong, in command. He'd certainly been in command of her body. She sighed at the thought of the way he'd bent her over the console and taken her from behind.

He'd said next time he'd come in her ass. A luscious shiver flowed down her spine at that thought. Too bad it had been a dream and not real.

Elayne glanced at the clock. It was only seven thirty, but she knew she wouldn't go back to sleep. Maybe Celina would already be awake. She doubted if Jasmine would roll out of bed before ten.

Coffee. She could think so much clearer after coffee.

Elayne threw back the covers. She gasped when she saw the black teddy and thong . . . the same outfit she'd worn in her dream.

Her head spun as she tried to figure out what had happened. She'd never seen this outfit in her life. She wore nice lingerie beneath her clothes, but slept in an oversized T-shirt and panties for comfort.

She didn't understand this at all.

Jonathan had a lot of explaining to do. She'd shower and dress, then hunt down the first officer and demand he tell her exactly what had happened last night.

Six

It surprised Elayne to find Jasmine sitting at a table on the upper deck. She'd assumed Jasmine would sleep in as late as possible. "Hey."

Jasmine looked up from the book she was reading and smiled. "Hi."

"You're up early."

Jasmine shrugged. "Couldn't sleep."

"Me either." She gestured over her shoulder at the buffet. "I'm gonna get some coffee. Want something?"

"I'm good."

Elayne's mouth watered when she looked at the amazing array of food. Fruit, ham, bacon, eggs, hash browns, English muffins, toast, bagels, and several different kinds of cheese. The blueberry bagels were too tempting to pass. She slathered half of one with cream cheese and poured herself a large mug of coffee.

She returned to the table, sitting down across from her

friend. Jasmine raised her eyebrows as Elayne took a big bite of her bagel. "Didn't we agree last night to have breakfast with Cee?"

"It's only a snack. I'm starved." Elayne washed down her bite with coffee. "Cee never has to know I started without her."

Jasmine chuckled. "You're the one who has to live with your conscience." She closed her book and picked up her glass of orange juice. "I assume your hunger is due to a wild night with Jonathan."

"You assume wrong. He had to work last night." She popped another bite of her bagel in her mouth and chewed it slowly. "In fact, I planned to talk to him first thing, but Andrew told me he's in the pilothouse. Passengers aren't allowed in the pilothouse. I told Andrew I wanted to talk to Jonathan as soon as possible."

"Trouble in paradise already?"

"There's no paradise, Jaz. This is strictly a shipboard fling."

"You and I agree on that. All I want is a shipboard fling, which I'm not getting with Chase. Yet. I refuse to give up."

"Good for you."

"I think Cee would like something more permanent. She's been throwing off those settle-down-with-one-guy vibes for a long time."

"Cee hasn't been burned like I have."

"Or had as much fun playing as I have. Why should I give up a good thing for one guy?"

Elayne raised her mug toward Jasmine. "Here's to the single life."

"Amen, sister." Jasmine clinked her juice glass against

Elayne's mug. "But since Cee doesn't agree with that senti-ment, we should do whatever we can to help her with Rand."

"You really think she's serious about him?"

"Have you seen the way she looks at him? Her eyes sparkle when he gets within twenty feet of her. If she hasn't fallen in love with him yet, she's on her way."

Elayne ate the last piece of her bagel. "Have you seen her this morning? Or Rand?"

Jasmine shook her head. "Nope."

"Maybe they're together."

"Maybe."

"Well, I think it's time to find out." Elayne pushed back her chair and stood. "Be right back."

Elayne hung up after her conversation with Celina and headed back toward her table. She saw Mara and Doretta sitting with Jasmine. Mara was young and sweet, and a bit starry-eyed over Barret. Poor girl. Elayne hoped Mara didn't fall for Barret. He wasn't worth her time, or her heart.

Doretta was in her late thirties and crazy in love with Ferris. She hoped everything worked out for them, even though she doubted it would. A long-distance relationship had no hope.

She liked both ladies very much. She wouldn't mind never seeing Glynnis again.

"Hi, ladies," Elayne said, taking the chair to Jasmine's right.

Doretta smiled. "Good morning, Elayne. I hope Mara and I aren't disturbing you."

"Not at all. We're waiting for Celina before we eat."

"*I'm* waiting for Celina," Jasmine said. "*You* already had a bagel."

"Half a bagel. And you don't have to broadcast that to the entire ship, Jaz."

Jasmine grinned. "I like causing trouble."

"I don't know why you're my friend."

"Because I'm adorable."

"Well, that's certainly debatable."

Mara and Doretta laughed, and Jasmine and Elayne joined them. Jasmine asked both ladies about where they lived and their jobs. Elayne sat back in her chair and listened to the stories, trying to ignore her rumbling stomach. Her "snack" hadn't been nearly enough to eat.

She hurried to her feet when Celina walked toward their table. "It's about time! I'm ready to pass out from hunger."

"What about the bagel and cream cheese you ate a few minutes ago?" Jasmine asked.

Elayne slapped Jasmine's shoulder. "Shh! You weren't supposed to tell her that."

"I didn't realize your food was a government secret."

Celina chuckled. "I'm sorry I made you wait a whole two minutes, Elayne."

"You're forgiven. This time." She looked at Mara and Doretta. "Would you ladies like to join us for brunch?"

"Thanks," Doretta said with a smile, "but we've already eaten. We're going to get ready for our trip to the island. See you later."

"The infamous island," Jasmine said, once the two ladies had left. "Rose told me about that."

Elayne led the way to the buffet. "So you can tell us. What island?"

"The company that owns the yacht also owns a small private island." She picked up a plate and began to fill it with fresh fruit. "We'll dock there this afternoon. There's volley-ball, swimming in the ocean, and a big cookout on the beach tonight."

"Sounds nice." Elayne bypassed the fruit and heaped her plate with scrambled eggs and ham. This was a vacation. She could eat healthy when she got home. "So why did you call it infamous?"

"Everyone is nude."

Celina paused while reaching for the pitcher of orange juice. "Everyone?"

Jasmine nodded. "Rose said most of the passengers didn't even bother to be dressed when they left the ship."

Elayne accepted the glass of orange juice Celina handed her. "Well, this is one gal who won't be playing volleyball in the nude. My girls would give me two black eyes."

"I'm not ashamed of my body." Celina picked up silverware and a napkin. "But I don't know if I can walk around nude in front of strangers."

"Sounds like fun," Jasmine said with a grin.

"It would to you." Elayne added a slice of toast to her plate. "You and Carol were always ready to try something new and daring back in college."

"Yeah, we were. I'll admit that. Carol is the perfect example of how short life can be. I want to experience everything I can. If that includes walking around nude in front of a bunch of strangers, I'll do it. We're on this cruise to have fun."

Celina exchanged a look with Elayne before following her friends back to their table. Elayne knew what that look meant without Celina saying a word—Jasmine would end up getting herself in trouble before the cruise was over. "You're really going to bare all in front of everyone?"

Jasmine shrugged. "Why not? When in Rome, yadda yadda."

"You have more courage than I do." Elayne spread her napkin over her lap. "I'd rather stay on the ship and attack Jonathan."

"Maybe if I walk around naked, Chase will notice me."

"Chase isn't the only single man on the ship, Jasmine."

"But he's the only one I want." Sighing heavily, she laid her fork on her plate. "There's something about him that . . . calls to me. I don't know how else to say it. He seems so sad. I want to make him feel better."

"Sex isn't the only way to make him feel better."

"Maybe not, but it's a great way to start." Picking up her fork again, Jasmine speared the piece of sausage and popped it into her mouth. "I love sex. It won't be any hardship on me to get Chase into bed."

"Speaking of bed," Elayne said, wiping her mouth with her napkin, "how was Rand?"

Celina smiled. "Incredible."

"I knew he would be." She propped her elbow on the table and rested her chin on her fist. "Is he huge?"

"Oh, yeah."

She laughed along with Elayne and Jasmine. Her laughter abruptly died when she leaned back in her chair.

"What's wrong?" Jasmine asked.

"I don't remember bumping into anything, but I must have. I have a bruise on my back."

"Let me see."

Celina leaned forward. Jasmine tugged down the back of her tank top and pulled her bra strap away from her back. "That isn't a bruise, Cee. You have a huge splinter in your back."

"I can understand rug burns," Elayne said, "but how did you get a splinter in your back?"

A chill skittered down Elayne's spine when she saw Celina turn pale. "All the color drained out of your face." She reached over and squeezed Celina's hand. "Are you okay?"

"Yes, I'm fine. I just . . ." She chuckled, but it sounded forced. "It's silly."

"What's silly?"

"I had a dream about Rand. He was a pirate. I was tied to a wooden post on the deck. He took me against that post. But it was only a dream, so I don't know how the splinter got in my back."

What happened to Celina didn't sound like a dream to Elayne. It sounded entirely too real . . . just like her own experience with Jonathan on the spaceship.

Celina looked from Elayne to Jasmine. "What? It was only a dream."

"Was it? I'm not sure." Jasmine blew out a breath. "I was fantasizing about Chase last night. I imagined him chasing me through a forest. When he caught me, he fell on top of me and started touching me. I woke up before he fucked me."

"So we both had erotic dreams. That isn't so unusual."

"Celina, I had leaves in my hair when I woke up this morning."

Elayne could see Celina swallow. "Leaves?"

Jasmine nodded. "I can't explain that any more than you can explain the splinter in your back."

Elayne pushed her plate to the center of the table. The lump in her throat kept her from taking another bite. "You gals are freaking me out here."

"Did you have a dream too?" Jasmine asked.

If she told them, maybe they could help her figure out what had happened. "Jonathan and I were on the bridge of a spaceship, flying through some unknown solar system. It had to be a dream. There's no way that could be real."

"Did you notice anything unusual when you woke up?"

Elayne drew her bottom lip between her teeth. Yes, she had definitely noticed something unusual when she woke up. "I always sleep in a huge T-shirt and panties. When I woke up this morning, I was wearing this one-piece silky thing. It was the same piece of lingerie I'd worn on the spaceship in my dream."

"It's the yacht," Celina said. "The yacht is making our fantasies come true."

Elayne frowned. "That's impossible."

"So how else do you explain what happened to us? To *all* of us?"

"I can't, but there has to be an explanation. A ship can't have any kind of power."

"We're in the Bermuda Triangle," Jasmine said. "Maybe that has something to do with it."

A sudden breeze blew a tendril of Celina's hair into her face. She pushed it behind her ear. "Rand told me a person never knew what might happen once the ship entered the Bermuda Triangle."

"So what are we supposed to do?" Elayne asked.

"I know what *I'm* going to do." Jasmine wiped her hands and laid her napkin beside her plate. "I'm going to the island and try my best to get Chase naked. That is my number one priority."

"What about the fantasies?" Celina asked.

"If they have to do with me fucking Chase, I'm all for them." She stood. "Later, ladies."

175

Once Jasmine had left, Elayne looked at Celina. "What are *you* going to do?"

"I'm going to find Rand and get more information about these fantasies. I want to know what to expect on the rest of this cruise."

That sounded like an excellent idea to Elayne. She drained her juice glass. "You find Rand, I'll find Jonathan."

Seven

Jonathan stepped inside Rand's cabin and closed the door behind him. Rand looked up from tapping on his laptop keys. "Hey."

"Sergey told me the navigation is fixed," Jonathan said as he sat in the chair across from Rand.

"Yeah. Everything is back to one hundred percent."

"I'm sorry I called you last night, but I figured you'd want to know what was happening."

"You figured right. I'm responsible for everyone on this ship. I want to be informed if we run low on toilet paper."

"That would be a biggie." Jonathan rested one ankle on the opposite knee. "So I didn't interrupt anything . . . important?"

Rand leaned back in his chair and linked his hands over his stomach. "Are you asking me if Celina and I were making love?"

"Inquiring minds . . ." Jonathan grinned.

Rand chuckled. "We'd finished round one. I had planned

to pour champagne all over Celina's body and lick it off, but I didn't get the chance."

That sounded very tasty to Jonathan. "Yum."

"She certainly is."

"Pretty hot?"

"Scorching. She's so . . . free. I had no doubt she'd be good in bed, but she surprised me. I felt . . ."

He stopped. Jonathan waited for his friend to continue, but Rand didn't. Jonathan tilted his head. "You felt what?"

"Nothing."

"Hey, man, don't be that way. You can talk to me about anything, you know that."

Rand stood and walked to the small refrigerator in his bar. "You want a beer?"

Jonathan figured Rand was stalling, perhaps trying to figure out exactly what to say. They'd been good friends ever since Jonathan started working on the yacht. If Rand needed to talk, Jonathan would listen without complaint. "Sure."

Rand removed two bottles. He twisted off the caps as he returned to his desk. He sat in his chair after handing Jonathan one of the bottles. "She's different, Jon."

"How?"

"I'm just like you, man. A woman comes on my ship and captures my interest. I meet her, I fuck her, she leaves, and I never think of her again. That's the way it's always been."

"That's the way we've wanted it."

"Yeah, but . . ." He seemed to be paying a lot of attention to his beer bottle. Jonathan figured Rand was still trying to figure out what to say and remained silent. "It wasn't fucking with Celina. It was lovemaking."

178

"You telling me there's a difference?" Jonathan had never considered that. He used the two terms interchangeably.

"A huge difference. I never realized that until last night."

"Such as?"

Rand sipped his beer. "Such as caring more about her satisfaction than my own. I've always tried to please my partner, but it's never meant something to me like it did with Celina. Watching her face when she came . . . It was special."

Jonathan thought he saw a hint of red creep into Rand's cheeks. That didn't happen often. Rand didn't get embarrassed or flustered. He accepted whatever happened and always made the best of a bad situation. This serious conversation about Celina had to mean Rand truly cared for her.

"Sounds like you're falling for her."

"Falling for her?" Rand asked, a shocked expression spreading over his face. "You mean, love?"

Jonathan nodded.

Rand shook his head. "Nope. Isn't going to happen."

"Why do you say that?"

"Because I don't want to fall in love. Love complicates things too much. I'm satisfied with my life the way it is."

Oh, yeah, Jonathan really believed that. Even as the words left Rand's mouth, he looked like he'd swallowed something sour.

His friend had fallen for Celina—hook, line, and sinker.

Rand frowned. "What?"

"Nothing."

"Don't say nothing. Tell me what you're thinking."

If Rand wanted to know what he was thinking, Jonathan wouldn't hesitate to tell him. "Okay. I think if you have strong feelings for Celina, you'd be a fool to let her go."

"I never said I have strong feelings for her."

"You didn't have to *say* it, Rand. I can read between the lines."

Rand shifted in his chair. "It's officially time to change the subject."

Jonathan watched him silently for a long moment, then asked, "Did Celina have a fantasy last night?"

A slow smile spread across Rand's lips. "Oh, yes."

"That's a wicked look. What happened?"

"I was a pirate."

Jonathan almost choked on his swallow of beer. "A *pirate*?"

"Yeah. It was wild." He leaned back in his chair. "What about Elayne?"

"Sex on the bridge of a spaceship."

Rand rubbed his chin. "I don't think a woman has ever had that fantasy."

"Elayne is definitely unique, and very hot. God, she has incredible tits."

"You can say that about all three friends. Jasmine has no trouble wearing very low-cut tops."

Jonathan grinned. "I noticed." His grin quickly faded. "She likes Chase. I wish he'd give her a chance."

"You think he's still scared?"

"Yeah." Jonathan ran a hand through his hair. "I understand his fear, but I wish he'd just . . . let go. He needs to learn how to live."

"I doubt if Jasmine is the right woman to teach him anything."

"Elayne told me Jasmine is spoiled rotten and only cares about herself, but that's what Chase needs. He isn't ready to get serious about a woman. Jasmine would be perfect to help give him the confidence he needs."

"The woman definitely oozes sex appeal."

"That she does. I'll keep working on Chase, try to convince him to give Jasmine a chance." Jonathan drained his bottle and set it on the desk. "All this talk of sex has made me horny. I'm gonna find Elayne."

"Good luck."

Stopping at the door, Jonathan flashed a grin at Rand over his shoulder. "I don't need luck. I have charm."

Jonathan took a few steps in the hallway before he stopped. Leaning against the wall, he blew out a huge breath. His best friend was falling in love. Jonathan never would've believed that could happen. He and Rand had gone skiing together, hung out in bars, gone fishing, shared women. There wasn't much they hadn't done together. If Rand became involved with Celina, all that would change. His friend would start thinking about minivans and kids' lunches.

The thought of kids' lunches made Jonathan shiver.

Jonathan had two sisters who had children. He adored his nieces and nephews. But at the end of the day, he could send them home with their mothers and get back to his peace and quiet. That was the way he liked it.

A movement to his right caught his attention. He turned his head to see Elayne walking toward him. She didn't look happy.

"Finally!" she said once she was within two feet of him. "I've looked all over this ship for you."

This woman only wanted a good time. Elayne was gorgeous, voluptuous, sexy. He could have a lot of fun with her, and she'd never demand anything of him. He took her hand, entwining their fingers. "You found me, darlin'."

"Don't *darlin'* me." She jerked her hand away from him. "You have a lot of explaining to do."

Jonathan had no idea what she meant. "About what?"

"About last night. What happened?"

"You're going to have to be more specific, Elayne."

She opened her mouth as if to speak again. Jonathan quickly held up one finger to stop her. "But not now. We're going to dock at the island in a few minutes and I have to get to the wheel."

"You were in that damn pilothouse all morning."

"I have a job to do. That comes first." Despite her frown, he gripped her upper arms and dropped a quick kiss on her lips. "There will be blankets at the exit. Grab one and find us a place on the island. I'll join you as soon as I can."

"Jonathan!"

He started backing down the hall. "No longer than twenty minutes, I promise."

Jonathan had another reason, besides his job, to avoid Elayne's questions now. He wanted to make sure Chase was going to the island. His friend had spent most of his time alone, despite Jasmine's attempts to get him naked. Jonathan doubted if Jasmine ever had trouble getting a man naked, but she wasn't having any luck with Chase.

Jonathan rapped twice on Chase's door before opening it. He found his friend stretched out on the bed, reading. Chase's attire of a T-shirt and faded jeans let Jonathan know his friend had no intention of going to the island.

Chase smiled. "Hey, Jon. What's up?"

"You tell me." He sat on the edge of the bed. "Why aren't you in swimming trunks? You're going to the island."

Chase's smile faded. "No, I'm not."

"Chase—"

"Save your lectures, Jon. I'm not going. That's final."

"Why not?"

"You know why not. I don't want people staring at me."

He climbed from the bed and crossed to the bar. Jonathan watched his friend take a bottle of water from the minifridge. "No one is going to stare at you, Chase."

"Yeah, right." Chase drained half the bottle in one gulp. "If I stay here, I can be sure no one stares at me."

"You can't hide forever."

"Watch me."

Jonathan rubbed his upper lip. He'd been working on Chase for over a month, trying to build up his confidence. Chase refused to believe what happened to him wouldn't make a difference with people . . . especially women.

"At least go up on deck and lie in the sun. Don't hide here in your cabin."

Chase screwed the lid back on his water bottle. "Everyone's going to the island?"

"Yeah, as far as I know."

"The crew too?"

"You'll be completely alone on the ship."

"Completely alone works for me."

Jonathan should deck his friend. Maybe knocking him on his ass would make him wake up. "We're docking at one. Give everyone fifteen, twenty minutes to get off the ship."

Chase nodded.

Jonathan made it to the door before Chase's voice stopped him. "Hey, Jon?"

He turned to face his friend.

"Thanks."

He really should deck Chase. Instead, he gave him a small smile. "Sure."

★ ★ ★

183

Elayne wanted to be mad at Jonathan for avoiding her on the ship, but knew she had no right to her anger. He had to do his job before anything else. But she was so confused about what she assumed had been a dream. Celina said the ship was making their fantasies come true. That wasn't even possible.

Something had happened last night; otherwise, she wouldn't have awakened in a piece of lingerie she'd never seen.

She needed to talk to Jonathan about it.

When she saw him walking toward her wearing a swimsuit that wasn't much bigger than a Band-Aid, all her anger and confusion vanished. She'd received a brief glimpse of his chest when they'd had sex, but she hadn't seen his entire body.

Oh, my.

He obviously worked out faithfully to have those washboard abs. His shoulders were broad, his chest lightly covered in blond hair. It narrowed down his stomach to his navel, then disappeared inside his suit.

She already knew the line widened to a nice nest at the base of his cock.

He dropped to the blanket beside her. "Hi."

"Hi."

"Nice spot." He leaned back on his elbows and stretched out his legs. "Good view of the game."

Elayne had no intention of paying attention to the volleyball game when she could stare at Jonathan. He crossed his ankles, which emphasized the bulge at his crotch. She'd love to peel back his suit right now and lick his balls, feel his rod grow hard in her mouth . . .

She lifted her gaze to his. His eyes twinkled with humor. He must have noticed where she'd been looking.

"See something you like?"

She wasn't about to let him know how much she wanted him, not until he answered her questions. "Don't be conceited."

"I wasn't being conceited. I simply asked you a question." He nodded toward his crotch. "If there's anything you'd like to play with, I won't object."

"You wouldn't object if I touched your cock right here in front of all these people."

"Cock, chest, ass. You can touch whatever you want to. Besides, everyone is playing volleyball. They won't notice us."

Elayne shook her head. "You're crazy, do you know that?"

"Not crazy, just horny."

He grinned, and Elayne laughed. "Is that supposed to make me feel sorry for you?"

"Does it?"

"No."

"Damn it."

She really liked him. Yes, he was so sexy it made it hard for her to breathe around him, but he was also funny and charming. She enjoyed talking to him.

It scared her how much she enjoyed it.

Elayne looked out at the bright blue water. Falling for Jonathan wasn't in her plans. He was a shipboard fling. That's all he could be. Celina and Rand lived a few miles apart. If they got together, they could easily see each other. Florida and Missouri weren't even close to each other.

"Hey." Jonathan cupped her chin in his hand and turned her face back toward his. "You okay?"

She could see the concern in his eyes. Not wanting him to suspect what she'd been thinking, she smiled. "Sure."

"I'm kidding about making love in public. If that makes you uncomfortable, I'd never ask it of you."

She touched his face, her fingertips gliding over his cheek. He was such an incredible man. "You've done that?"

He nodded.

"And it doesn't bother you for other people to see you in such an intimate situation?"

"People come on this cruise expecting good food, freedom, and lots of sex. It took me a few cruises to . . . let go. After that . . ." He shrugged. "When everyone around you is naked, it's easy to shed your inhibitions."

Elayne glanced toward the volleyball game. Ian still wore his shorts. Doretta, Mara, and Ferris wore swimsuits. Glynnis, Barret, Boyd, Vaughn, Anna, Nicola, Sergey, and Andrew were all nude. "Your crew seems very comfortable without clothes."

"They're used to it."

She studied the group of people again. "I don't see Samir."

"He's helping Henri get everything ready for the cookout tonight."

A squeal drew Elayne's attention back to the game. Glynnis and Barret were on the same team, each trying to return every serve. Elayne watched Glynnis jump up to hit the ball. Her breasts didn't even bounce.

"Glynnis has so much silicone in her boobs, I'm surprised she can walk upright."

Jonathan laughed. "Not exactly natural-looking, are they?"

"No. *You* probably like them, since you're a breast man."

His gaze dipped to her chest. "I am definitely a breast man, but I like real ones."

"Even ones affected by gravity?"

"Elayne, your breasts are perfect."

She snorted with laughter. "Hardly perfect."

"They are to me. Big and firm with beautiful nipples."

"You haven't seen my nipples."

"I have a great imagination." He tugged out the front of her one-piece swimsuit and peeked inside. "Oh, yes. Definitely perfect." He slid his finger over the top of her breasts. "You could pull your suit down to your waist so I can enjoy the view. You wouldn't be *totally* nude."

His hopeful expression made her laugh. "You look like a three-year-old begging for a cookie."

"You can't blame a guy for trying." He released her suit and cradled her jaw in his hand. "How about if I beg for a kiss instead?"

Elayne smiled. "Now that I won't mind doing in public."

Jonathan kissed her softly, sweetly. Elayne sighed. She did so love the way he kissed, as if he couldn't get enough of her taste. His tongue swept across her lips, his teeth nipped the bottom one. She opened her mouth, her own tongue parting the seam of his lips to venture inside his mouth. A deep growl came from Jonathan's throat before he tilted his head and deepened the kiss.

Elayne went willingly when Jonathan lowered her to the blanket. One of his legs slipped between hers while he continued to kiss her. He cupped the back of her knee and pulled her leg over his hip. The new position left her open for the gentle thrust of his cock against her mound.

Privacy would be a very good thing right now.

Jonathan kissed the sensitive spot beneath her ear. "Why don't we take our blanket into the woods?"

She'd planned to ask him about her spaceship dream. Right now, that didn't seem nearly as important as having Jonathan in her arms. She nodded. "I think that's an excellent idea."

Eight

Jonathan held Elayne's hand as he led her deep into the woods. He took a path he knew well, one he'd followed several times. Elaine knew he'd played with other women. She didn't want anything serious, and neither did he. A good time. That was all he wanted from her.

It seemed so cold.

He thought of what Rand had said about the difference between fucking and lovemaking. If that were true, then he'd fucked all the women in his past. Once they walked off the ship, he never gave them another thought. He doubted if he'd forget Elayne that quickly. There was something about her, something that drew him. She turned him on, no doubt about that, but he also liked talking to her. Their teasing on the beach had been fun.

He found the perfect spot among the trees to spread out the blanket. Turning to Elayne, he held out one hand to her. She placed her hand in his. Jonathan dropped to his knees, bringing Elayne with him. He tunneled his fingers into her hair and lowered his head. Before their lips touched, he stopped. He looked at her face, her eyes. Those dark brown eyes drew him closer, mesmerized him.

"What?" she asked softly.

"I just want to look at you. You're so lovely."

A blush bloomed in her cheeks as she smiled. "Thank you."

He caressed her temples with his thumbs. "Aren't you used to men complimenting you?"

"No."

"Then the men you know are fools."

He kissed her, his lips gently caressing hers. He didn't deepen the kiss. He didn't use his tongue. He simply . . . absorbed the taste of her.

She clutched at his waist, then her hands slid around his back. Those soft hands traveled up and down his spine. He inched closer until he could feel her breasts against his chest, her mound against his cock.

Her tongue peeked out of her mouth to brush his bottom lip. Jonathan took that as a signal that she needed more from him. Wrapping his arms around her, he parted his lips and darted his tongue into her mouth. She moaned, her fingernails digging into his skin. The pleasure-pain sent a surge of desire through his cock.

He nipped at her bottom lip, licked the corners of her mouth. "I love to kiss you."

"I love it too. Don't stop."

"I don't plan to." He followed his words with another kiss, his tongue diving into her mouth over and over. Elayne's hands drifted down to his buttocks and squeezed. One hand crept forward to touch his shaft through his suit. Her fingers stroked up, down, up again.

"Easy, baby. You want me to last longer than two minutes, don't you?"

"I don't think you'll have any trouble lasting longer than two minutes."

"I will if you keep using that magic hand."

A wicked smile curved her lips. "Magic is fun."

So was she. The more time he spent with her, the more he wanted to be with her. "Well, if you're going to feel around . . ." He fingered the shoulder straps of her swimsuit. "It's only fair I get to do the same."

"I wouldn't want you to think I'm not fair."

Jonathan tugged the straps down her arms to her elbows. The bodice of her suit fell away from her breasts. He looked for a long moment, then cradled the full mounds in his hands. So soft, yet so firm.

"Oh, yeah. Beautiful nipples."

He dipped his head and licked each firm tip. They grew even harder under the caress of his tongue. He drew one into his mouth to suckle, giving it his attention for several moments before switching to the other one.

"Jonathan," Elayne breathed.

Her breathless voice urged him to suckle harder. With his lips still wrapped around her nipple, he lowered her to the blanket. Elayne shifted until her arms were free of the straps. She clasped his head, holding him close to her breast. "Oh, God, that feels so good."

Jonathan rose to his knees and straddled her body. "Put your arms over your head."

She did as he said. Jonathan continued to knead her breasts

and lightly twist her nipples. Elayne arched her back and closed her eyes. She bit that luscious bottom lip when he pulled on her nipples.

"Does this hurt?"

"No." She opened her eyes. His blood rushed faster through his veins when he saw the lust in her eyes. "I love it."

Jonathan leaned over and laved a nipple while thumbing the other. He could see Elayne's pulse pounding in her throat. He loved how responsive she was to him, but he wanted to give her more. He wanted to take her higher than she'd ever been.

Moving to her side, he gripped her swimsuit at her waist. "Lift your hips."

He tugged her swimsuit down her legs and tossed it aside. He drank in the sight of her, from her toes to her face first, then back to her breasts and pelvis. One fingertip ruffled the hair on her mound. "Your body is incredible."

"So is yours." She reached out to touch him. Jonathan quickly shifted so she couldn't reach him.

"Uh-uh. Arms over your head."

"I want to touch you too."

"Not yet. This time is for you. Open your legs for me."

He waited until she'd lifted her arms over her head again before sliding his hand between her thighs. She was warm and wet and swollen. His cock jerked in his suit. He wanted so badly to thrust into her pussy right now.

Jonathan mentally told his dick to behave. His own needs had to wait until he satisfied Elayne.

He slowly pushed two fingers inside her. Watching her face, he moved them as he pressed upward. There. Elayne's sudden gasp and low moan told him he'd definitely found her G-spot. He rubbed the sensitive area with his fingertips as he continued to watch her face. Her eyes drifted closed, her lips parted. She began to pump her hips in the same rhythm that he caressed her.

She was so beautiful like this.

Her breath hitched. She arched her hips and released a low moan. The walls of her pussy contracted around his fingers, as if to pull them even farther inside her. He continued to gently caress her G-spot until she relaxed on the blanket again and opened her eyes. A cat-that-ate-the-canary smile turned up her lips.

"Feel good?" he asked.

She nodded. "Wonderful."

Jonathan pulled his fingers from her and lifted them to his mouth. He licked off every bit of her juices.

The scent and taste of her destroyed the last of his self-control. Jonathan stood, shucked off his swimsuit, and knelt between Elayne's legs. She placed her feet on the blanket and let her knees fall open. Unable to resist the lure of her wet flesh, he leaned over and ran his tongue over her clit and labia.

"Delicious" wasn't a strong enough word to describe how she tasted.

Straightening to his knees again, he hooked Elayne's legs over his arms and slid into her. She took him so perfectly, as if their bodies were made for each other. He pumped slowly, evenly, taking his time in the buildup. His balls were so tight, he could fuck her fast and come in a minute. With another woman, he'd consider that. After all, she'd already come once while he hadn't yet.

Elayne's pleasure mattered much more to him than his own.

Her arms were still over her head. Her breasts jiggled with

each thrust into her channel. While he greatly enjoyed watching her breasts move, he wanted to touch her more. Releasing her legs, he reclined on top of her and gathered her into his arms.

He heard her soft sigh a moment before she wrapped her arms around his neck. Jonathan continued to thrust slowly. He lifted his head from Elayne's shoulder and looked into her eyes. Her gaze passed over his lips, his eyes, his hair, and back to his eyes. She gave him a small smile.

"It feels good," she whispered.

"Yeah." He kissed her, as gently as he thrust into her body. "It feels really good."

Elayne tunneled her fingers into his hair. "I'm so close. Move a little faster."

He slipped one hand beneath her buttocks and lifted to give more stimulation to her clit. Elayne's lips parted, her eyes closed. Jonathan couldn't resist biting her neck when she arched it. He sucked the skin over her pulse while she shivered.

The contractions in her pussy milked his own climax from him. Jonathan lay still, his lungs struggling for breath. Sweat trickled down his spine to pool at his lower back. Elayne's skin felt damp against his. He didn't care. He didn't want to move from her arms.

Ever.

He raised to his elbows. Elayne's eyes were at half-mast, her cheeks flushed. She looked like a woman who had been thoroughly loved. "How do you feel?"

"Wiped."

He chuckled. "Is that a good wiped or a bad wiped?"

"Definitely good."

He kissed the tip of her nose. "Am I too heavy?"

"No." Her hands drifted down his back to his buttocks. "You're perfect."

A compliment like that deserved another kiss, this time on her mouth. Jonathan palmed her breast as he kissed her yet again. He couldn't seem to get enough of touching her, kissing her.

Jonathan ended the kiss with a soft nip to Elayne's bottom lip. "I'll be right back."

Elayne rolled to her side and watched Jonathan walk farther into the woods. What an amazing ass, all tanned and toned. It gave her the perfect place to grip while he fucked her.

He was an incredible lover. It'd been a long time since Elayne had been with a man so unselfish, so thoughtful of her needs. Her first husband had been that way in the beginning, until he began to love his scotch more than her. One backhand when he'd been drunk was all it had taken for her to pack up and leave him. He'd apologized, swore he loved her, swore it would never happen again. Elayne knew better. She'd watched the same thing happen to her sister. Elissa's bastard husband had put her in the hospital before she'd finally realized all his promises of love and reforming were only words.

Jonathan appeared from among the trees. Elayne sighed softly. It was such a pleasure to watch him. His cock was no longer erect, but still nice. She remembered Jasmine saying that some men were "growers" and some were "show-ers." Jonathan actually fit into both categories.

How lucky for her.

He dropped back on the blanket. "You were staring at my cock."

"Yes, I was."

"I like a woman who's honest." He stretched out his legs and propped up on one elbow, facing her. "If you want to play with it, I won't mind."

"I think I'd rather lie here and recuperate."

"What a lightweight. Two orgasms, and you're done."

"Give me a few minutes, and I'll be ready to go again. Can you say that?"

"I can *say* it. Doesn't mean I can *do* it."

Elayne reached over and drew one finger down his chest to his navel. "I have no doubt you recuperate quickly."

He lifted her hand and kissed her palm. "I do have to get back to the ship soon, but I'm all yours after the cookout."

Elayne had read about the cookout in the ship's brochures. The crew made a big bonfire on the beach, and Henri prepared traditional Western fare. It sounded like a lot of fun. No one had to actually dress up in Western clothes, although she wouldn't mind seeing Jonathan that way. She could easily picture him in a pair of leather chaps and a cowboy hat . . . and nothing else. His cock would stand up straight and hard in the chaps' opening. She'd drop to her knees and take him in her mouth, suck him until he begged her to let him come . . .

He lifted her chin with one finger. "I think I lost you."

Heat rushed to her cheeks when she realized she'd been fantasizing. "Sorry. Just thinking."

"About me, I hope."

"See, there you go being conceited again." She softened her scolding with a smile. "Actually, I was thinking about tonight. I can't come to the cookout with you. I'm having dinner with Celina and Jasmine."

"Aren't they coming to the cookout?"

"I don't know where we'll eat, but we promised to have dinner together tonight."

"If you want to eat on the ship, that's no problem. Henri will prepare anything you want." He caressed her chin with his thumb. "I'm disappointed I won't be eating with you."

"We can have dessert together."

"Yes, we can." He released her chin and cradled her breast. His thumb whisked across her nipple. "Maybe something with whipped cream on top."

"You have a thing for whipped cream?"

"I do when it's spread on nipples."

His casual comment reminded Elayne how many times he'd been with a woman just like this. He'd seduced them, then probably forgot them the next day. It would be the same with her. That's what she wanted—a shipboard fling with no promises, no commitments. She wanted to take memories of a good time and great sex home with her. Nothing else.

A hollow feeling formed in the bottom of her stomach at the thought of never seeing Jonathan again after Sunday.

No. I can't fall for him. I won't *fall for him. All love does is complicate things. I learned that lesson a long time ago. I have to keep everything casual.*

He continued to caress her nipple. Elayne glanced at his groin. His cock grew with each pass of his thumb over her flesh.

"Have you recuperated yet?"

His touch stoked her desire back to life. She scooted closer to him and wrapped her arm around his neck. Before their lips met, she whispered, "Oh, yes."

Nine

Nothing was going the way Elayne planned.

The second round of lovemaking with Jonathan had been even more powerful than the first. He'd held her and caressed her after their orgasms, his touch caring and loving. She found herself wishing for more, that they could see each other after the cruise.

She'd immediately put a stop to those thoughts. She refused to care for Jonathan. He was her own private stud on this cruise. That was all she would allow.

She needed a drink.

Samir came out of a door behind the main salon bar as she stepped up to it. He smiled. "Can I get you a drink, Ms. Wyatt?"

"A glass of Merlot, please."

"If you wish to get comfortable, I will bring it to you."

"Thank you, Samir."

Elayne curled up in a corner of the love seat. Leaning her head back, she closed her eyes and thought about this afternoon. Jonathan had talked to her after they'd made love the second time. He'd told her about how he'd applied for the job on the ship, how he and Rand had become good friends almost immediately. He'd started out as a steward and worked his way up to first officer. He'd talked about his small house on the water, and how he couldn't imagine living anywhere else. She'd even been able to pry a bit about his family out of him. She'd learned he had two sisters he adored, and his dad had passed away three years ago.

Elayne hadn't been nearly as open about her family.

Samir brought her glass of wine on a tray. Elayne smiled at him as she took it. "Thanks."

"If there's anything else you need, I'll be happy to get it for you."

He disappeared through the door behind the bar as Celina entered the salon and walked toward her. "Hi."

"Hi." Elayne held up her glass of wine. "Want some? I can call Samir back."

Celina shook her head. "I'm fine." She joined her friend on the love seat. "Where's Jasmine?"

"I haven't seen her since breakfast. If she went to the island, I never saw her there." Elayne sipped her wine. "Did you go to the island?"

Celina nodded. "I found a private place to sunbathe. I'm not quite ready to walk around the other passengers in my birthday suit."

"I'll second that." She drained her glass and set it on the low table in front of her. "I didn't see you."

"You were too wrapped up in Jonathan."

"Yeah, that's probably true," she said, her voice flat. That was exactly what she didn't want, yet her emotions seemed to have other ideas.

Celina touched her arm. "What's wrong?"

Before Elayne could answer Celina's question, Jasmine came bouncing into the room, a huge smile on her face. She flopped down in the chair opposite the love seat. "Oh my *God*. I just had the most intense orgasm I've ever had in my *life*."

Jasmine's interruption gave Elayne the perfect excuse to change the subject. She knew the concerned look in Celina's eyes meant a round of questions, questions that Elayne wasn't prepared to answer. She forced herself to grin. "Do we dare ask her?"

"I doubt if we'll have to ask her. She'll tell us anyway."

"You're damn right I will." She looked over her shoulder at the bar. "Where's that hunky Samir? I need a drink."

As if he'd read Jasmine's mind, Samir appeared behind the bar. "Ladies, would you care for a drink?"

"You bet. I want one of those pink things you made yesterday." Jasmine glanced at Celina and Elayne. "How about it?"

"I'll take another glass of wine," Elayne said.

"I can't be a party pooper if you two are drinking. I'll have one of the pink things too, Samir."

He smiled. "Coming right up."

Once he had turned to prepare the drinks, Jasmine leaned forward in her chair. "You will not believe what Chase did to me."

"Chase? You mean you finally got him into bed?"

"Well, yes and no. We were on my bed, but we didn't exactly have sex."

"How can you not exactly have sex?" Celina asked.

Jasmine's smile was positively wicked. "He blindfolded me and—"

She stopped and her gaze darted to her left. "Nicola's coming."

Elayne watched Nicola approach them. Once again dressed in her perfect white uniform, she looked completely different than the nude woman who had played volleyball on the beach.

"Excuse me, Ms. Britt," Nicola said. "I apologize for interrupting."

"No problem. What can we do for you?"

She faced Celina. "The captain asked me to give this to you, Ms. Tate."

The redhead held out a small envelope to Celina. She frowned. "It's from the captain?"

Nicola nodded. "Yes, ma'am. He asked me to wait for a reply."

Celina withdrew a single sheet of paper from the envelope. She read it silently, which made Elayne crazy with curiosity. She peeked over Celina's shoulder. "What does it say?"

Samir approached with the drinks. He began setting them on the table as Celina answered Elayne's question. "Rand invited me to dinner tonight in his suite."

Elayne noticed Samir glance at Celina, a look of disbelief on his face. She wondered why Rand's invitation would amaze the steward so much. Nicola looked equally surprised.

"What?" Celina said to Samir. "You look shocked at Rand's invitation."

The stewardess and steward glanced at each other. "It is none of our business, Ms. Tate," Samir said. "Enjoy your drinks."

"Wait."

Celina's command stopped Samir before he turned to walk away. "I'd like to know why you and Nicola seem surprised that Rand would invite me to have dinner with him."

"It's just that . . ." Nicola clasped her hands together in front of her. "The captain has never done that, Ms. Tate. He's dined with several passengers, but he's never invited one to his suite."

"Are you sure?"

"Oh, yes, ma'am. I've worked for the captain for two years."

"And I for three," Samir said. "Nicola speaks the truth."

Celina reread the message. Elayne could almost hear the battle going on in her friend's head. She'd seen the way Celina's eyes lit up when she spoke about Rand. She was falling for him, and she didn't want to. The men on this ship were single and all planned to stay that way. Why shouldn't they, when their single life gave them so much pleasure?

"Ms. Tate?" Nicola said. "What shall I tell the captain?"

"I'm supposed to have dinner with my friends."

"Oh, pish." Elayne waved one hand as if that would erase Celina's comment. "You don't give another thought to Jaz and me. We'll be fine."

"Besides," Jasmine said, "maybe Elayne and I will have dinner with a couple of hunky guys."

"Damn straight. You should enjoy Rand while you can. You'll only have him for a couple more days."

Celina stuck the note back in the envelope and smiled at Nicola. "Please tell the captain I would be pleased to have dinner with him."

Elayne decided casual would be the way to dress to dine on the beach. She picked out a pair of walking shorts and a simple green T-shirt, deciding that would be perfect for a cookout. She slipped on canvas flats, fluffed her fingers through her hair, and opened her cabin door.

She stepped into a Western saloon. Elayne blinked twice, not believing the scene in front of her. She saw a bar to her right, complete with an ornate mirror behind it and bottles of liquor on shelves. Wooden tables and chairs dotted the floor to her left. A winding staircase stood straight ahead, the steps leading to an upper floor. There were no people in the room, but she could easily imagine a man playing the piano against the wall, and customers playing poker at the tables. The entire room would be filled with cigar smoke.

I've walked into a time warp.

Elayne turned and opened the door, expecting to go back into her cabin. Instead, she entered a bedroom. A large canopy bed took up the middle of the room. Frilly white curtains covered the windows. A mirrored dresser sat on the wall to her left, a rocking chair next to it. The room looked like something from the 1800s.

Goose bumps rose on her flesh as fear skittered down her spine. This whole thing was beyond weird. She had to be dreaming, but it didn't feel like a dream. Stepping forward, she touched the bedspread with her fingertips. She felt each nub of the chenille.

Elayne crossed her arms over her stomach. That's when she noticed that she no longer wore her T-shirt and shorts, but a long cotton dress with a deep square neckline. Her breasts spilled over the top of the bodice.

A door opened to her right. Elayne turned toward it. Jonathan stood in the doorway, wearing a brown cowboy hat and leather chaps . . . and nothing else.

He slowly moved toward her. His cock lengthened and thickened with every step. By the time he was within four feet of her, it stood straight up with a clear drop of pre-cum on the tip.

She remembered her fantasy from the island, when she'd pictured Jonathan dressed exactly like this. It was as if he'd read her mind. "Why are you dressed that way?"

"Because it's what you want."

"How do you know that?"

He stepped closer, close enough so he could run his fingertips over the top of her breasts. "No more questions." He slid his palm inside the bodice and squeezed her breast. "Just enjoy this."

Her breath caught at his caress, yet she wasn't ready to give up. "Jonathan, I need to know what's happening."

He leaned forward and kissed her neck, then nipped her earlobe. "What's happening is," he whispered, "we're going to make love."

"Jona—"

His kiss cut her off before she could say anything else. She almost pulled away, then his tongue swept over her lips. Elayne melted and wrapped her arms around his neck. It didn't matter how he knew what she wanted, as long as he kept kissing her.

His hands traveled over her breasts, her waist, her hips, her buttocks. He returned to her breasts, kneading the mounds, playing with the nipples. Elayne ran her hands up and down his back. She could feel his muscles shift beneath her fingertips. Her hands drifted down to his buttocks. She dug her fingernails into his firm flesh when he twisted her nipples.

"Too much?" he asked against her lips.

"No." She tilted back her head to give him room to nibble at her neck. "Never too much."

He pulled her dress down to her waist, then cradled her bare breasts again. Thumbs and forefingers tugged at her nipples until they were hard. "I love playing with these."

"I love it too, but it makes my legs weak."

"I can stop."

"Don't you dare!"

Jonathan chuckled. "Maybe you should drop to your knees so you don't fall."

He nudged his cock against her mound. Elayne fought back a grin at the devilish light in his eyes. "How gentlemanly of you to be so considerate."

"That's me. Mister Considerate."

She cradled his shaft in one hand and his balls in the other. "Such a gentleman should be rewarded."

She kept a tight grip on him as she knelt on the floor. A drop of clear liquid trickled from his slit. Looking up into his eyes, she licked off the drop. Jonathan inhaled sharply, then let his breath out slowly. Clasping the sides of her head, he pushed his cock closer to her mouth. "Yeah. Lick me."

Elayne circled the head with her tongue. More liquid seeped from the slit. She lapped it up before dragging her tongue down his length to the base. She slowly repeated her journey back to the head. She made one more trip down and back before taking the tip in her mouth.

Jonathan slid his fingers into her hair. "Damn, that feels good." He pumped his hips, gently fucking her mouth. "Can you take more?"

Instead of answering his question with words, Elayne drew his cock farther into her mouth. She slid her lips down his rod an inch at a time. Up, down, establishing a rhythm with him as he moved his hips. She could hear his breathing deepen, could tell that his desire grew from the increased movement of his hips. He had to be close to a climax.

She pulled back slightly, then licked one finger and pushed it into his ass. Jonathan froze, then his hips jerked as he groaned loudly. His warm semen filled her mouth.

Elayne swallowed before letting his softened cock slide from her mouth. It had barely passed her lips when Jonathan gripped her upper arms and hauled her to his chest. His arms wrapped around her as his mouth covered hers in a voracious kiss.

The floor disappeared beneath her feet. Elayne tightened her arms around Jonathan's neck when he lifted her. He continued the deep, drugging kisses while he carried her to the bed. His firm body pressed her into the soft bedspread. She heard the sound of fabric tearing, then the brush of cool air across her skin. Glancing down, she saw that Jonathan had literally torn her dress from her body.

She gasped when he pushed her legs apart and up so they almost touched her breasts. She had no chance to utter a word before he drove his tongue into her pussy.

"Oh, God!"

He lapped at her clit, her labia, her anus. He suckled her clit for several moments, then returned to her anus. Elayne's back arched off the bed when he began tongue-fucking her ass.

Elayne had always enjoyed anal play, but rarely had a man spent so much time pleasuring that sensitive area. Jonathan seemed in no hurry to stop. His growl vibrated against her anus, sending waves of sensation through her body. She hooked her arms under her knees and pulled her legs closer to her chest.

He licked his way back to her clit. "You like my tongue in your ass?"

"Yessss."

"So do I." He laved her clit several times, then thrust his tongue inside her ass again. Elayne would swear her toenails curled, the pleasure was so intense. "I'd like my cock here even more."

Her pussy clenched when she thought about Jonathan sliding his rod into her ass. It'd been a long time since she'd had anal sex. She'd relented if her lover wanted it, yet had never truly enjoyed it. She believed it would be different with Jonathan. "I want your cock there too."

His eyes flashed fire. "Roll over."

Elayne rolled to her stomach. She felt the mattress shift when Jonathan moved. He wrapped his arm around her waist and lifted to slide a pillow beneath her stomach.

"Oh, yeah. I like that ass in the air." He pulled her cheeks apart and licked her anus again. "Spread your legs more."

She heard a drawer open as she rearranged herself on the pillow. Jonathan's cool, slick finger circled her anus. He slowly pushed it inside her. "Relax. Take a breath and blow it out."

She did as he said, and he pushed a second finger inside her. Moaning, Elayne arched her back.

"That's the way. Show me you want this."

She did want this. She couldn't believe how hot it felt to have his fingers inside her ass. He began to pump them, getting her ready to take his cock.

Jonathan removed his fingers. Elayne lowered her forehead to her crossed arms, waiting for what he would do next.

The head of his cock touched her anus. He slowly pressed forward, until it slipped past her entrance. Elayne took another breath and released it. His cock slid in another inch, then another. He pulled back, pushed forward, repeating the action until she could feel his balls against her pussy.

Gripping her hips, he thrust steadily into her. "You okay, baby?"

"Yes." A single word was all she could manage with her heart beating so hard. She reached back with one hand and grabbed his thigh. "Faster."

"Damn." His thrusts picked up speed. "I wish you could see my dick in your ass."

Elayne wished she could see it too. Something that felt so good had to look incredible.

Jonathan leaned over her body and cradled her breasts. "Touch yourself. I want you to come while I'm fucking you."

Sliding her hand between her thighs, she gathered the cream seeping from her channel and spread it over her clit. Jonathan fondled her breasts as he pumped into her. The faster he pumped, the faster she rubbed her clit.

She shoved two fingers into her pussy when the orgasm gripped her.

Jonathan growled deep in his throat. "Yeah. Oh, *yeah.*" He squeezed her breasts as his body shuddered.

Elayne's knees shook. Afraid they would give out on her, she slowly stretched out on the bed. Jonathan followed her, his hands still cradling her breasts, his cock still inside her ass.

"Legs finally gave out?" he asked.

"Definitely."

His chuckle vibrated against her back. "Zapped your strength, huh?"

"Yes, but I loved it."

"So did I." He kissed her shoulder. "I'm not ready to let you go. Any objections to my staying with you tonight?"

The thought of waking up in Jonathan's arms made her smile. "None at all."

Ten

*J*onathan scooted closer to Elayne. She didn't move. Her deep, even breathing told him she was still asleep. He wrapped his arm around her waist and palmed her breast. His cock woke up at the feel of the soft weight in his hand.

He'd discovered the first time he'd touched Paula Hobbs's small breast that he liked girls a lot. Paula had been happy to help him lose his virginity at sixteen. Since then, women had flitted through his life. One had never interested him enough to think about the next date, much less forever.

Elayne made him think of forever.

He kissed her neck, her shoulder. She shifted on the bed, her bare bottom brushing against his groin. Jonathan closed his eyes, silently telling his cock to behave. Right now, he only wanted to hold her.

"Well, something is awake," Elayne said, her voice groggy.

Jonathan chuckled. "I have no control over that."

She turned her head on the pillow and smiled at him. "You have amazing control when you're using it."

"I do my best."

"Your best is very good."

Her compliment earned her a kiss. Jonathan enjoyed it so much, he kissed her again. He hadn't wanted to wake her. Since she had awakened on her own, he saw no reason why they shouldn't make love.

Elayne rolled to her back. The covers slipped off one breast. She pulled up the sheet beneath her arms. Jonathan tugged the covers back to her waist. "Hey, don't spoil my view."

She laughed. "You really are a breast man, aren't you?"

"Oh, yeah." He ran his hand over both breasts. Her nipples peaked beneath his caress. "These are beautiful."

He leaned over to take one jutting tip into his mouth. Elayne sighed. "I love when you do that."

"I love doing it." Moving between her legs, he drew the other nipple between his lips. She placed her feet on the bed and let her knees fall open, creating a cradle for his hips. Jonathan continued to suckle her nipples as he rubbed his cock up and down her slit. Her labia moistened with her cream, letting his shaft glide easily through the folds. "I love doing everything with you."

He slid his shaft into her pussy. He groaned, and so did she. He moved slowly, his thrusts slow and easy. Elayne raised her hips off the bed, meeting each of his thrusts. Needing to go deeper, Jonathan slipped his hands beneath her buttocks and lifted her closer to him.

"God, I love fucking you," he growled in her ear. "I can't get enough."

His movements increased, until he pounded into her. Elayne's fingernails dug into his shoulders. Her choppy breathing and soft moans signaled the start of her climax. Jonathan pushed a finger into her ass.

Elayne threw back her head. "Jonathan!"

He pushed a second finger inside her as she shuddered. Jonathan waited a few moments for her to catch her breath, then began moving again. He slid his fingers in and out of her ass as he pumped his cock in and out of her pussy. His orgasm began to build in his balls. He fought it, wanting Elayne to come again before he did.

"Yes. *Yes!*" Elayne cried. "Right there. *God!*"

The contractions in her channel grabbed his rod, her anus grabbed his fingers. Jonathan dropped his head to Elayne's shoulder. The pleasure galloped up and down his spine and exploded out the end of his cock.

He kissed the spot beneath her ear that he knew was so sensitive. "I love fucking you."

She chuckled. "You've already said that."

"It's worth repeating." Jonathan raised to his elbows. He liked the satisfied look he saw in her eyes. "Everything with you is worth repeating."

She cradled his cheeks in her hands and drew him closer for a tender kiss. "I feel the same way about you."

"Then there's no reason this has to end. I want to keep seeing you after the cruise."

Her satisfied look quickly changed to trepidation. "What?"

"I feel things for you I've never felt for a woman. I don't want that to stop."

"Jonathan, we can't possibly keep seeing each other. I live in Missouri, and you live in Florida."

"We'll work it out."

"You don't even *know* me."

"It's a good way to *get* to know you."

"No. It isn't possible."

Her flat refusal surprised him. He thought she'd at least consider his suggestion. "Don't you want to see me after the cruise?"

"Let me up please."

"Answer my question first."

"Jonathan, let me up," she said, her voice firm.

Hesitating a few seconds before obeying, Jonathan pulled out of Elayne and moved to her side. She scrambled off the bed and went into the bathroom, shutting the door behind her.

He fell back on his pillow, throwing one arm over his eyes. He didn't understand what had just happened. They were incredible together, the best sex he'd ever had. He knew Elayne enjoyed it too. Her intense orgasms were proof of that. She shouldn't hesitate to want to see him after the cruise.

They lived over a thousand miles apart, but airplanes traveled between the two states every day. He made an excellent living and knew Elayne did too. They could take turns traveling until she decided to move in with him. With her credentials and background, she wouldn't have any trouble getting a job as a CFO in any big company in Florida.

Elayne quietly opened the bathroom door. Jonathan lay on the bed, one arm over his eyes, the sheet draped over his pelvis. His deep tan looked even darker against the pale blue sheets. Her breath caught every time she looked at his handsome face and incredible body.

He moved his arm and looked at her as she walked back to the bed. Slowly, he sat up and leaned against the headboard. She sat on the bed facing him, drawing the sheet over her lap.

"You okay?" he asked softly.

She nodded. "You surprised me."

"Maybe I could've said it differently, but I was honest."

"I know you were." Elayne picked up the edge of the sheet and worked it through her fingers, over and over. "I've loved my time with you. Please don't think I haven't. But we live too far apart to see each other after the cruise."

"Is there something wrong with airplanes?"

"No, of course not. I fly all the time."

He reached over and covered her hands with his. "I'm not ready to give you up."

His sweet words touched her heart and brought a lump to her throat. She turned over one hand and entwined her fingers with his. "I've enjoyed every moment with you. You're handsome and sexy and an amazing lover. But it's only a fling, Jonathan. That's all I wanted when I took this cruise."

He looked down at their clasped hands. "Things can change. You might not plan for something, but it happens anyway."

"That's true, but you're also in charge of your own life. I like my life the way it is." She raised his hand to her face and rubbed it across her cheek. "We have another day together. Let's enjoy it, okay?"

Disappointment filled his eyes, but he finally nodded. "Okay."

Elayne opened her cabin door that evening after the gentle knock to see Jonathan on the other side. Her stomach fluttered at the sight of him. She didn't want to react so strongly to Jonathan. Her heart had other ideas.

"Hi," he said.

"Hi."

He brought his hands from behind his back and held up a bottle of champagne. "I thought our last night together deserved something special."

Our last night together. Those words sent a shaft of pain directly into her heart.

Ignoring that pain, she opened the door wider. "Come in."

Jonathan walked to the bar. Elayne followed him, watching as he opened the bottle of champagne and poured some into two flutes. He handed one glass to her, then held up his own.

"To my lovely companion. I've enjoyed our time together more than I can say."

Elayne touched her glass to his. Tears burned her throat, and she had to swallow before she could speak. "So have I."

He took a sip of his wine, then leaned forward and kissed her gently. Elayne tilted her head when he moved his lips to her jaw. "You smell good," he whispered.

"Thank you."

Elayne had wanted to look her best tonight for Jonathan. After her dinner with Celina and Jasmine, she'd showered and put on the prettiest dress she'd brought. On an impulse, she had packed samples of her company's new cosmetic and cologne line. One sniff of the musky scent and Elayne knew she had to wear it for Jonathan.

He wrapped his arm around her waist as he kissed her neck. "You feel good too. I like having you in my arms."

His mouth covered her again. Elayne sighed when his tongue touched hers. He nipped her bottom lip, slid his tongue across it, licked the corners of her mouth. He kissed her so passionately, she didn't understand why he jerked away from her.

"God damn it," he muttered. He set his glass on the bar and turned away from her. "I can't do this."

"Jonathan?"

He spun back around to face her. "I want more than sex

from you, Elayne. I want *you*. What can I do to make you understand that?"

She'd hoped they would spend their last night together without a confrontation. He'd just dashed her hopes. "I told you I wanted a fling, nothing else."

"I know you did, but things changed between us. At least they did for me."

"Jonathan—"

"I love you."

His declaration stole the air from her lungs. "What?"

"I've never said those words to another woman." He plucked her glass from her hand and set it next to his. "I can't let you simply walk away from me tomorrow and never see you again."

To have a man as handsome and caring as Jonathan love her should make her jump for joy. Instead, she felt like crying. "It isn't possible."

"It *is* possible. I don't understand why you won't at least give us a chance. If you don't love me, I understand that. This has happened really fast for us. But let's spend time together, get to know each other." He gave her a crooked grin. "I'm really a great guy."

She couldn't help chuckling at his boyish expression. "Yes, you are."

"Then why—"

"Jonathan, I've been divorced twice."

"What does that have to do with us?"

"I was burned both times. I don't want to go through that again."

"I would never hurt you, Elayne."

She remembered Kenneth's saying the same thing, only a

214

week before he backhanded her. She didn't believe Jonathan would ever physically hurt her, but there were other ways to be hurt.

"All I'm asking for is a chance." He took her hands in his. "I'll make the first trip. I'll fly to St. Louis and spend a couple of days with you. Then you can come back to Florida to see me."

"Jonathan, you make it sound like I can simply hop in a car and be at your house in twenty minutes. I have a very demanding job that takes up an enormous amount of my time. I travel a lot. Besides, you work on the weekends. How would we be able to spend time together?"

"I'll take some time off. I do earn vacation time. Don't you?"

"Yes, of course—"

"Then what's the problem? Why are you throwing up roadblocks before we even get started?"

She looked into his eyes. She saw love, and eagerness, and pain. She was hurting him, and she didn't want to.

She had to tell him the whole truth.

Elayne walked to the closet and drew a small photograph from her purse. Returning to Jonathan, she handed the photo to him. He looked at it, his eyebrows drawing together in confusion. "Who is this?"

"That's Joel and Dylan. Joel is eight, Dylan is six." She drew in a breath for courage. "They're my sons."

His gaze snapped to her face. Elayne wasn't surprised to see the shock in his eyes. His face paled beneath his tan. "Your . . . *what*?"

"My sons."

"You have two sons?"

She nodded. "From my first marriage. They're the only good things Kenneth ever gave me."

Jonathan looked like he might collapse at any moment. Elayne took his hand and led him to the bed. She sat on the side and drew him down to sit beside her. "I married Kenneth right out of college. We had Joel a year later. I was young and in love and totally oblivious to what should have been so obvious.

"Kenneth liked to play poker with his friends. I didn't mind. It gave me some time alone with my baby. What started out as a few beers turned into scotch and water, then straight scotch. By the time I became pregnant with Dylan, Kenneth was drinking heavily. We began to argue about it. He'd become defensive and say having a drink or two wasn't hurting anyone. The night he hit me, I—"

"Wait a minute. He *hit* you?"

Elayne nodded. "We were arguing about his drinking, and he backhanded me."

Rage filled Jonathan's eyes, and his jaw clenched. "That son of a bitch. No man has the right to hit a woman. Ever."

She squeezed his hand. "He only did it once. I packed up my boys and left him the next day."

"Where did you go?"

"To my parents' house. My mom took care of the boys while I worked. That's where they are now, with my parents. They love staying with their grandparents. Mom and Dad spoil them rotten."

"That's a grandparent's job." He turned his hand over and entwined their fingers. "What about your second marriage?"

"It started out great, just like with Kenneth. But Winston soon decided having a wife who made a large salary gave him the right not to work at all. I would have gladly supported him if he couldn't find a job, but that wasn't the case. He simply didn't want to work. It became old very quickly to come home and find it a mess while he watched TV all day." Her throat tightened as the painful memories filled her head. "He didn't love my boys, not the way he should have. He told me he wanted his *own* child. He'd promised to love Joel and Dylan as if *they* were his own." Tears filled her eyes. "He didn't do that."

The sympathy in Jonathan's eyes touched her heart. How easy it would be to fall in his arms right now.

Elayne cleared her throat. "So you see why I'm not interested in getting involved with another man."

"I understand you were hurt, but I'm not those guys, Elayne. I'm me, and I love you."

"But it isn't only me. I'm part of a trio. My boys mean everything in the world to me. I can't take the chance of hurting them again."

"I wouldn't hurt you, or your boys."

"Can you honestly tell me you want a ready-made family?"

His hesitation spoke louder than words. Elayne stood. She didn't take two steps away from the bed before Jonathan stood and grabbed her arm. "Okay, I'll admit the thought of taking on two young boys wasn't part of my plan when I fell in love with you. But give me a chance with them, Elayne. Let me meet them and see how we get along."

She shook her head firmly. "I won't put them through the hope of having a dad, only to have that hope ripped away from them when you decide you aren't ready to be a father."

"You don't know it'll be ripped away. You don't know that I won't fall in love with your sons the second I see them."

"I can't take the chance! Don't you see that? I can't hurt them. I *won't* hurt them."

"Are you going to stay alone the rest of your life because you're afraid your sons might be hurt?"

"Yes, if that means protecting them."

He gripped her upper arms and drew her closer to him. "You don't have to be alone ever again. I'm here for you, and your sons."

He lowered his head as if to kiss her. Elayne backed away. She'd weaken if he kissed her. "I think you'd better go."

Jonathan frowned. "Go?"

"There's no reason to draw out our good-bye."

"I want to make love to you."

Elayne shook her head. "I'd rather you go now."

The frustration and pain in his eyes tore at her heart. She didn't want to hurt him, but she had no choice. Her sons came first.

"You won't give us a chance?" he asked, his voice husky. "I'll accept it if things don't work out, but at least give us a chance."

"I can't." She'd fall apart if he didn't leave soon. "Please go."

Jonathan lowered his head. Elayne thought he might continue to plead with her. Instead, he sighed deeply and walked to the door. He turned the knob, then looked back at her.

"I'll always love you. Remember that."

He closed the door softly behind him.

Jonathan watched Rand leave the pilothouse before he faced Chase. He'd straightened out one friend by ordering Rand to go after Celina. Now it was time to convince Chase to go after Jasmine. "Okay, it's your turn."

"Don't pull that shit on me. It won't work. I'm not going after Jasmine."

"Why not?"

"Because it would never work between us."

"You don't know that until you give it a chance."

"I'm not willing to give it a chance."

Jonathan couldn't believe what idiots his friends could be. "For a guy with a near-genius IQ, you can be incredibly stupid."

Chase jumped down from his stool. "End of discussion, Jon."

"Okay, okay." Jonathan held up his hands, palms forward. He still thought Chase was wrong, but didn't want to anger his friend. "I give up. I won't say anything else about Jasmine."

"Good."

"You're coming to my house, right?"

Chase nodded. "I need to pick up some things at a store. I'll head for your house in a couple of hours."

"That gives me time to finish up on the ship. See you later."

Once Chase left, Jonathan picked up the clipboard Rand had used and slipped into the captain's chair. He had his own paperwork to finish before he left the ship. He flipped through a couple of pages, looking for the form he needed to complete.

The words blurred as an image of Elayne flashed through his mind. His chest suddenly felt heavy, his throat tight. He wondered how long it would be before he could take a breath without the pain in his heart.

He wished things could've been different for Elayne and him. He wished she would've given them a chance. Understanding her decision to push him out of her life didn't make it any easier to accept.

Knowing she had two small sons no longer terrified him the way it had last night. He hadn't given a lot of thought to being a father, but he loved being an uncle. He liked kids, even the little hellions. If they were anything like their mother, he'd fall in love with Joel and Dylan on first sight.

He'd never get the chance to meet them. That realization hurt almost as much as losing Elayne.

Jonathan cleared his throat and focused on the form. He had a job to finish, then a guest to entertain. Since he and Chase were both miserable because of women, Jonathan figured a guys' night out was in order. Some fast food that had no nutritional value at all along with several bottles of beer would be perfect.

He'd forget Elayne . . . at least for a few hours. He had no doubt it would take a long, long time to get her completely out of his mind.

He smelled her perfume.

Jonathan thought at first he was imagining it, but soon realized that musky scent could only be Elayne. Slowly, he stood, laid the clipboard in the chair, and turned. She stood in the pilothouse doorway.

His heart kicked into overdrive.

"Let's take a chance," she said softly.

Two steps, and she was in his arms. Jonathan didn't try to speak. He doubted if he could get one word past the lump in his throat. Instead, he cupped her face and covered her lips with his, pouring all the love he felt into his kiss.

Elayne touched his cheeks, his chin, his lips. "I don't know how things will work out."

"Neither do I. All we can do is try."

"My boys come first."

"Always."

This time she kissed him, until Jonathan's cock grew hard and his knees threatened to buckle.

"I don't want a long-distance relationship," Elayne said. "I travel a lot in my job. I don't want to travel to see the man I love."

"So I'll move to Missouri."

Elayne blinked and her mouth slackened. "What?"

"I don't want a long-distance relationship either. I want you in my bed every night. If that means I move to Missouri, that's what I'll do."

"What about your job? You said you didn't want to work anywhere else but on this ship."

"There are huge riverboats that travel up and down the Mississippi. Want to bet I can charm my way into a job?"

Elayne chuckled. "I have no doubt you can charm your way into anything." She touched his lips again, her fingertips gently stroking them. "You'd do that for me?"

"I'd do anything for you." He took her hands and kissed both palms. "We won't rush into anything. For now, I'll travel to see you. I'll meet your sons. I'll get to know them, and they'll get to know me."

"They'll love you."

"I hope so, because I adore their mother."

He took her in his arms again and kissed her. Elayne wrapped her arms around his neck and pressed her body to his. He felt her beautiful breasts against his chest, her mound against his cock. He moved his hips from side to side, caressing her with his hard shaft.

He nipped the pulse pounding in her neck. "Hey, lady," he growled into her ear. "You ever made love in a pilothouse?"

She pulled back and looked at his face. "I don't recall seeing that on my agenda."

"It's never been on mine either. Passengers aren't allowed in the pilothouse."

"So I'm breaking the rules?"

"You are. Lucky for you, I know the captain personally and can make sure you won't be punished."

Elayne fingered the top button of his shirt. "I certainly don't want to be punished. Maybe we should go somewhere else."

"My house is fifteen minutes from here. When does your plane leave?"

"Five thirty."

"That gives us plenty of time. There are no rules at my house. Whatcha say?"

She smiled. "I say that sounds like an excellent idea."

Jasmine

One

Join me to remember our good friend,
Carol St. Claire.
Carol died while celebrating life.
She would not want us to grieve, but to celebrate life also.
Meet me on the S.S. Fantasy *on Thursday, April 10,*
Port of The Everglades, Fort Lauderdale.
Jasmine Britt

The perfect words. The perfect lettering. The perfect paper. Her mother would've approved if Jasmine had decided to show the invitation to her.

She hadn't. The least amount of time spent with her mother, the better.

Jasmine ran one finger over the raised letters. She didn't understand why Carol had to die. She'd tried to talk to her mother, hoping she could share her feelings with the woman who had given her life. Raquel Britt had been much too busy with her luncheons and her charity affairs to offer comfort to her daughter. Only her grandfather understood. He'd held Jasmine while she'd cried over losing her best friend.

Now he was gone too.

Jasmine blinked back the tears that were trying to fall. No grieving. She'd grieved over Carol with her grandfather, and over her grandfather alone. Carol wouldn't want anyone to be sad. She'd expect her friends to party.

That was exactly what Jasmine planned to do.

Pushing her sadness to the back of her mind, she glanced at her watch. Celina and Elayne had promised to board the ship by ten thirty. It was almost eleven o'clock. Jasmine was late, as usual.

"Shit," she muttered as she gathered up her purse. Just once, she wished she could get her act together and be on time. At home, she'd even set all the clocks in her apartment ten minutes fast to trick herself into being prompt. It didn't work. In the back of her mind, she knew those clocks were fast and she ran late anyway.

She hurried through the terminal and down the dock to the S. S. *Fantasy*. A client had told Jasmine about the yacht. An online search had given her more information. Usually booked up months in advance, a private party had canceled their trip for this weekend. Jasmine had quickly put down the necessary deposit to hold the reservation.

Very nice. She looked up at the gleaming white-and-blue ship with a smile. What a perfect place to celebrate Carol's life.

Somewhere in the world, cocktail hour had begun. A drink was the first thing on Jasmine's agenda. After all, she was here to party.

A steward met her at the entrance and offered to take her

luggage to her cabin. Jasmine smiled her thanks at the handsome man in the white uniform. She watched him walk away, her gaze focused on his ass. *Mmm, nice.* The ocean wouldn't be the only scenery on this trip.

She passed another crew member, this one a woman. Her name badge read *Nicola*. She smiled and tipped her head at Jasmine. "Do you need some help?"

"Where can a gal get a drink?"

"I suggest the upper salon bar. We'll be setting sail soon, and the view is incredible."

After getting instructions from Nicola, Jasmine headed for the salon. Another handsome young man stood behind the bar. He appeared to be in his mid-twenties, with the dark coloring of someone from the Middle East. "Hi," she said, sliding onto a tall chair.

"Good morning," he said in a lilting accent that made Jasmine think of hot steamy sex. "Would you care for a drink?"

She would, but now that she was here, she should probably wait for Celina and Elayne. She glanced at his name tag. "I'd love one, Samir, but I'm waiting for my friends."

"I will prepare something special for you and your friends, Ms. Britt."

It surprised Jasmine that he knew her name. "You have the passengers memorized already?"

"The crew is here to serve you."

Well, that brings up interesting ideas. Jasmine wondered if Samir ever fucked the passengers. She propped one elbow on the bar and rested her chin on her fist. "You're very cute."

He smiled and tipped his head. "Thank you."

"Are you single?"

"The entire crew is single."

Jasmine smiled. "How convenient." She reached across the bar and drew a figure eight on the back of his hand. "Are you off-limits to the passengers?"

"I am here to serve you."

This cruise was getting better and better. She leaned forward to give Samir a good view of her cleavage. His gaze dropped to her breasts. "I want a good time on this cruise, Samir. A *really* good time."

A movement to her right caught her eye. Jasmine turned her head as Elayne slid onto the next chair. Delighted to see her friend, she reached out to give her a one-arm hug. "Hi!" She pulled back so she could look at Elayne's face again. "I'm so happy to see you!"

"Me too, Jaz." She glanced at the man standing behind the bar. "Have you been flirting with Samir?"

"Shamelessly."

He laughed. "It has been a joy talking to you, Ms. Britt."

"'Ms. Britt' is so formal." She touched his hand again, her fingertips gliding over his skin. He had nice hands with large fingers. She'd bet he knew exactly what to do with those fingers. "Call me Jasmine."

"The captain prefers we respect our passengers by using their last names." He looked from Jasmine to Elayne and back again. "May I prepare a drink for you ladies?"

A tug on her hair kept Jasmine from answering. "He can't handle both of you at once," Celina said.

Jasmine grinned over her shoulder. "He'd have a lot of fun with both of us at once." She slid from her chair and grabbed Celina in a fierce hug. "Hi, Cee."

"Hi back." Celina tightened her arms around her friend. "It's so good to see you."

"You too." Jasmine released her but kept a firm grip on Celina's hands. Tears filled in her eyes. "You look wonderful."

"If I look so wonderful, why are you crying?"

Jasmine waved away Celina's question. "Silly sentimentality." She wiped a tear from her cheek. "Okay, enough of that. We're here to party and have a good time. No crying allowed."

"Right. No crying allowed."

Celina looked at Jasmine from head to toe. "You're gorgeous."

"I know," Jasmine said with a grin.

Celina laughed with her friend, then looked at Elayne. "So what's the plan?"

"The plan right now is for this hunk to make us something wicked to drink." Elayne turned her hundred-watt smile on Samir. "Isn't that right?"

He returned her smile. "Absolutely. Anything you want, I'll make. What's your pleasure?"

"Surprise us."

"I'll make you ladies something very special. Why don't you relax in one of the sitting areas?"

"Good idea." Elayne slid off her chair. "Let's get comfy so we can talk."

Celina led the way to a grouping of two armchairs and a love seat. She sat in one of the chairs. Jasmine chose the love seat, Elayne sat beside her. She hadn't seen her friends in a couple of years, yet she felt completely at ease with them. It had always been that way among the four friends. They'd formed a bond their freshman year in college, one that had lasted for over ten years.

"I'm already loving this," Jasmine said with a contented sigh. "Four days of pampering. I won't want to leave the ship."

"How did you find out about this yacht?" Celina asked.

"One of my clients told me about it. She took the cruise when her divorce was final. When I heard about Carol . . ." She stopped and blinked several times to hold back her tears. Just saying Carol's name hurt. "Hearing about Carol's death made me realize how short life truly is." She looked from Celina to Elayne and back again. "We're best friends. No matter how busy our lives are, we should never go so long without getting together."

"Amen to that," Elayne said.

"And I figured we three single women would have a blast on a sex cruise."

Samir arrived with their drinks. He'd topped off the pink and frothy beverages with a skewer of tropical fruit. He placed the tray on the low table in front of the love seat. "Here you are, ladies. Enjoy."

"What did you make for us?" Elayne asked.

"Something special." He tipped his head and smiled. "Call me when you're ready for a refill."

Elayne picked up one of the drinks as Samir walked away. "Damn, he has a fine ass."

Jasmine picked up her own drink. She thought the same thing, but wasn't going to admit it to Elayne. She had her own thoughts about Samir and needed to discourage her friend from going after the hunky bartender. "Don't you think he's a little young for you?"

"Hey, we're only thirty-one. That's hardly over the hill. He's probably . . ." She tilted her head and wiggled her mouth back and forth. "Twenty-three, twenty-four, with all the stamina of youth." She shivered playfully. "Mmm, don't you just *love* stamina?" Picking the skewer out of her glass, she bit off a fat cherry. "I wouldn't mind using some of that youth for a few hours."

So would Jasmine. Stamina was good. A man who knew how to pleasure a woman was even better. "I'd rather have someone with more experience. A man who knows how to touch a woman to give her the most pleasure." Jasmine swirled her straw through her drink before taking a sip. "Wow, this is good. I wonder what he put in it?"

"You mentioned this being a sex cruise," Celina said. "What are you talking about?"

Jasmine had wondered when one of her friends would latch on to what she'd said earlier. "My client—Rose—said it's known as the sex cruise. All the passengers are single. There are no limits or rules. If you want to fuck a guy out on deck in front of everyone, no one will say a word about it."

Elayne's eyes widened. "Are you serious?"

"Absolutely. Rose said one night she was in a four-couple orgy in the salon on the main deck. Said it was H-O-T."

Celina slowly swished her straw through her drink. "That's what the brochure meant."

"What brochure?" Jasmine asked.

"The one in the cabin. Didn't you read it?"

She shook her head. "I haven't been to my cabin yet."

"There were several brochures in my cabin. One of them described the ship, showed a map, pictures of the crew. It said the crew is here for our comfort, but will disappear when we don't need them. It also said that the passengers are supposed to enjoy each other."

Elayne grinned wickedly. "Sounds like fun."

"I'm all for fun." Jasmine shifted on the love seat and crossed her legs. "That's the whole point of this trip—to have fun and celebrate Carol's life. That's what she would've wanted."

Celina took another sip of her drink. "What does one of these cruises cost, Jasmine?"

"It doesn't matter. I can afford it."

"It *does* matter. It's wonderful of you to think of honoring Carol's memory this way, but Elayne and I should help with the expenses."

Jasmine waved her hand. The cost didn't matter. She could easily afford this cruise, plus a lot more. "Look, I make a ton of money at my job. My grandfather left me his entire estate. I have to spend the money *somewhere*. What better way to spend it than on my two best friends? Besides, I can call it entertaining clients and write it off my taxes."

Elayne laughed. "Honey, if you can write a sex cruise off your taxes, I want to meet your accountant."

Celina laughed, then raised her glass. "A toast, ladies." She waited until they'd lifted their glasses also before speaking again. "To Carol. Wherever she may be now, I know she's either skydiving or scuba diving or racing a motorcycle."

Her voice caught on the last word. Jasmine held her breath, not wanting to cry. Carol had died in a motorcycle race. "And to friendship, the special kind that lasts forever."

Jasmine touched her glass to the other two. She agreed with everything Celina said, but it was time to start having fun. It's what Carol would have wanted. "And to the sex cruise!"

"Yeah, baby!" Elayne said with a grin. "I am ready for some fun." She emptied her glass with one gulp. "Where's that hunky Samir? I need another one of these."

Her eyes widened and her lips parted in a silent "O." Jasmine turned her head to see what had fascinated her friend so much. A handsome man strode toward them, wearing the same white uniform as the rest of the crew. He stood at least six feet tall with a swimmer's build.

"Damn," Elayne whispered.

He stopped by their seating area and smiled at each of them. "Ladies. I see Samir has been taking care of you."

"Yes, he has," Celina said.

"Good. We want our passengers to be happy. I'm Jonathan Hurn, the first officer, at your service." He looked directly at Elayne. "Don't hesitate to ask if there's anything I can do for you."

Elayne's gaze traveled over his body, stopping at his groin. "I'm sure there are *lots* of things you can do for me."

One corner of his mouth tilted up in a rakish grin. "That's why I'm here . . . to see to your comfort and pleasure."

Elayne licked her bottom lip as she peeked at his groin again. "Exactly how . . . involved do you get in your passengers' pleasure, Jonathan?"

"As involved as you might want."

Jonathan's gaze dipped to Elayne's breasts and lingered for several seconds. Jasmine's D-cup breasts garnered a lot of male attention. She imagined Elayne's larger breasts would garner even more.

"Would you like a tour of the ship?" he asked Elayne.

"I'd love it." She set her empty glass on the table and stood. "See you later, girls," she said without one glance at them.

"Well," Jasmine said, once Elayne and Jonathan had left, "I think we've been abandoned."

"I think you're right."

"He could've offered to give *all* of us a tour of the ship."

"I'm pretty sure you and I disappeared the moment he saw Elayne."

"Especially her boobs."

Celina chuckled. "True."

"So since we've been totally ignored, I vote for a swim. Let's change and meet at the pool."

"Deal."

Two

$\mathscr{C}$hase set his empty suitcase in the bottom of the small closet. He'd brought very few clothes, so had refused Anna's offer to unpack for him. After an obligatory appearance on deck to please Jon, he planned to spend most of the cruise in his cabin. Alone.

He didn't know why he'd let his friend talk him into coming on this cruise. His answer when Jon invited him had been a firm no. There was no way he could afford to take the cruise. Jon had pleaded with him to come, saying his cruise was a gift. Chase didn't want charity and had told Jon that. His friend had finally worn him down. A man could only take so much begging before he had to give in.

He still felt guilty that Jon was paying for everything.

Flopping down on the bed, Chase stared at the ceiling. Self-pity had been a constant companion lately. He hated it. He didn't want to feel sorry for himself, but he couldn't stop it. So much had happened to him during his life, more than three people should have to endure. The last six months had been pure hell.

Chase slowly ran his hand over his chest. He could feel the ridge of the scar through his T-shirt.

When he realized what he was doing, he snatched his hand away from his chest. Disgusted with himself for letting the self-pity grab him again, Chase quickly rose from the bed. The sooner he made the appearance on deck for Jon, the sooner he could come back here and hide for the rest of the cruise.

Jasmine stopped by the railing and adjusted the cups of her bikini over her breasts. The minuscule bits of fabric barely covered her areolas. That was exactly what she wanted. She liked when people looked at her. Both men and women stared at her when she passed them in her tight, low-cut clothing.

Slipping on her sunglasses, Jasmine continued to the pool area. Only one person lay on a chaise by the pool—a naked man. Jasmine stopped in her tracks. Her gaze traveled over his blond hair and tanned skin. He lay on his back, one arm thrown over his head. His legs were parted, letting her clearly see his impressive cock and balls.

Nice package.

There was no reason why she couldn't have two men on the cruise. She could fuck Samir, then this guy. Or vice versa. After all, she was here to party.

"Hi," she said, dropping down to sit by the edge of the pool.

He lifted his head and looked at her. A smile spread over his lips. His green eyes sparkled with interest. "Well, hello."

"I'm Jasmine Britt."

"Barret Ackerman. Nice to meet you, Jasmine."

"You too." She stretched out her legs and leaned back on her hands. She knew the position emphasized her breasts. Barret's gaze whipped to her cleavage and lingered there. "Is this your first cruise?"

He seemed to be having trouble tearing his gaze off her breasts. Jasmine arched her back a bit. She saw Barret swallow and smiled to herself. "Uh, no. It's my fourth."

"Your *fourth*?" She knew firsthand what this cruise cost. The man must be rolling in dough to be able to afford four of them. "You must really enjoy them."

"I do." He finally dragged his gaze back to her face. "I like the route we take. The island is great. The food is the best I've ever had." He shifted and lifted one foot to rest on the lounge, letting his knee fall to the side. His new position gave Jasmine an even better view of his balls. "I like the freedom. I only wear clothes at dinner."

"You like to be naked."

"Don't you?"

Jasmine nodded. "I do."

"So why are you wearing a swimsuit?"

To tease, she thought, fighting a smile. Jasmine rolled to her stomach and propped up on her elbows. "I'm getting a feel for the ship. I don't know what's allowed and what isn't." That wasn't true. Rose had already told her *anything* was allowed. Barret would have to work to see her naked.

But not *too* hard.

"I'll be glad to help you figure out what's allowed and what isn't," Barret said with a wolfish grin.

I'll bet. "Thanks. I appreciate that."

His grin widened. "I also like the fantasies. Talk about hot!"

"Fantasies?" Jasmine didn't understand what he meant. "What fantasies?"

Celina joined them, dropping her tote bag on the chair next to Barret. "Hey, Jaz."

"Cee, hi. This is Barret. We've been getting to know each other. Barret, my good friend, Celina."

Barret smiled, showing straight white teeth. "Hi, Celina." His gaze quickly passed over her body. "It's a pleasure."

Jasmine noticed the straightening of Celina's back and the way her smile slipped. Her friend obviously didn't think much of Barret. However, Celina had always been polite and quickly smiled again. "For me too, Barret."

He gestured toward the lounge next to him. "Sit, please. Would you ladies like a drink?"

"I'd love one," Jasmine said. "Samir made something for us earlier that was to die for."

"Then I'll have Samir make you another one." He flashed his blinding smile again as he walked away.

Jasmine rolled to her side and watched Barret walk away. She sighed heavily. He might have the morals of an alley cat, but he looked amazing. "What a body. Did you see the size of his cock?"

"Everyone on the ship saw the size of his cock." Celina tugged a lounge closer to Jasmine. "That's what he wants."

"Yeah, probably." Jasmine returned to her stomach and propped up on her elbows again. "He told me this is his fourth cruise. He loves everything about it . . . the route, the food, the freedom. His clothes come off as soon as he boards, and he doesn't get dressed again until the ship returns to the dock. Well, except for dinner. How hot is that?"

"You did say this is a sex cruise. Sex is easier without clothes."

"That's true. And naked is always nice." She pushed her sunglasses to the top of her head. "Barret said something I don't understand."

Celina stretched out on the lounge and crossed her ankles. "What's that?"

"Right before you got here, he said he especially liked the fantasy part of the cruises. I didn't get the chance to ask him what that means."

"It's in the brochure I told you and Elayne about when we were in the salon. It said something about the passengers' most erotic fantasies coming true. I asked one of the stewardesses about it, but she wouldn't tell me anything. She said the captain would explain everything at dinner."

Jasmine frowned. "How are our fantasies supposed to come true?"

"I don't know. Anna wouldn't tell me anything. She said she preferred to honor her captain's wishes."

"Well, now I'm curious. I think we should find the captain and ask him."

"I already did."

Jasmine's eyebrows shot up. Celina wouldn't have had time to talk to the captain before she came to the pool. "And when did you talk to the captain?"

"He came to my cabin before we set sail."

"Oh, really?" Smiling wickedly, she sat up and scooted closer to Celina's lounge. She wanted to hear all the juicy details. "Tell me everything."

Celina laughed. "There's nothing to tell. He came to my

cabin and welcomed me aboard. I assumed he did that with all the passengers."

"Not me. I haven't even seen him yet. What does he look like?"

"Dark hair, brown eyes, deep tan. Tall, great body. *Very* handsome."

Jasmine sighed dramatically. He sounded perfect. "I think I'm in love."

She saw jealousy flare in Celina's eyes. Jasmine had no trouble going after the man she wanted unless a friend had already spoken for him. Celina was definitely interested in the captain. Jasmine thought that was great. Her friend needed to let loose and have a good time on the cruise. Fun was the whole point of the trip.

"We probably shouldn't bother him now," Celina said. "I mean, he's busy with sailing the yacht."

"I guess. Well, there's always dinner, right? He's supposed to explain everyth—"

She stopped. All the breath left her lungs, making it difficult to breathe. She forced enough oxygen into her mouth to mutter a soft, "Damn."

A man stood at the rail, gazing out over the water. The wind tousled his shaggy brown hair. He wore a simple white T-shirt, faded jeans, and deck shoes. Tall and slim with broad shoulders, he had the kind of build Jasmine loved. She licked her lips. She'd love to start at his toes and kiss all the way to the top of his head . . . stopping at strategic places in the middle.

Forget Samir and Barret. She wanted *this* man.

"Lots of hunks on this ship, aren't there?" Celina asked.

Jasmine heard her friend's question. Barely. She was too involved with staring at the handsome man to listen to Celina.

Celina waved her hand in front of her friend's face. "Yo, Jaz!"

Jasmine jerked and swiveled her head back to Celina. "Huh?"

"I said, there are a lot of hunks on this ship."

"There certainly are." Jasmine's attention swung back to the dark-haired man. She definitely wanted to get to know him better. "He looks like he could use some company."

"And you're just the person to help him out, right?"

Jasmine grinned. "You know me so well." She stood and adjusted her bikini so the top showed the greatest amount of cleavage. "I'll see you later."

He leaned on the railing as she walked closer to him. The position drew his jeans tighter across his ass. Jasmine didn't understand why he'd be wearing jeans on the ship and not shorts or a swimsuit, but she couldn't complain about the way they made his ass look. He was actually a little slimmer than she usually liked, but those shoulders and arms made up for it. He must work out every day to have that physique.

Her tummy fluttered when she pictured him lifting weights, his skin glistening with sweat . . .

It was time to get a man into her bed.

She stepped up to the railing next to him. "Hi."

He jerked, as if she'd startled him, before turning his head her direction. "Hi."

"I'm Jasmine Britt."

Clearing his throat, he straightened from the railing. At five-eight, Jasmine didn't consider herself short for a woman. He was at least six inches taller than she. Her tummy fluttered again.

"Chase Cummings."

Chase. What a great name. It made her think of running through the woods, with him in pursuit. She'd tease him by almost letting him catch her before sprinting away again. Then when he *did* catch her, he'd fuck her until she came at least twice. Maybe even three times.

It sounded like such fun.

"Is this your first cruise, Chase?"

He nodded. Jasmine waited, but he didn't say anything. Wanting to hear his sexy voice, she tried again. "It's my first time too. I think I'm going to love it. My two best friends from college are with me."

Still silent, Chase looked out over the water again. Jasmine pursed her lips. The man must be incredibly dense not to realize she wanted his attention. Experience had taught her the quickest way to get a man's attention was with sex. She laid one arm on the railing and leaned on it, pushing her breast almost completely out of the bikini cup. "Have you met the other passengers yet, Chase?"

He looked at her. Jasmine had to bite her bottom lip to keep from smiling when his gaze dropped to her breasts. "A few."

"How did you hear about the cruise?"

"From Jonathan."

"The first officer? You know him?"

"We've been friends a long time."

"What a coincidence. He's with Elayne right now. She's one of my friends." She laid her hand on his arm. His muscle jumped beneath her fingertips. "I guess the four of us will be spending a lot of time together."

She couldn't say he jerked his arm away from her touch, but it was close. Chase straightened and took two steps backward. "Excuse me, Jasmine. I have something to do."

Disappointment curled inside her. She wanted to spend more time with him. "Sure. I'll see you later."

He nodded once, then walked away. Jasmine watched him until he disappeared from her sight. What an absolutely edible man. She didn't understand his avoidance of her, but it didn't matter. Whatever Jasmine wanted, she always got.

And she wanted Chase Cummings.

Three

Jasmine switched two place cards on the table and smiled. That was better. Now she could sit next to Chase during dinner.

"What are you doing?" Elayne whispered in her ear.

Jasmine yelped and whirled around to face Elayne. Eyes wide, she laid one hand over her pounding heart. "Don't scare me like that!"

"Sorry." She didn't look sorry. Jasmine thought her friend looked very pleased with herself. "I repeat, what are you doing?"

"Nothing."

"Looks to me like you were switching place cards."

"Now why would I do that?" she asked, all innocence.

Elayne pressed her lips together, as if to keep from laughing. "Why don't you tell me?"

Jasmine looked at her for several seconds before releasing her breath in a huff. She'd been caught, so might as well confess. "Okay, I switched my place card with Glynnis's. It isn't a crime."

"Why did you do that?"

"Because I want to sit next to Chase at dinner."

"Who is Chase?"

"Remember? He's the guy . . . Oh, that's right. You weren't at the pool with me and Cee. You were off with Jonathan." Perfect. A chance to change the subject *and* get some juicy details. "So, how was he?"

"He was incredible, but don't change the subject. Who is Chase?"

"I'm surprised Jonathan didn't tell you about Chase. They're best buddies."

"Jonathan and I were busy. Talking wasn't at the top of our list. Let's try this again. Who is Chase?"

"Chase Cummings. I met him this afternoon. Ohmigod, Elayne, he is so gorgeous! He has curly brown hair and deep brown eyes. He's about six-one or -two with broad shoulders and a nice tight butt." She shivered. "I get wet just thinking about him." *And hot and bothered and very horny . . .*

"I didn't get the chance to talk to him much today. I figured if I sit by him at dinner, we'll have lots of time to get to know each other. Then after dinner, I'll haul him back to my cabin and fuck his brains out."

"Another conquest for you."

Jasmine grinned. "I'm so blessed."

"So you've decided Chase will be your fling of the weekend."

"Yep. I'll make him so happy, he won't want to give me up on Sunday."

"Maybe he'll make you so happy, you won't want to give *him* up."

Jasmine snorted. "Yeah, like *that's* ever going to happen. This gal doesn't give her heart to *any* man. I want a good time, that's all. That's what this trip is about." She took Elayne's hands and held them out to the sides. "You look incredible." The black sheath showed off her legs and a generous amount of her breasts. "Very hot dress."

"Thanks."

A man and woman walked in, arm in arm. Jasmine didn't recognize them, but Elayne apparently did. She smiled as the couple walked up to them. "Hi."

"Hi," the woman said, also smiling. "Elayne, right?"

"You win the prize."

"Oh, good. I love prizes." She slid her hand down to clasp the man's standing next to her. "This is Ferris Grover. We met on the ship last month. Ferris, this is Elayne and . . ."

"Jasmine, one of my best friends."

"Hi, Jasmine. I'm Doretta."

"You two met last month?" Jasmine asked.

Doretta nodded. "We enjoyed each other's company very much, but I live in South Carolina and Ferris lives in Oregon. So we decided to take another cruise and get to know each other better."

It was a lot of money to get to know each other better. It would've been cheaper for one of them to fly across country and stay in the finest hotel than pay for the cruise again. Jasmine shook her head. Love made people do really stupid things. That was one of the reasons she wanted nothing to do with it. A man was good for two things—sex and presents. Anything else, she didn't need or want.

More people filed into the room, including Celina and the captain. Her friend's eyes glowed with pleasure. She knew from Anna that the captain had been at the wheel all afternoon. That meant he and Celina couldn't have had sex yet. Jasmine had no doubt they would before the night was over.

So would she, as soon as she cornered Chase.

He walked into the room behind a clothed Barret. Chase wore a simple white button-down shirt and khakis, yet looked incredible. She imagined slowly releasing each of those buttons on his shirt. She'd spread the garment and kiss the center of his chest, then drop kisses down his stomach until she reached the waistband of his pants. By the time she unzipped them, his cock would be hard and ready for her mouth.

Jasmine could hardly wait.

Chase looked her way. He acknowledged her with a slight nod. That was enough for her to prove his interest.

She found her place at the table. Chase stood by his chair and waited until she sat before sitting next to her. He uttered a soft, "Good evening."

"Good evening." She slid the silver ring off her napkin. "I've heard the food is delicious. I hope so. I'm starving."

"I'm sure it will be." Chase took his own napkin and laid it in his lap. Jasmine assumed he would continue to talk to her. He remained silent.

A challenge. Jasmine loved challenges.

"I'm an investment broker. What do you do for a living?"

"Paint."

"Canvases or houses?"

"Both."

"You're an artist?"

He nodded at Boyd when the steward offered him wine. Jasmine waited for Chase to answer her question. He didn't.

Samir set Chase's salad in front of him. Chase picked up his salad fork, speared a piece of tomato, and popped it into his mouth. If Jasmine had discouraged easily, Chase's attitude would have her slinking off to her room. She'd never been one to slink. She picked up her own salad fork. He was going to be a bigger challenge than she'd thought. No matter. She'd win him over. She had no doubt about that.

By the time Boyd picked up her empty plate, Jasmine was getting discouraged. Her attempts to draw Chase into a conversation resulted in more one-word answers, or no answers at all. He either remained quiet or spoke to Jonathan on his left. Tired of being ignored, she'd turned to speak to Ian on her right. Every time she looked at him, his gaze fell to her cleavage and stayed there. She'd purposely worn a low-cut dress to entice Chase. He ignored her, while Ian's expression clearly said he'd be happy to play with her breasts the rest of the evening.

Jasmine wanted a man, but not *that* much.

The captain stood and everyone turned to him.

"Ladies and gentlemen, I want to officially welcome you aboard the S. S. *Fantasy*. The evening is yours to do anything you wish. A movie will start in the main salon at ten. The pool and hot tub are especially pleasant at night beneath the stars. A dessert bar is available on the upper deck. My crew and I will do everything in our power to make sure your cruise is enjoyable. Please don't hesitate to call on any of us at any time if you need something.

"Please excuse me as I have to return to work. You are welcome to stay here as long as you wish."

He looked directly at Celina. "Until later."

Jasmine easily recognized the private signal between her

friend and the captain. They planned to meet later, after he'd finished whatever captain duties he had to finish. The goo-goo eyes Elayne and Jonathan threw at each other clearly indicated they'd be together later also.

Jasmine refused to be the only one who didn't get the man she wanted into bed tonight.

Chase closed the door to his cabin before flipping on the light switch. He turned, his gaze falling on the bed. The covers had been pulled back to expose pale blue sheets. A gold foil-wrapped chocolate lay on each pillow. Fresh flowers in a crystal vase sat on the nightstand. He could smell their fragrance from where he stood.

They didn't smell nearly as good as Jasmine.

Ignoring her hadn't been easy. Not only did she smell good, she looked like a siren in that low-cut dark green dress. Her dress had fastened behind her neck, baring her shoulders and back. Twin straps had barely covered her breasts. Her long hair flowed halfway down her back. He'd imagined lifting her hair away from her neck. He'd lick her tan shoulder, then kiss his way to the sensitive spot behind her ear.

Closing his eyes, Chase pressed his hand against his thickening cock. Jon had told him he should let go on the cruise, find a woman and keep her in bed most of the time. That was easy for his friend to say. Jon hadn't gone through everything Chase had.

Self-pity tried to sneak its way back into Chase's mind. He firmly pushed it away. He refused to go down that path anymore.

A gentle knock on the door surprised him. He certainly wasn't expecting anyone. The only person who might come by would be Jon. His friend would barge right in without knocking.

Chase opened the door to see Jasmine on the other side. He forgot to breathe as his gaze passed over her body. She still wore that clingy, low-cut green dress. Something that sexy should be illegal.

"Hi," she said with a sultry smile. "May I come in?"

He should say no. Chase knew he should say no. Instead, he stepped to the side so she could enter.

She sauntered past him. He closed the door and leaned against it, trying to appear calm and relaxed. Inside, his heart pounded.

"I was going to the dessert bar with Celina and Elayne." She sat on the edge of his bed and leaned back on one hand. "I decided dessert with you would be better."

"I'm not much for sweets."

"No?" Jasmine stretched out on the bed, resting on one elbow. "What *do* you like, Chase?"

He'd like to go back and relive his life so he'd know what to do right now. He had a beautiful woman in his cabin, on his bed, obviously interested in him, and didn't know what to do. "I'd like to go to bed."

A wicked smile turned up her lips. "Works for me."

Shit! "I mean, it's been a long day. I'd like to go to bed. Alone."

"You don't have to go to bed alone, Chase." She rose from his bed, graceful as a ballerina. Chase swallowed as she strolled up to him. "Not as long as I'm here."

She slid her hands up his chest and around his neck. Chase opened his mouth to tell her no. He didn't get the chance to say a word before she kissed him.

Her lips slid across his. Her scent teased his nostrils, her taste teased his tongue. She moaned and stepped closer, pressing her breasts against his chest. He was caught between the door and her body. She nipped at his bottom lip, licked each corner of his mouth.

The woman definitely knew how to kiss.

Chase was a moment away from returning her kiss when he came to his senses. Reaching behind his neck, he grabbed her wrists and pulled her arms away from him. "That's enough."

Instead of discouraging her, her smile widened. "Hardly. I've only begun."

"You've begun and ended." Chase stepped away from the door, and her. "You need to go."

Her smile slowly faded. "Go?"

"Yes. Please leave."

"You are kidding, right?"

"Do I look like I'm kidding?"

She studied his face for several moments. "No, you look very serious."

Chase walked back to the door and opened it. "Good night."

Jasmine stood in the same spot, still studying his face. "You really want me to go?"

Her tone clearly said she wasn't used to men turning her down. Too bad. Chase didn't have any other choice but to turn her down. "Yes, I really want you to go."

Jasmine lowered her head, sighed, and looked back into his eyes. "Good night."

Chase closed the door behind her. Telling Jasmine to leave hadn't been easy. He could still taste her on his lips, smell her perfume in the air. She obviously wanted him. Her actions had made that clear since the moment he met her.

But Chase knew she wouldn't want him anymore if she knew the truth.

He'd turned her down. She'd been in his cabin, ready and willing to fuck him, and he'd turned her down. Jasmine couldn't believe it. A man had *never* turned her down. She'd brushed aside many men who didn't please her, or no longer pleased her. Throwing one away was easy when there were so many more in the world. But to have a man ask her to *leave*? That did not happen.

She should forget all about him. He had to be an idiot to turn down a woman so willing to share his bed.

She placed one hand over her fluttering stomach. An idiot wouldn't make her tummy do backflips.

She headed for the upper deck. Chocolate would be a poor excuse for sex, but it's all she had right now.

She saw Celina and Elayne sitting at a table. Bypassing the dessert bar—for now—she headed for their table.

"Damn, damn, damn," she huffed as she flopped down in the chair opposite Celina.

"What's wrong?" Celina asked.

"Chase. I don't understand him. I practically attacked him, and he pushed me away. A man has *never* ignored me like he does." She blew out another breath. "He's so . . ." Jasmine stopped. Leaning forward, she plucked one of the chocolate-covered strawberries from Celina's saucer and popped it in her mouth. She chewed slowly before speaking again. "He's gorgeous, for sure, but he's also . . . mysterious. There's something going on with him that he won't tell me."

"Like what?"

"I don't know. He seems . . . sad and alone. Something happened to him, something that hurt him badly."

"Isn't he Jonathan's friend?" Elayne asked.

Jasmine nodded. "Think you can get Jonathan to spill the beans to you?"

"I can try." Her lips turned up in a wicked grin. "Of course, we haven't talked much yet."

"Bragging is so unbecoming, Elayne."

"You'd be the one bragging if Chase had fucked you."

"Yeah, I would." She tossed her long hair over one shoulder. She should be in his bed right now, his cock buried deep inside her. "I don't know what it is about him that draws me, but it's definitely there. I can't stop thinking about him."

"Love at first sight?" Elayne asked, taking the last bite of her cheesecake.

"Oh, puh-*leese*. I do *not* fall in love."

"There's a first time for everything."

"Not for this gal. All love does is complicate a good time."

"You sound like Elayne." Celina looked from one friend to the other. "I didn't know you two were so cynical about men."

"You haven't been married." Elayne wiped her mouth and laid her napkin next to her empty saucer. "Love hurts. All the hearts and flowers stuff from romance novels is crap. Sure, it starts out great. Hormones are raging and the sex is hot. Once that calms down and you have to face real life, it isn't fun anymore. I should've learned that with my first husband. But no, I had to fall for Winston and dig myself another hole."

Celina touched Elayne's hand. "You were happy with Winston."

"Yeah, at first, until I figured out he was content to stay home and drink beer while I worked. Uh-uh. I don't mind that I earn more than a lot of men, but I won't support him. Marriage is supposed to be a partnership. Neither of mine was."

Jasmine eyed Celina's other strawberry. Before she could snatch it, she saw the captain approaching. He stopped at their table. "Ladies," he said with a smile. "I see you've been enjoying the dessert bar."

"The lemon cheesecake was incredible." Leaning forward, Elayne rested her forearms on the table. "Any chance of getting the recipe?"

"You'll have to speak to the chef about that. Henri is very protective of his recipes."

"Maybe I can convince him to share with me."

Rand laughed. "I have no doubt that if anyone can get Henri to give up one of his recipes, it would be you, Ms. Wyatt."

"You are a charmer, aren't you, Captain?"

He dipped his head. "I do my best."

He turned his attention to Celina. "Ms. Tate."

"Captain."

"Would you like to see my ship now?"

"Yes, I would." She looked at Elayne and Jasmine. "I'll see you later."

Elayne grinned. "Have a good time."

Jasmine frowned while she watched Celina walk away with the captain. Elayne had already been laid. Celina was about to be. The man she wanted had pushed her away. How disgusting. "I need a drink. Wanna go to the bar with me?"

"You're on."

Four

Jasmine glanced at the illuminated clock on the night-stand—2:13. Muttering under her breath, she rolled to her back and stared at the ceiling. Damn Chase for rejecting her. She couldn't sleep, and it was all his fault. If he hadn't pushed her away, she'd be exhausted from orgasms instead of wide-awake from frustration.

Slipping her hands beneath the sheet, she cradled her bare breasts. Her hard nipples nestled into her palms. Jasmine closed her eyes as she slid her hands over her nipples in small circles. Each pass over the firm tips sent a zing between her thighs. Her pussy clenched and began to weep.

"Chase," she whispered.

She imagined him leaning over her, his pelvis pressed tightly to hers. He wouldn't fuck her, not yet. First, he'd play with her. He'd circle his hips, brushing his erection up and down her slit. Over and over he'd tease her, until she begged him to take her. Still he'd tease her, rubbing her clit with his hard cock, whispering that he wanted her to come.

Jasmine slid one hand between her open thighs. Her warm cream covered her fingers. She pushed two fingers into her channel, then began to rub her clit. She pictured Chase's face, his dark brown eyes looking into hers, as she caressed herself. She saw him sit back on his knees and reach for the snaps on his jeans. He'd release one and press his hand against his shaft. A cocky grin would turn up his lips as he released another snap. She'd be able to see the skin beneath his navel through his jeans' opening.

Pinching one nipple, she rubbed her clit faster, harder. Chase would unfasten another snap. He'd pull his jeans apart. His hard rod would be released, standing up against his belly. Then . . .

"Oh, God!" Jasmine bucked as the orgasm galloped through her body. "Yes! Chase. *Yes!*"

She continued to caress her clit until the final waves of her climax passed through her body. Breathing hard, she rolled to her side and tucked her knees close to her chest. As soon as her heart stopped pounding, she'd be able to sleep.

Ten minutes later, sleep still hadn't claimed her. With a heavy sigh, Jasmine rolled to her back again. She opened her eyes, expecting to see the ceiling in her darkened room. Instead, she saw a canopy of leaves.

Leaves?

She sat up and looked around. Trees surrounded her . . . thick, tall trees with vines hanging from the branches. She could hear birds chirping in the trees and the sound of rushing water nearby. The ground felt damp beneath her butt. Looking down, she saw that she sat on a bed of moss. The next thing she noticed was her clothes. A pair of loose khakis covered her legs, a tight brown tank covered her torso. Dark brown hiking boots made her feet look huge.

She wouldn't be caught dead in hiking boots.

Jasmine pushed herself to her feet. She turned in a slow circle, gazing at the entire area. The air felt sticky and hot, like a place in the tropics. Sweat formed over her mouth and between her breasts. She'd never been a fan of heat. She'd take the cold of Chicago in the winter rather than hot and humid any day.

Crappy dream, Jaz. You could've at least dreamed you're stranded in a snowbound chalet in Switzerland.

A twig snapped to her right. Dream or not, the sound sent goose bumps scattering across her skin. Someone—or some-*thing*—headed her way.

She didn't plan to stick around and find out which.

Jasmine turned to her left and took off at a fast walk. More twigs snapped behind her. Her fast walk escalated into a jog. Moving faster wasn't possible because of the thick foliage that surrounded her. She plodded through moss. Leaves and vines hit her face. She couldn't hear anything following her over the pounding of her heart, but she sensed it was there.

She tripped over a large root. Not able to catch herself, she fell in a patch of moss. She took only a moment to catch her breath before she tried to scramble to her feet. A sudden weight on her back pushed her down into the soft moss.

"Where do you think you're going?" a husky voice growled in her ear.

Fear gave her strength. Jasmine bucked, trying to knock off the man sprawled over her. Instead of being knocked off, he chuckled.

"Quite the little tigress, aren't you?"

Jasmine froze. She immediately recognized his voice. Chase lay on top of her. "What are you doing?"

"Exactly what you want."

One moment she lay on her stomach, the next Chase had flipped her to her back. He held her wrists next to her head. Still trying to catch her breath, Jasmine looked up at him. He wore camouflage pants and a raggedy black T-shirt. With him holding her arms and his legs nuzzled between hers, she couldn't move.

A slow heat began to burn in her belly.

He straightened his arms so his torso no longer touched hers. The new position pressed his pelvis even more firmly between her thighs. She could feel his cock hardening against her mound.

"Is this what you want?" He circled his hips. Jasmine bit her bottom lip when his rod brushed her clit. "You want this inside you?"

"Yes." She tried to jerk her wrists out of his hands, but his hold was too strong. "Let me touch you."

Chase shook his head. "I'm in charge. You do whatever I say."

A delicious shiver skittered down her spine. Jasmine had always been in charge, had always been the leader during sex. To put herself completely in Chase's hands was very exciting.

"I'm going to let your arms go, but don't move them."

"Okay."

She lay still, her hands palms up by her head. Chase leaned over her, resting his hands on the ground next to her waist. He used his knees to push her legs farther apart. "Yeah, like that. Open for me."

"Take off my pants, and I'll show you how fast I can open."

He chuckled, low and wicked. "You're impatient."

"I'm horny."

He pressed his cock against her pussy. Jasmine moaned and arched her hips to get more of that delicious friction. She pumped her hips in time to his thrusts. Each movement caressed her clit. Each movement drove her desire higher.

She cried out when he tunneled his hands beneath her tank and squeezed her breasts. "Chase!"

"Damn, these feel good." He pushed her breasts together and ran his thumbs over the nipples. "Nice and firm."

He continued to touch her nipples, rubbing his thumbs back and forth, then in circles. Jasmine had never come simply from having her nipples rubbed, but she soon decided this could be the first time.

Her eyes drifted shut in pleasure. He kept caressing her breasts as he rubbed his shaft up and down her slit. Jasmine liked the friction, the slow climb to orgasm. Placing her feet on the ground, she let her knees fall open. His pumping increased. Jasmine opened her eyes again and looked into Chase's deep brown ones. She could see the heat there, the desire. His jaw clenched, a muscle jumped in his temple. He was obviously as close to coming as she. Jasmine lifted her hips and thrust against him, searching for that extra stimulation on her clit.

She found it a moment later. Squeezing her eyes shut, she threw back her head and keened through her release.

Heart pounding, lungs struggling for air, Jasmine slowly opened her eyes. Expecting to still see the lush forest overhead, she was surprised to see the ceiling of her cabin instead.

"What the hell . . ."

Jasmine quickly sat up. Dawn's light through her portholes gave her enough illumination to see around her cabin. Feeling fuzzy, she shook her head to clear it. She must have been dreaming. But it had seemed so *real*. She would swear she had felt Chase's hands on her breasts, his pelvis arching against hers. Her body still tingled from the orgasm that had raced through her.

She doubled up her fist and hit the mattress. Damn it, she didn't want to *dream* about Chase . . . she wanted to *be with* him. She couldn't remember any man ever affecting her so strongly. She needed to spend time with him, to find out exactly how she felt about him. It wasn't love. She knew that without a doubt. But it was something . . . something she wanted to explore.

Jasmine knew she wouldn't be able to go back to sleep. It was probably too early for the crew to start serving, but perhaps she could con someone into making her a cup of coffee. She could sit on the upper deck, enjoy her coffee, and read until Celina and Elayne joined her for breakfast.

She crawled out of bed and stumbled to the bathroom. A nap later today would definitely be in order. Maybe she could convince Chase to take one with her . . . after they made love.

She liked that idea very much.

A glance in the mirror at her matted hair caused her to flinch. She'd often thought about cutting the long mass, but hadn't been able to make herself take that final drastic step. Regular trims were as far as she could go. The way it looked today, it was past time for a trim.

Picking up her brush, she began to work the tangles out of her hair. A particularly nasty one had her cursing under her breath. Leaning closer to the mirror, she peered at the clump in her hair. Small twigs were buried in the strands, along with several leaves. She picked them out one by one and laid them on the counter.

Twigs and leaves. She stared at the small pile and wondered how she'd gotten them in her hair while she slept. She'd been in a forest in her dream, but that had been a *dream*. Dreams weren't real.

Unless it had been her fantasy coming true and not a dream.

Rose had mentioned the fantasies. She'd said she had no explanation for her fantasy about Victorian England coming true, yet it had. Every detail she'd imagined in her mind had actually happened, much to her delight.

Jasmine touched one of the twigs with her fingertip. Only part of her fantasy had come true last night. She'd imagined Chase running after her in the woods, but he hadn't fucked her the way she'd wanted. She'd only had one orgasm instead of the two or three she'd expected to have.

Instead of feeling frightened at something she couldn't explain, she looked forward to the adventure. Chase wouldn't get away from her so easily next time. She'd make sure *all* her fantasy came true.

Jasmine had spent hours and hours with her etiquette teacher, Mrs. Bachman. One of those lessons had been how very rude it was to eavesdrop. Jasmine remembered that lesson so clearly. That didn't mean she couldn't ignore it.

She watched Jonathan rap twice on Chase's door before opening it. Tiptoeing up to the door Jonathan had left ajar, she leaned in to listen.

"Hey, Jon. What's up?"

"You tell me. Why aren't you in swimming trunks? You're going to the island."

"No, I'm not."

"Chase—"

"Save your lectures, Jon. I'm not going. That's final."

"Why not?"

"You know why not. I don't want people staring at me."

How interesting. Jasmine could understand people staring at Chase since he was so good-looking. Any other reason made no sense to her.

She heard a door open and bottles rattle. "No one is going to stare at you, Chase."

"Yeah, right." He paused for several seconds. Jasmine leaned a bit closer to the open door.

"If I stay here," Chase said, "I can be sure no one stares at me."

"You can't hide forever."

"Watch me."

"At least go up on deck and lie in the sun. Don't hide here in your cabin."

Another pause. Jasmine held her breath while waiting for Chase to speak again.

"Everyone's going to the island?"

"Yeah, as far as I know."

"The crew too?"

"You'll be completely alone on the ship."

"Completely alone works for me."

Jasmine grinned. *Too bad, Chase. My plans don't include your being alone.*

★　★　★

Chase leaned his head back on the lounge and closed his eyes. The sun felt good on his face. He'd love to take off his T-shirt and get some sun on his chest too. Despite Jon's assuring him he'd be alone on the ship, Chase couldn't take the chance of someone seeing him.

He wasn't ready for that.

"Hi, Chase."

He inhaled sharply when he heard Jasmine's voice. Lifting his head, he peered at her over the top of his sunglasses. She stood a mere three feet away. Her hair was pulled up in a high ponytail. Her shiny gold bikini couldn't contain more than half a yard of fabric.

She looked hot and sexy and beautiful.

"Mind if I join you?"

He'd answer her as soon as he could make his tongue work again. "You didn't go to the island."

"No. I'm not much on volleyball."

She turned her back to him and bent over. She wore a thong, which left her buttocks completely bare. Chase's mouth went dry as he thought of reaching over to her, running his hand across that firm, tan flesh . . .

She adjusted the lever on the lounge so the chair was flat. After spreading out a large towel, she lay down on her stomach. She crossed her arms and used them as a pillow, her face turned toward him. "The sun feels good."

Chase closed his eyes. He hated being a wimp. Jasmine wanted him. He'd seen shock and disappointment in her eyes last night when he'd asked her to leave his cabin. A simple yes from him, and she would have been in his bed the rest of the night.

Maybe she didn't want *him* as much as she wanted another

conquest. Self-confidence oozed from the lady. She was obviously used to getting what she wanted. Or *who* she wanted.

When Jon had explained the fantasies to him, Chase had laughed at his friend. A ship—an inanimate object—didn't have the power to make fantasies come true. Finding himself drawn into Jasmine's fantasy last night proved his friend had been telling the truth. The romp in the jungle had been fun, as well as arousing.

Jon had also explained how Chase could alter the fantasy. Chase had gone along with running after Jasmine in the woods, but had refused to finish it the way she'd wanted. He had cradled her breasts and rubbed his cock against her mound through their clothes, the way she'd imagined, but had stopped short of fucking her. It had been frustrating as hell for him, yet delicious to watch her as she climbed toward orgasm. After she came, he drew her back out of the fantasy to awaken in her cabin.

"Chase, would you put some lotion on my back please?"

He opened his eyes to see Jasmine holding out a bottle of suntan lotion. Her eyes were narrowed against the bright sunshine so he couldn't see them, but he thought he saw her lips twitch in a mischievous grin. She was baiting him, just like dangling a nice juicy worm before a largemouth bass.

Go for it, man. You know you want to touch her more than you want your next breath.

Chase rose from his chair and sat on the edge of hers. She smiled at him over her shoulder. "Thanks. I appreciate it."

He took the bottle from her and poured a generous amount of lotion in his palm. He rubbed his hands together to distribute the lotion evenly, then laid his hands on her upper back.

Using gentle, even movements, he spread the creamy liquid over her skin.

Her back rose and fell with her deep breath. "You have a nice touch, Chase."

Chase poured more lotion into his palm and began to spread it on her lower back. The scent of coconut drifted up from her sun-warmed flesh.

"Untie the straps please. I don't want white lines."

Those tiny straps wouldn't leave much of a white line. Chase hesitated a moment, then did as she asked. Pushing her ponytail aside, he untied the strap around her neck first and let the ends fall to the lounge. The strap across the middle of her back came next. Other than for a scrap of cloth that barely covered her mound, she was nude.

Trying to ignore her state of undress, Chase continued spreading the lotion across her entire back. He stopped when he reached the thin piece of elastic circling her hips.

"The backs of my legs too please."

"You can do that yourself."

"I can, but it's easier if you do it. Please?"

It *wasn't* easier for him to do it. She had no idea how diffi-cult it was for him to touch her like this and not want more.

He'd wanted more for months.

Chase drizzled a line of lotion on each leg. Starting at her ankles, he smoothed the lotion over one leg to the top of her thigh. He repeated the journey on her other leg, then stopped. He wasn't sure if he should continue or not.

"You aren't through," Jasmine said. Then, in a breathy voice, "Please."

Five

Jasmine turned her head so her forehead rested on her arms. Holding her breath, she waited for Chase to spread the lotion over her buttocks. She would swear ten minutes ticked by before he touched her. His slick hands slid over her skin, almost reverently. He took much longer to spread the lotion over her butt than he had over her back and legs.

She didn't mind at all.

Her breath hitched when he ran one finger along the thong between her cheeks.

"You have an amazing ass, Jasmine."

He lifted his hands. Moments passed while Jasmine waited again for what he would do next. She was about to raise her head to see if he'd left when she felt the tiny nip on her left cheek.

A firmer bite on her right cheek made her squirm. He squeezed both buttocks, then began to knead them. More bites, more kneading, until Jasmine was ready to scream at Chase to fuck her.

"Spread your legs," he commanded.

A man didn't tell her what to do. A man obeyed her, not the other way around. Yet she was willing to do whatever Chase ordered. She spread her legs.

He lay on top of her, his denim-covered cock nestled against her ass. Jasmine let one foot fall to the deck to give him more room to move. He thrust between her legs, the way he had in her dream last night.

"Chase," she sighed.

"What?"

"I want more."

"I know you do." His fingertips pressed the sides of her breasts. "So do I."

She arched her hips and smiled when she heard him groan. Finally, she would get exactly what she wanted from him. "Fuck me, Chase."

He stopped thrusting. "Not here." He rose to his feet and held out one hand to her. "In your cabin."

Jasmine rolled to her side and shaded her eyes with one hand. Chase's gaze immediately slipped to her bare breasts. "Why not here? No one's on board."

"I don't want to take a chance on someone interrupting us."

He continued to hold his hand out to her. Jasmine wouldn't mind if someone interrupted them. No one had ever watched her having sex. She thought it would be hot.

"Jasmine. Let's go."

She would always choose Chase over having an audience. Placing her hand in his, she let him pull her to her feet.

Chase kept glancing at Jasmine as he led her toward her cabin. He couldn't believe he was doing this, that he was actually going to have sex with her. If he disappointed her, he'd be mortified.

He caught himself before he rubbed the scar on his chest. He couldn't think about that. All his thoughts had to be focused on Jasmine.

He shut the door behind them and leaned against it. Unsure what to do, he watched her approach the bed. She turned to face him, a seductive look on her face. *She* knew what to do. She knew all the words, all the gestures, all the moves. Chase felt like a kindergartener next to her.

Relying on instinct, he stepped closer to her. Those incredible breasts deserved his attention. Chase cradled both in his palms and tested their weight. He whisked his thumbs across her nipples. She inhaled sharply, then exhaled slowly. Her obvious pleasure at his touch drove him to caress her nipples again. They hardened and grew larger with each pass of his thumbs.

Beautiful.

He took a step back when Jasmine clasped the bottom of his T-shirt, as if she planned to remove it. Her lips pursed in a pout. "I want to see you."

"You will. Later."

He drew her into his arms and lowered his lips to hers. Finally, finally, he could kiss a woman the way he'd wanted for so long. He framed Jasmine's face and tilted it to get the angle he wanted. A nip on her lower lip, a swipe of his tongue across the upper. She parted her lips and touched the tip of his tongue with her own. Chase lifted her face and deepened the kiss. His tongue drove deep into her mouth, over and over. He felt Jasmine's hand slide beneath his T-shirt and up his back. Her hands began to drift around his sides. That's when he ended the kiss. She couldn't touch his chest . . . not until he'd had the chance to explain.

Scooping her up in his arms, he walked the few steps to the bed and lay her in the middle. After slipping off his sandals, he followed her down and reclined on top of her as he kissed her again. She clutched at his shoulders, gripped his hair. Little noises came from her throat . . . ones of passion, of pleasure.

His little tigress had been let loose.

Taking her hands, he pressed them to the bed next to her head. He straightened his arms, copying his position in her fantasy last night. "I want to play. Are you game?"

Her eyes widened a moment, then turned sultry. "What do you have in mind?"

Chase released her hands. He pulled open the nightstand drawer and rummaged through the contents. He found what he wanted and held them up for Jasmine to see. "Ever been handcuffed to the bed?"

"I'm usually the one who handcuffs the guy."

An image flashed through Chase's mind, one of his wrists cuffed to the bedposts while Jasmine rode his cock. The thought made his rod twitch. "Not this time."

She didn't argue with him. Chase fastened one of the fur-lined cuffs around each of Jasmine's wrists, then the other end around the round bedposts. An extra length of chain between the cuffs kept Jasmine's arms bent by her head instead of un-comfortably stretched.

Chase straddled her hips, bent over, and kissed her mouth. Her lips were so warm, so soft. He kissed her again and again, unable to get enough of her taste.

With his mouth still covering hers, he cradled her breasts. Jasmine released a loud moan and arched her back. Her tongue dove into his mouth. Chase bit it lightly, making Jasmine moan again.

"God, you're a good kisser," she rasped.

She couldn't possibly know how much her comment pleased him. He continued to knead her breasts, thumb her nipples. Jasmine's breathing became more choppy the longer he caressed her.

It was time for more.

Chase moved away from Jasmine so he could open the nightstand drawer again. "What are you doing?" she asked.

"You'll see." He located a red silk scarf and drew it from the drawer. He held it up so she'd know exactly what he planned to do. "Or maybe you *won't* see."

Jasmine clenched her fists. "I've never been blindfolded."

Chase wouldn't do anything that would make her uncomfortable. The way she squirmed on the bed, he didn't think the idea of being blindfolded bothered her. "Then it'll be a first for you."

He kissed her deeply before fastening the scarf around her eyes. She whimpered, but Chase suspected it was from desire and not fear. "You okay?"

"Yes." He saw her throat work as she swallowed. "What are you going to do?"

"Make you come."

Hearing him say the words was almost enough to send her over the top. Jasmine's belly quivered in anticipation.

He lightly licked her left nipple. She couldn't feel any part of his body touching her, only his tongue. Her right nipple received the same gentle lap. Then nothing. She waited, but he didn't lick her nipples again.

She gasped when he licked her navel.

"You have a very sexy belly button, Jasmine."

Jasmine tilted back her head, trying to peek under the edge of the scarf. She couldn't see anything. With her wrists cuffed, she was completely at his mercy.

Her pussy wept, and her clit throbbed. She wanted him inside her so badly, she'd probably come if he did nothing more than blow on her pussy. "Chase, you're making me crazy!"

"Am I? I think I like that." He grasped the elastic band of her thong. "Lift your hips." He slid her thong down her legs and off her feet.

Jasmine didn't hear anything except Chase's heavy breathing. She could feel him looking at her, examining every part of her exposed body. She'd always been proud of her body but couldn't help wondering if his silence meant he found her lacking. "What's wrong?"

"Nothing's wrong." One finger skated across her bare mound. "You shave your pussy."

"Don't you like that?"

"Yeah." His voice sounded choked. "It's . . . Damn."

He pushed on the inside of her knees. Jasmine spread her legs at his silent command. The mattress shifted. Denim grazed her legs as he moved between them. She didn't understand why he hadn't undressed. "Why are you still wearing clothes?"

A gentle kiss on her mound, and she forgot her question. Chase lifted her legs until her feet were flat on the bed. Her knees fell open. More kisses fell on her skin, gentle brushes of his lips followed by whisks of his tongue. His fingers slid through the cream covering her feminine lips.

"You're beautiful here." He circled her clit, and she moaned. "All pink and wet. You smell incredible."

She lifted her hips when he lapped at her sensitive flesh. He spread her lips and licked up and down her labia. His touch was both tentative and arousing. Jasmine wanted so badly to touch him, to bury her fingers in his wavy hair as he licked her.

"Open the cuffs, Chase. Let me touch you."

He ignored her request and continued to nuzzle her slit. He laved her clit, the opening to her channel, her anus. Jasmine's heart pounded in her ears. She couldn't remember ever wanting a man as much as she wanted Chase right now.

"Chase, fuck me! *Please.*"

"Not until you come."

He placed his lips over her clit and suckled. The orgasm started in her toes and ran up her legs to engulf her whole body. "Yes! Oh, *yes!*" She pressed her pussy against his mouth, trying to draw out the pleasure as long as possible.

Jasmine collapsed on the bed, her breathing heavy. Her heart beat so strongly, she wondered if Chase could see the movement in her chest.

Soft, wet lips covered hers. She inhaled sharply at the taste of herself on his mouth. Releasing her breath with a long moan, she parted her lips and returned his kiss. She thought she heard the rattle of the handcuffs, but was too involved in the kiss to care.

A swipe of his tongue ended the kiss. The mattress shifted with his movement. Jasmine expected to hear Chase remove his clothes. Instead, she heard the gentle click of the doorknob.

Jasmine waited, certain she hadn't really heard the door close. Chase couldn't have left her, not before they made love. And certainly not handcuffed to the bed.

"Chase?"

No answer. Jasmine slowly lifted her hands. The cuffs fell away from her wrists. She quickly sat up and jerked off the blindfold. She was alone in the room.

Jasmine scrambled off the bed and dashed to the door. She almost pulled out the doorknob in her haste to turn it. She didn't see Chase in the short hallway.

Her first instinct was to run after him. She ignored that instinct and returned to the bed. Lying on her back, she stretched her arms over her head and smiled. Chase wanted to play. Fine. As long as he kept on giving her such powerful orgasms, he could play all he wanted to . . . as long as he understood that she got to play too. Next time, *he'd* be the one handcuffed to the bed.

Jasmine bounced into the main salon, a huge smile on her face. Her body still hummed from her climax, even after the long, cool shower. She flopped down in the chair opposite the love seat where Celina and Elayne sat. "Oh my *God*. I just had the most intense orgasm I've ever had in my *life*."

Elayne looked at Celina and grinned. "Do we dare ask her?"

"I doubt if we'll have to ask her. She'll tell us anyway."

"You're damn right I will." She looked over her shoulder at the bar. "Where's that hunky Samir? I need a drink."

As if he'd read Jasmine's mind, Samir appeared behind the bar. "Ladies, would you care for a drink?"

"You bet. I want one of those pink things you made yesterday." Jasmine glanced at Celina and Elayne. "How about it?"

"I'll take another glass of wine," Elayne said.

"I can't be a party pooper if you two are drinking. I'll have one of the pink things too, Samir."

He smiled. "Coming right up."

Once he had turned to prepare the drinks, Jasmine leaned forward in her chair. "You will not believe what Chase did to me."

"Chase?" Elayne's eyebrows disappeared into her curly bangs. "You mean you finally got him into bed?"

"Well, yes and no. We were on my bed, but we didn't exactly have sex."

"How can you not exactly have sex?" Celina asked.

Jasmine smiled wickedly. She couldn't wait to give her friends all the details. "He blindfolded me and—"

She stopped and her gaze darted to her left. "Nicola's coming."

"Excuse me, Ms. Britt," Nicola said. "I apologize for interrupting."

"No problem. What can we do for you?"

She faced Celina. "The captain asked me to give this to you, Ms. Tate."

The redhead held out a small envelope to Celina. She frowned. "It's from the captain?"

Nicola nodded. "Yes, ma'am. He asked me to wait for a reply."

Celina withdrew a single sheet of paper from the envelope. She read it silently while Elayne peeked over her shoulder. "What does it say?"

Samir approached with the drinks. He began setting them on the table as Celina answered Elayne's question. "Rand invited me to dinner tonight in his suite."

Jasmine picked up her drink. She tuned out the conversation while thinking back to her time with Chase. It'd been amazing, but also . . . different. There had been times when

Chase's touch had been tentative, almost as if he didn't know what to do. His touches, his kisses, had all been gentle. Most of the men she'd been with had become more aggressive as she'd neared orgasm. Chase hadn't. He'd continued to lick her and touch her as if she were a precious treasure.

She liked that.

Chase was so different from any other man she'd known. He hadn't asked her any of the where-do-you-live-what-do-you-do-for-a-living questions. She'd asked him a few questions last night at dinner, but hadn't learned much about him. She planned to change that tonight.

In the past, she couldn't wait for the man to leave her bed. All that touchy-feely after-sex conversation had never been her style. The man had been there to satisfy her. She'd never cared if he lived in a mansion or an alleyway, or if he had brothers and sisters. Once she'd had all the orgasms she could get from him, she'd sent him on his way. She wouldn't do that with Chase. She *wanted* the touchy-feely after-sex conversation with him.

"I'm supposed to have dinner with my friends."

Jasmine snapped back to the present to hear Celina's comment to Nicola. She was about to tell Celina not to worry about her and Elayne, but Elayne beat her to it.

"Oh, pish." Elayne waved one hand as if that would erase Celina's comment. "You don't give another thought to Jaz and me. We'll be fine."

"Besides," Jasmine said, "maybe Elayne and I will have dinner with a couple of hunky guys."

At least *she* would. Then after dinner, she'd have Chase for dessert.

Six

Chase knew he'd never see Jasmine again after the cruise. Singles came on this cruise to have a good time and fuck each other's brains out. That's what Jonathan had told him. Chase had seen evidence of that shortly after casting off. He'd stumbled onto Mara and Barret having sex in the main salon. Neither of them had been the slightest bit embarrassed for him to catch them. Barret had grinned wickedly and asked Chase if he wanted to be next.

He and Jasmine were together simply to make each other feel good. Still, he felt he should tell her the truth. He had to be honest with her before they were intimate.

All he had to do was figure out how to tell her.

She sat at her place at the dining table. She didn't notice him when he walked into the room for she was speaking to Elayne across the table. Her friend must have said something funny. Jasmine laughed, a rich tinkling sound that traveled straight to his balls.

Leaving her cabin today without sinking his cock into her sweet pussy had been torture.

She glanced in his direction. Her eyes narrowed into that sultry look she'd given him in her cabin . . . that look that made his knees weak and his dick hard.

Chase held her gaze as he walked to his chair. He clapped Jonathan on the back when he passed his friend. "Hey, Jon."

"Hey, Chase. Everything okay?"

"Yeah. It's great." He sat in his chair and looked at Jasmine. Her hazel eyes appeared golden in the dim lighting. "Good evening."

"Good evening." She leaned closer to him. Her soft breast pressed against his arm. "You owe me," she whispered.

Trying to ignore the feel of her firm flesh, Chase shook out his napkin and laid it in his lap. "What do I owe you?"

"We didn't finish this afternoon."

He looked directly into her eyes. He clearly remembered the way her body had shivered when she'd climaxed. "*You* did."

Jasmine shook her head. "That was only the appetizer. I want the whole meal, plus dessert."

"Wine, Mr. Cummings?" Samir asked.

Chase nodded. Samir splashed a deep red wine into Chase's glass. He took a healthy sip to avoid commenting on what Jasmine had said. He didn't know if he could give her the whole meal, much less dessert.

Even with his doctor telling him he could do anything he desired, a knot of fear still tightened Chase's stomach. He'd had to be careful for so many years. He didn't know how to simply let go and be a normal, healthy man.

He watched Jasmine as she sipped her wine. This woman made him feel things he'd never experienced, never believed he *could* experience. If she wanted the full meal, he'd do his damnedest to give it to her.

"Would you join me on the deck after dinner?"

Her smile lit up her eyes. "I'd like that."

A tingle traveled up Jasmine's arm when Chase took her hand. She'd always thought holding hands was hokey, something sentimental couples did. Touching Chase in such a simple way seemed right.

He led her to the railing on the upper deck. Tugging her in front of him, he wrapped his arms around her waist. Jasmine crossed her arms over his and leaned back into his body. She liked standing here with Chase, looking out over the calm water. She didn't speak, but didn't feel the need to.

"Would you like another glass of wine?" Chase asked.

Jasmine shook her head and drew his arms tighter around her waist. "I had one at dinner. That was enough."

He kissed her nape. Jasmine sighed softly. Normally, she would've already dragged her man to her cabin to ravish him. Right now, she was content to stand in Chase's arms, feel his heartbeat against her back.

He kissed the side of her neck. "What are you thinking about?"

"How good it feels in your arms." She reached back and encircled his neck with one arm. "I'm not thinking about tearing off your clothes. That's a first for me."

His warm breath tickled her ear when he chuckled. "Have I lost my appeal already?"

"No way. I just . . ." She stopped, unsure what to say. That was a first for her too. Jasmine was never at a loss for words, never had any problem saying what was on her mind. It made her mother cringe for Jasmine simply to say what she was thinking before worrying about the consequences.

"You just what?"

"Nothing." She turned and slid her arms around his neck. "I think I'm ready to tear off your clothes."

"That was a quick about-face."

"I'm a spur-of-the-moment gal." Standing on tiptoe, she ran her tongue across his bottom lip. "How would you like to get me naked?"

"I'd like that a lot."

Jasmine held Chase's hand and led the way to her cabin. She flipped the light switch inside the door. Both lamps came on, their soft light illuminating the bed. Either Anna or Nicola had already turned down the bed and added the little pieces of chocolate to the pillows. Leading Chase to the bed, Jasmine picked up one of the chocolates. She unwrapped the treat and held it up to his mouth. He took it, nipping her fingers as he did so. Holding her gaze, he slowly chewed the piece of dark chocolate.

"Good?" she asked.

"Very."

Jasmine picked up the second piece of chocolate and handed it to Chase. He unwrapped it and held it up to her mouth, copying her actions. Before she could take it, he popped it in his own mouth and began chewing.

"Hey!"

Chase grinned. "I like dark chocolate."

"So do I, and that was my piece."

"Too bad."

Jasmine tried so hard not to laugh. Seeing his impish grin made that impossible. She laughed, until the serious look in his eyes caused her to stop. "What's wrong?"

"Nothing's wrong. I like to hear you laugh." He touched her cheek, then pushed her hair behind her ear. "You should do it more often."

Her heart thudded in her chest. A thousand butterflies took flight in her stomach. She looked into Chase's deep brown eyes and couldn't look away. He whisked his thumb over her lips. She parted them. He dipped his thumb inside, gathered up the moisture from her mouth, and spread it over her lips.

Then he kissed her.

Soft. Tender. Loving. The barest touch of his tongue against hers. A gentle nip, a soothing lick. His kisses were so sweet, tears sprang to Jasmine's eyes. He swept his hands slowly up and down her spine. At the third pass, he unzipped her dress. He didn't stop the kiss as he peeled the silk from her shoulders and down her arms. It fell in a puddle at her feet.

Jasmine stood still while Chase looked at her. A tiny white thong and strappy gold high heels were the only things she wore.

"You're so beautiful, Jasmine."

He made her feel beautiful, and desired. The outline of his hard cock in his pants proved he wanted her. Seeing the outline wasn't enough. She wanted to see *everything*.

She reached for his belt. He took her hands and lifted them to his mouth, kissing the back of each one. "Not yet."

"You've seen my body. I want to see yours."

"You will, soon." He gave her one more searing kiss. "Get on the bed for me."

Jasmine peeled off her thong and sat on the edge of the

bed. She reached down to slip off her high heels. Chase's voice stopped her.

"Leave them on."

She sat up again and looked up at him. He stood with his hands clenched at his sides, lust heating his eyes. His gaze shifted from her breasts to her mound and back again. Chase looked as if he would pounce on her at any moment.

That worked for her.

"In the middle of the bed," he said. "On your hands and knees."

She turned and took the position he'd ordered. Jasmine's nipples puckered, her clit gently throbbed in anticipation of what he would do next.

"Spread your legs more."

If he didn't touch her soon, *she* would pounce on *him*. She could feel the moisture dampening her channel. She was so ready to take his cock deep inside her.

A shoe hit the floor. Jasmine looked over her shoulder in time to see Chase remove his other shoe. Finally, she would see his body.

He twirled his index finger upside down. "Turn around."

"No way. I want to watch."

"Nothing else comes off until you turn around."

Jasmine frowned. "You know, that bossy attitude of yours is getting old."

He didn't say anything, but his expression said it all. It would be his way or no way. Guilt tugged at Jasmine's heart for the men she'd treated the same way. Now she knew how they felt when she'd made all the demands.

With a huff, she straightened and stared through the door into the bathroom.

She almost turned back around when she heard the rustle of clothing. Instead, she lowered her head to her bent arms and waited.

She gasped at the swipe of his tongue across her anus. Her pussy clenched. She had to have him *now*. "God, Chase, please fuck me!"

"I want you to come first."

"I'll come, I promise! *Please*."

He ran his tongue down her labia to her clit and circled it with the tip of his tongue. He blew on her wet flesh. Jasmine arched her back to get closer to that delicious sensation. She was already so hot, it wouldn't take much more to make her come.

Chase continued to lick her pussy . . . first gently, then harder, then gently again. He'd pay attention to her clit, but not quite long enough to tip her over the edge. His tongue slid back and forth between her clit and her anus, discovering sensitive nerve endings she didn't realize existed.

He darted his tongue into her ass. Jasmine shattered. The tingling started in her toes. It slowly traveled up her legs, then whooshed through her body so quickly, stars exploded behind her eyes.

Her knees trembled. *Everything* trembled. Certain she would collapse at any moment, Jasmine started to straighten her legs so she could lie down.

"Uh-uh. Stay on your knees."

"Chase, I *can't*. My legs feel like overcooked spaghetti."

"I like the view. Stay on your knees."

She didn't know why she wasn't telling him to go to hell. That's exactly what she'd do with any other demanding man. There was something different about Chase, something that . . . called to her. She didn't obey his commands because he made them. She obeyed because she wanted to.

She rose back up to her knees.

A drawer opened. Plastic tore. The mattress dipped. Jasmine held her breath when she felt the tip of Chase's cock touch her entrance. He pushed the head inside her, pulled back, pushed again. She blew out a long breath as his shaft slid all the way inside her.

"My God," Chase whispered, his voice rough. He gripped her hips and didn't move. "This feels . . . I can't . . . *God.*"

He began to slowly pump, his rod gliding easily along her wet channel. Jasmine lifted her hips a bit more so Chase's cock would rub her G-spot. She pushed back at him as he fucked her, her movements gaining speed along with his thrusts. He pumped harder, faster, his fingers digging into her hips. Jasmine closed her eyes and tightened her internal muscles.

"*Shit,* Jasmine!"

Her second climax engulfed her a moment before Chase jerked and groaned loudly.

He leaned over her and cradled her breasts in his palms. His hot breath flowed over her neck. "That was . . ."

"Amazing."

"Yeah." He squeezed her breasts. "Amazing."

Jasmine wondered if her bones had dissolved. She couldn't hold herself up any longer. Chase's shaft slipped from her body as she fell facedown on the bed.

She could feel Chase move away from her. There was silence for a moment, then she heard water running in the bathroom. She'd have the chance to see him naked when he came out of the bathroom. It was a good thought, except she didn't have the strength to open her eyes.

She pried her eyes open in time to see the room plunged into darkness. Chase removed her shoes, then touched her back in a gentle caress. "Come here. I want to hold you."

"What makes you think I can move?"

He chuckled. "Want some help?"

"No. I'll do it."

It took her more than one try, but Jasmine managed to turn around and slip between the sheets with Chase. He wrapped her in his arms, her back to his chest. One hand cradled her breast, one lay on her thigh. Soft kisses fell on her shoulder. Jasmine smiled. She liked that Chase wanted to cuddle. She couldn't remember the last time she'd wanted to cuddle with a man after sex. For her, it was usually wham-bam-thanks-now-get-out-of-my-bed-so-I-can-be-alone.

"What time is it?" she asked.

"The clock is behind me. It's probably around midnight. Maybe a little after. Why? Do you have an appointment?"

"No. Just curious."

His thumb flicked her nipple. "Do you want me to leave?"

"No! Don't go."

He tightened his arms around her. "Okay."

Jasmine's muscles felt deliciously weak. Snuggling closer to Chase, she sighed and closed her eyes.

Seven

Chase awoke to feel Jasmine's warm mouth wrapped around his cock.

He was already hard, but his shaft hardened even more when her tongue circled the head. She licked the very tip of him, slid her lips down the length. Her tongue bathed his tight balls before she took his cock in her mouth again.

Ten more seconds, tops, and he'd come.

Chase lifted the sheet. The sight of Jasmine sucking his shaft almost made him come on the spot. He didn't want to stop her, but knew he must. "Jasmine." He touched her head. "Stop."

She grunted and kept on licking him. Chase's eyes rolled back in his head. Oh, God, it felt so good!

He cradled her face and tried to pull her mouth away from him. "You have to stop."

"I don't want to." Looking in his eyes, she swirled her tongue around the head like an ice cream cone. "I want to taste you."

She took him deep, his entire cock disappearing inside her mouth. Chase closed his eyes and arched his hips. There was no way he could stop now. His orgasm built in his balls and galloped through his rod to explode in her mouth.

Chase tried to think, to focus. The pleasure Jasmine gave him was unlike anything he'd ever felt. He'd never believed he'd have the strength for sex, or anything else. He could easily be dead now instead of lying in bed with a beautiful woman.

Jasmine crawled up his body and laid on top of him. She crossed her arms on his chest and propped her chin on them. A wicked grin curled her lips. "You taste good."

Chase burst out laughing. His little tigress could also be an imp. "I'm glad you approve."

"I do. In fact . . ." She circled his mouth with one fingertip. "I wouldn't mind a repeat."

He should talk to her before they made love again. He'd meant to do that last night, but his dick had been in control instead of his brain.

She kissed him, slow and long. Chase caressed her back and buttocks while they kissed. He loved the silkiness of her skin, the feel of her breasts pressed to his chest. Her mound cushioned his hardening cock.

She shifted against him, her lower body rubbing his. "I think there might be something to play with down there."

"There might be."

She nipped his bottom lip. "Maybe I should investigate."

"Maybe you should."

Jasmine gave him another searing kiss on his mouth. She kissed his chin, his Adam's apple, the hollow of his throat. She slid down his body as she continued to drop kisses. Chase closed his eyes, lost in the pleasure of her touch.

"What's this?"

Chase opened his eyes at her question. She lightly touched the top of the scar that ran down the center of his chest.

He couldn't postpone their talk any longer.

"It's a scar from an operation. Actually, several operations."

The puzzlement in her eyes didn't surprise him. "What happened?"

"Do you want the detailed version or the summary?"

"I want whatever you'll tell me."

Jasmine moved to his side. Chase sat up and leaned against the headboard. He almost pulled the sheet up to cover his chest, then decided that would be silly. She'd already seen part of the scar. He had no reason to hide it.

She touched his arm, her fingertips gliding over his skin. "What happened?"

Chase decided a simple statement of the facts would be enough. He didn't need to tell Jasmine all the details. "I was born with a heart defect. My heart didn't pump the way it was supposed to. I went through a series of operations to repair the problem. Each operation helped for a while, but I'd end up back in the hospital needing more surgery. I was put on the transplant list. I got a new heart six months ago."

Her gaze dropped to his chest. She reached forward and tentatively touched his scar. "Are you okay now?"

He nodded. "My doctor said I can do what any other healthy twenty-nine-year-old guy can do. I'll be on medication the rest of my life, but I'll gladly pop some pills in order to stay alive. And I have to have regular checkups."

He lifted her hand from his chest and entwined their fingers. "I won't live to be an old man, Jasmine. My body could reject the heart. Even with a heart that works now, I'm more susceptible to infections because of the antirejection drugs. I have to pretty much take one day at a time."

"That's all any of us can do, Chase."

"I know that, but it's different for me. A lot of people say they'll follow their doctor's orders, then go on and do whatever they want. I can't do that. I *have* to follow what he tells me."

"You just told me he said you can do what any other guy can do."

"Yeah, pretty much, now. I started working out four months ago, which I'd never been able to do. I'll never compete in the Mr. Universe contest, but I'm finally building up some muscle."

The concern in her eyes made Chase decide it was time to tease. He crooked his arm. "Wanna feel my biceps?"

She giggled, which was exactly what he wanted, before she tunneled her hand beneath the sheet. "I'd rather feel other things."

Chase moaned softly when she wrapped her hand around his cock. "That's nice."

"Yes, it is. I like touching you." Her hand dipped down to his balls and gave them a gentle squeeze. "At least your heart problem didn't affect your sex life."

He covered her hand to stop her exploring. "Yeah, it did."

She frowned. "I don't understand."

"Jasmine, last night was the first time I'd ever had sex."

He wasn't sure how she'd react. He definitely didn't expect her to laugh. "Oh, Chase, that's funny!"

"You find virginity funny?"

"You weren't a virgin. It isn't possible."

"I'm pretty sure everyone is a virgin to start with."

"I know that, but not you. You knew exactly what to do . . . how to kiss me, how to lick my pussy, how to fuck me. That takes experience."

"You weren't the first woman I'd kissed, but I'd never done anything else."

The skepticism in her eyes clearly showed she didn't believe him. "Chase, I've been with a lot of men. Some were very experienced, and they didn't perform oral sex a tenth as well as you did."

Her praise pleased him. He'd worried about satisfying her, about doing everything wrong. "I read a lot. I watched videos. Not porn. Well, yeah, some of those. But I watched instructional videos. I followed my instinct. I watched how you reacted, listened to the sounds you made when I touched you or moved a certain way. I could tell when you liked or didn't like something. I just had to pay attention to your body."

"You should give lessons to other men about paying attention. Some are so wrapped up in themselves, they don't give a damn about their partners." She propped up on her elbow and rested her head on her fist. "Does the scar embarrass you? You never go out on deck without a shirt."

"I don't want people pitying me. Or worse, asking a bunch of questions."

"Maybe they ask questions because they care." She ran her finger down the length of his scar. "That's why I asked when I saw it, because I care."

The thought of Jasmine caring about him sent warmth all through his body. Chase quickly pushed aside the pleasant feeling. He couldn't get involved with her, or any woman. It wouldn't be fair.

Jonathan had told him to let go, to finally accept that he could do all the things he couldn't while growing up. That included sex. Chase had spent four months working up the courage to do as his friend suggested. He knew that's why Jonathan had been so adamant about the cruise. Six single women looking for sex, plus the two stewardesses, would mean Chase could experience what most guys did by their eighteenth birthday.

He'd never suspected Jasmine would make it so perfect.

"You know what?" Jasmine asked, scooting closer to him.

"What?"

"I'm famished. Let's order breakfast and eat it in bed."

Chase touched her hair, his fingers tunneling through the long strands. He considered himself lucky to have met a woman as sexy and lovely as Jasmine. She wanted a good time with a man, not any kind of promise for more after the cruise. They'd go their separate ways on Sunday with no regrets.

He smiled. "Works for me."

Jasmine popped the last strawberry into her mouth and moaned in pleasure. "Oh, my *God,* that's better than sex." She looked at Chase, sprawled naked on the bed while he ate a piece of toast. "Well, almost better than sex."

Humor shone in Chase's eyes as he chewed. "I don't think you can have an orgasm from food."

"Depends on what you do with the food."

"Now I'm intrigued. Care to elaborate?"

"Nope." She wiped her hands on her napkin. "There are some secrets a gal gets to keep."

"You're no fun."

"Oh, darlin', I'm tons of fun. That's why you're in my bed." She picked up the tray that had been piled with their breakfast and set it on the floor. Turning back to Chase, she stretched out beside him. "We've satisfied one hunger. Care to satisfy another?"

His lips quirked with a grin. "Whatever do you have in mind?"

"I'll bet I can think of something."

She covered his lips with hers. Chase claimed he had no experience with women, but she couldn't tell that from his kisses. He knew exactly how to move, when to use his tongue, his teeth.

A lifetime of his kisses wouldn't bother her at all.

Jasmine slipped her hand to the inside of his thigh. She slid her hand up and down, exploring the different textures of his leg . . . the crisp hair that tickled her fingertips, the muscle that flexed beneath her touch, the puckered skin of a scar.

She ended the kiss and looked at the inside of his thigh. A long scar ran down the length. Puzzled, she looked into his eyes.

"They had to take a piece of the vein during surgery."

He said everything so matter-of-factly, as if he hadn't suffered from a life-threatening condition that required more than one major surgery. "That's why you haven't worn shorts or a swimsuit."

Chase nodded.

Her chest tightened as she touched the scar on his leg again. She couldn't imagine the pain he'd endured. "Was it horrible? All the surgeries and the healing afterward?"

"I wouldn't recommend it to anyone. I'd rather be lying on a tropical beach instead of a hospital bed."

Jasmine knew medical care was expensive. Something like this must've cost hundreds of thousands of dollars. "Are you okay financially? Did you have medical insurance to cover the surgeries?"

His eyes narrowed and his lips thinned. Money was obviously not the right thing to mention. "That's none of your business, Jasmine."

No, it wasn't, but she wanted to make it her business. She made a ridiculous salary at her job, plus she'd inherited her grandfather's estate not long ago. She had plenty of money to help Chase with his medical expenses. Rising to her knees, she took both his hands in hers. "I can help you. Whatever you owe, I can pay. It'll be a gift."

She tightened her hands on his when he tried to pull away from her. "Don't go all macho on me, Chase. It doesn't make you less of a man to accept help."

"I don't want your pity."

"I'm not offering pity. I'm offering my help."

He jerked away from her and rose from the bed. She started to scramble after him. One stern look stopped her. She sank back to her knees and watched him tug on his jeans.

"I don't want your money. I don't *need* your money."

She didn't believe that. He would've told her if money wasn't a problem instead of getting defensive. "Chase, I care about you. Let me help."

"You want to help? Leave me alone."

"I can't do that." She grabbed his arm before he could pull on his shirt. "Look at me." She dug her fingernails into his arm until he winced. "Look at me, Chase."

He sighed heavily, then turned his head toward her, a thunderous expression on his face.

"Do I feel sorry for you? Yes. I'm sorry you had to go through so much pain. Do I pity you? No. You're a strong man who wants to make it on his own. I respect that. Making it on your own doesn't mean you have to suffer when someone wants to help you."

"Why do you want to help me? Because we fucked?"

"Because I *care*." She hadn't realized how much until now. Knowing she could help Chase meant a lot to her . . . more than she thought it would. He'd started out as another conquest, a man to satisfy her desires. He'd quickly changed into a man she enjoyed being with, a man who made her laugh, who made her feel good simply by his presence. She wanted to be with him, and for a lot longer than a four-day cruise.

Jasmine climbed off the bed to stand before him. She laid her hands on his chest and looked into his eyes. "I'm falling in love with you."

His posture relaxed. The anger drained away from his eyes, to be replaced by sadness. He pulled her hands from his chest and held them. "No, you aren't."

"I know how I feel—"

"You feel sorry for me. You just said that."

"It's more than that. I want to be with you."

"You don't know anything about me. You don't even know where I live."

"So tell me. I want to know everything about you."

"Jasmine, you're a beautiful, sexy, desirable woman. You can have your pick of any man out there. There's no reason for you to think about getting involved with me." He squeezed her hands. "I'm a poor painter. I'm up to my eyes in debt. Despite getting a new heart, I could die before my thirtieth birthday."

"I'm willing to take the chance."

"*I'm* not. I wouldn't ask any woman to take a chance on me. It wouldn't be fair to her."

"Chase, you can't stay alone forever." She could feel him slipping away from her and didn't know how to stop it. "Life doesn't come with guarantees. You have to take happiness when you find it."

"I'm happy to be alive. I don't know if I can ask for any more than that." Releasing her hands, he cradled her face. "I enjoyed every moment with you. Thank you."

Tears filled her eyes. For the first time in her adult life, she wanted more from a man than just a good time in bed, but he didn't want her. "Please don't leave me."

He kissed her softly, then grabbed his shoes and left her cabin. He didn't look back.

Eight

Hiding had never been Jasmine's style. She'd always be-lieved in meeting her problems head-on. They couldn't be solved if she ignored them.

She didn't know how to solve the problem with Chase.

Three hours of crying in her cabin hadn't helped her decide what to do. If she didn't make an appearance on deck soon, Celina and Elayne would come looking for her.

Not even extra makeup could hide her puffy eyes. Jasmine decided to wear her largest sunglasses to cover up the evidence of crying.

Satisfied she looked as good as she could, she headed for the top deck to find Celina and Elayne. She spotted them sit-ting at a table close to the railing. Straightening her shoulders, she strode to their table and slid into the chair between them. "Hey."

Her lower lip trembled. No matter how hard she tried to fight them, the stupid tears simply wouldn't stop. A glass of tea sat at her place. She picked it up and sipped it, hoping to hide her distress from her friends.

"You okay, Jaz?" Celina asked.

So much for fooling anyone. She set her glass back on the table. "Oh, I'm just peachy."

"What's wrong?" Elayne asked.

"I did something incredibly stupid." Her lip trembled again, and tears seeped from beneath her sunglasses. "I fell in love."

She saw the look her two friends exchanged. They both knew she'd sworn men were for a good time, that she had too much fun being single to ever tie herself to one guy. How quickly one's life could change.

"I assume you're talking about Chase," Celina said.

Jasmine nodded. "He's such a great guy. Life has kicked him in the teeth way too many times. I want to help him. I could give him so much if he'd just let me."

Elayne pressed a paper napkin into Jasmine's hand. "Are you sure he won't let you?"

Jasmine pushed up her sunglasses and wiped the tears from her cheeks. "I told him how I feel about him. He said I couldn't love him, that I only felt sorry for him."

"Why would he say that?" Celina asked.

"Because he's had a lot of medical problems. Some of them almost killed him." Fresh tears filled Jasmine's eyes. She hadn't cried so much since her grandfather died. "He pushed me away. He literally pushed me away from him."

Elayne reached over and squeezed Jasmine's hand. "I'm sorry, Jaz."

"Yeah, me too." She blew her nose and wadded her napkin into a ball. "But you know what? I'm not going to think about

Chase anymore. If he doesn't want me, it's his loss. It's our last night on the ship. I'm going to have dinner with my two best friends, then find me a hunk to spend the night with. Barret has been after me since I first met him."

"Not Barret, Jaz," Celina said. "He's a user."

"He's hot, and that's what I need tonight. You have Rand. Elayne has Jonathan. Ian has been drooling on Glynnis the last two days. Lamar and Tony are gay. Ferris is with Doretta. Unless I hit on one of the crew, Barret is it."

"Then hit on one of the crew. I'd rather see you with Samir or Sergey than Barret."

"We don't always get what we want, do we, Cee?" Jasmine pushed back her chair and rose. "I'm going to take a hot shower and put on my sexiest dress. I'll see you two at dinner."

She hurried away, not wanting her friends to see her burst into tears. She walked with her head down, so didn't see Barret until she literally ran into him.

"Whoa!" He grabbed her upper arms to steady her. "Where's the fire?"

"I'm sorry. I wasn't watching where I was going."

"I gathered that." He leaned down and peered into her face. "You okay?"

She forced a smile so he wouldn't notice her tears. "I'm great." How perfect that she'd found Barret. Her decision to be with him tonight had to be right, despite the churning in her stomach. "Actually, I was looking for you."

He grinned. "I like the sound of that."

"I was wondering if you'd like to get together later . . . say, after dinner."

He stepped closer and brushed his naked cock against her mound. "What's wrong with now?"

Jasmine caught herself before she jerked back from him. "I have something to do now. Let's say eleven o'clock at the hot tub."

"I'll look forward to it."

Before she could stop him, he leaned forward and kissed her. Jasmine closed her eyes and parted her lips. His tongue dove into her mouth and wrapped around hers. One hand released her arm and slid down her back to her butt. He pulled her against his hardening cock.

Normally, Jasmine would arch against a man when she felt his growing shaft. This time, she stood still while he kissed her. He was good, but she had no desire to deepen the kiss or take it any further. She told herself that her lack of feeling was because Chase had so recently hurt her. Later, in the hot tub with Barret, her desire would return.

He dipped his fingers into her cleft between her buttocks. "Sure you don't want to fuck now?"

"I can't." She kissed him to soften the rejection. "I'll make it up to you later."

She turned and quickly walked away. Tears blurred her vision. She had to blink several times to see. *Damn Chase!* She'd offered her heart to him, and he'd rejected her. She should've kept their relationship strictly sexual. Love 'em and leave 'em had always been her motto. If she'd remembered that, she wouldn't be hurting now.

It was her last night on the cruise. She'd have dinner with her two best friends, then fuck Barret until he passed out. That would show Chase she didn't need him.

Chase picked at his crab salad. The food was excellent, as always, but he had no appetite. He couldn't get Jasmine out of his mind. He hadn't meant to hurt her. He hadn't thought he *could* hurt her. She was an experienced woman. Her actions the first time they met had been bold and brash. She was used to going after what she wanted and getting it. For some weird reason, she'd decided she wanted him.

He wished it could be different, that they actually had a chance at a relationship. He wouldn't put any woman through the uncertainty of a life with him . . . a life that could end at any time.

"Yeah, with Jasmine," Barret said.

Hearing Jasmine's name drew Chase's attention to the other end of the table. Barret sat to the left of Rand, with Ferris on his other side. The wicked grin on Barret's face made Chase uneasy. He didn't like the cocky model at all.

"I've wanted to sink into that pussy ever since I saw her," Barret said to Ferris.

Chase stared into his salad. Jasmine had said she loved him only a few hours ago, yet she'd made a date with that bastard. He would put his hands on her, touch her soft skin, kiss those full lips.

Apparently, her love wasn't any stronger than a dandelion in a breeze.

"She agreed to meet me at the hot tub at eleven," Barret said. "I can hardly wait to get my hands on those tits."

Chase didn't want to hear any more. He pushed back his chair and stood. With a final glare at Barret, he strode away from the table.

"Chase!" Jon called out.

Chase didn't stop. He didn't want to face his friend right now. He didn't want to face anyone.

"Chase, wait up."

Sighing, Chase stopped. He knew Jon would follow him all over the yacht if necessary so he could have his say.

"What happened back there?" Jon asked.

"I didn't want to hear anything else that came out of Barret's mouth."

"I was talking to Ian and didn't hear Barret. What did he say?"

"He's meeting Jasmine later at the hot tub." Chase laughed without a trace of humor. Needing to work off some of his rage, he began to pace. "She told me she loves me. She certainly changed her mind quickly."

"She did what?" Jon grabbed Chase to stop him. "Jasmine said she loves you?"

"Yeah. This morning in her cabin."

"This morning . . ." He released Chase's arm. "So the two of you . . . ?"

"Made love. Yeah."

Jon glanced at Chase's chest. "Does she know about your heart?"

"I told her everything."

"That's good, man. That's exactly what I wanted to happen. You needed to let go and realize you're okay and can live a normal life."

"However long that life lasts."

"Chase—"

"Don't lecture me, Jon. I'm being realistic. Yeah, I have a new heart, but it isn't *my* heart." He flopped down in a chair. "There are so many things that can go wrong, I'd need a legal pad to list them all."

"Just because they *can* go wrong doesn't mean they *will*." Jon sat in the chair opposite Chase. "Elayne and I have talked a lot about her friends. She said Jasmine has always been self-ish when it came to men. She took what she wanted and sent them on their way. If she says she loves you, she means it. You can't throw that away."

"How am I supposed to get involved with a woman, know-ing I could leave her a widow at any time?"

"You're no different from anyone else. Hell, man, I may get hit by a drunk driver on my way home. There's no guarantee I'll live longer than you."

"But the odds—"

"Fuck the odds. Be one of the survivors, Chase." He tapped his temple. "A lot of healing is mental. I don't have to be a doctor to know that."

Everything Jon said made sense. Still, Chase hesitated to give in so quickly. "I'll think about it."

"Good." He slapped Chase on the knee. "I gotta get back to the other guests. Let me know what you decide, okay?"

"Sure."

Chase stayed in the chair long after Jon left. Memories flooded his mind . . . images of his childhood, the hospital stays, the recuperations. He'd been bitter as a teenager, mad at God since he couldn't physically do all the things his friends did. As he'd grown older, he'd realized his anger only hurt himself. He couldn't play football or run track, but could still enjoy other things.

Like art.

He'd turned to drawing as his escape. Stick figures and doo-dling had advanced into scenery and people. He'd especially enjoyed sitting in the park and sketching people as they played with their kids or walked their dogs. Sometimes he'd transfer a sketch to an oil painting on canvas.

He wouldn't need a sketch of Jasmine to paint her. He'd see her clearly in his mind for the rest of his life.

Chase rose and wandered toward the upper deck. He stayed in the shadows, wanting to see but not be seen. Barret sat in the hot tub, his arms stretched out along the sides. A wolfish grin exposed his phony white teeth.

"Well, hello," Barret said.

Jasmine stepped closer to the tub. As Chase watched, she untied the swimsuit cover-up she wore and let it fall to the deck. She wore nothing beneath it.

Barret's grin widened while his gaze moved over her. "Damn. You have an incredible body."

Chase felt as if his new heart were crumbling. He had no intention of sticking around to watch Jasmine have sex with another man. He turned and walked away.

Jasmine climbed into the hot tub and sat across from Barret. She couldn't work up the courage to sit next to him yet. Everything inside her screamed for her to leave before she did something she'd always regret.

He frowned. "Why are you way over there?"

"I like the jets over here."

"Then I'll come to you."

She was about to tell him not to, but he was too fast for her. He slid next to her, encircling her shoulders with one arm. "Much better."

She summoned a smile that she didn't feel. "Yes, much better."

Barret tilted up her chin and kissed her. Jasmine wanted to keep her mouth closed, but his tongue pushed its way inside. She managed not to struggle in his arms, but it wasn't easy.

She sat still and accepted his plundering kisses, even though she felt nothing.

He cradled her breast and thumbed her nipple. "Damn, you've got great tits." He nipped her earlobe, darted his tongue into her ear. "I want to fuck them first, then your ass."

Jasmine shivered in revulsion. She couldn't do this. She couldn't sit here and let this animal paw her. She pushed him away from her and scrambled out of the tub.

"Hey, what are you doing?"

"I'm sorry, Barret. I changed my mind."

She reached for her cover-up. Barret climbed out of the tub and grabbed her arm before she could touch it. He jerked her upright. Jasmine looked up into furious green eyes.

"I don't know what the fuck you're trying to pull, but it doesn't work with me."

She tried to tug her arm from his grip. "Let me go, Barret."

"What are you, a cock-tease? You get a guy all worked up, then say no?"

"I said I was sorry. Please let me go." Her own anger rose when she couldn't get loose from his grip. "I suggest you let me go before I kick you in the part of your anatomy you prize so highly."

"You cunt." He threw her arm away from him. "I wouldn't fuck you if you begged me."

"Fat chance of that happening."

Jasmine snatched her cover-up and hurried away from him. She needed a shower to wash any traces of Barret's touch from her body.

She was so incredibly stupid. She didn't know what made her think she could simply pick up any guy for sex when her heart belonged to Chase. He was the only man she wanted to touch her, kiss her . . . the only man she wanted in her life.

Bypassing her cabin door, she continued down the hallway to Chase's room. She stood outside the door for several seconds, trying to work up the nerve to knock. Maybe he would let her stay with him tonight. They didn't have to make love if he didn't want to, but she so desperately wanted to be held.

In less than twelve hours, she'd say good-bye to her friends and head back to her life in Chicago. She'd stay busy with work and friends, but she knew her short relationship with Chase had changed her. Jumping into bed with any man she met would no longer be possible. She couldn't imagine feeling desire for another man besides Chase. He was in her heart, and would stay there for the rest of her life.

Taking a breath for courage, she knocked lightly. Moments passed with no answer. She knocked again, a bit louder. Nothing.

Jasmine rested her forehead against the door. Tears flowed down her cheeks, and her throat burned. "Chase," she whispered. "Why couldn't you love me too?"

Nine

Two weeks later

Jasmine stood outside the door and stared at the black numbers on it. Chase was on the other side. She only had to knock, and she'd see him.

She had no idea if he'd want to see her.

It had taken her two weeks to work up the courage to contact Jonathan for Chase's address. Jonathan hadn't budged at first, saying he wouldn't betray his friend's confidence. Jasmine understood that, and respected Jonathan's desire to protect his friend. Never one to give up, she'd proceeded to call Jonathan every day and beg him to help her. Jonathan finally gave in. He told her he couldn't take her begging any longer, not when it was mixed with Elayne's urging him to help Jasmine.

She'd been astonished to discover that Chase lived in Fort Wayne, less than two hundred miles from Chicago.

She took a deep breath, blew it out slowly, and knocked.

Footsteps became louder as someone walked to the door.

Jasmine laid her hand over her churning stomach. *Please don't slam the door in my face.*

Chase opened the door. His eyes widened in surprise. "Jasmine."

She gave him a tentative smile. "Hi, Chase." She waited for him to invite her in. When he continued to stare at her, she took the initiative. "May I come in?"

"I'm sorry. Come in."

She stepped into a small but neat living room. A dark green couch sat against one wall. Matching armchairs flanked the couch to create a "U" shape. The bare wood floors looked old, but clean and polished. Cream curtains hung from the windows. The entire room was smaller than a closet in her condo.

Chase slipped his hands into the front pockets of his paint-spattered jeans. "How did you find me?"

"Through Jonathan. Please don't be mad at him for telling me where you live. With Elayne and me both working on him, he didn't have a chance to say no."

Chase chuckled. "Yeah, I can understand that." He cleared his throat. "Would you like a Coke or something?"

"No, I'm fine."

The tension in the room pressed down on her chest. She hadn't expected him to drag her into his arms and make passionate love to her as soon as she walked in the door, but his obvious discomfort hurt her deeply. She'd hoped time away from her would make him realize he cared for her.

"What are you doing here, Jasmine?"

Making a fool of myself. "I was hoping we could talk."

"About?"

"What happened between us on the cruise."

He said nothing, leaving her to flounder by herself. She'd worked out everything in her head so she'd know exactly what to say to him. Now, standing here looking into his brown eyes, all the words disappeared. She wanted to hold him, tell him she loved him, beg him to give them a chance.

She needed a moment to compose herself before she dissolved into tears. She laid her purse on the coffee table. "May I use your bathroom?"

"Sure. It's at the end of the hall." He pointed to a doorway to her right.

"Thanks."

Chase stepped forward so he could watch her walk down the hall. Only after she closed the bathroom door did he release his breath. She looked incredible. She wore a pair of dark denim jeans and a simple gold T-shirt, but still carried herself like royalty.

He wandered into the kitchen, took a bottle of water from the refrigerator, and swallowed half of it. He'd suspected Jasmine was wealthy before Jonathan told Chase she'd paid for her friends' cruises. Some online research had confirmed his suspicion about her wealth. A person couldn't live on Lakeshore Drive in Chicago and not have big bucks in the bank. The difference in their finances only intensified Chase's belief that he and Jasmine couldn't be together.

The bathroom door opened. He screwed the lid back on his bottle and replaced it in the refrigerator. He waited for Jasmine to come back to the living room. Several moments passed, but she didn't appear. His apartment was too small for her to get lost.

Chase's stomach dropped to his feet. His studio. He'd left the door open.

He hurried down the hall to the extra bedroom. Jasmine stood in the middle of the room, staring at the three-foot-by-four-foot canvas that bore her likeness.

Swallowing the lump in his throat, Chase moved to Jasmine's side. Tears streamed down her face. "It's beautiful," she whispered, her voice husky.

Chase looked at the canvas. He'd painted Jasmine on the bed in her cabin on the yacht. She lay half on her side, half on her stomach. Her left leg was exposed, as well as her left buttock and back. Her hair lay tousled over her shoulder. The side of one plump breast peeked from beneath the pale blue sheet. Her eyes were closed. A serene smile touched her lips.

She reached out as if to touch the painting. Chase quickly grabbed her wrist. "No, don't touch it. It's wet."

"Chase, this is . . ." She wiped the tears from her cheeks. "My God, it's incredible. It looks just like me." She turned her head and looked at him. "You did this from memory?"

Chase nodded. "It isn't finished yet."

"What more could you possibly do? It's perfect."

"It needs some tweaking here and there."

"Were you working on it when I arrived?"

"Yeah."

Jasmine gazed at the painting again. "It's good enough for a gallery as is." She tapped her chin. "I have a client who owns a small, but successful, art gallery. You have other paintings, right?" She continued before Chase could comment. "I'll bet he'd set up a showing for you." Smiling broadly, she clapped her hands. "Oh, Chase, that would be perfect! Where's my purse? I have Frank's number on my cell."

"Hold it." He grabbed Jasmine's arm before she could scurry by him. "You're going way too fast here."

She frowned "Why? You have other paintings, don't you?" She glanced around the room. Her face lit up when she saw the canvases facing the far wall. Slipping from his grip, she hurried over and knelt on the floor in front of them. She turned the first one around, removed the cloth protecting it, and gasped loudly.

"Oh, Chase, this is wonderful."

He sat on the floor next to her. The two-foot-by-three-foot painting she held was of a young girl on a swing in the park. He'd caught the laughter in her eyes and the joy on her father's face as he pushed her in the swing.

"I had no idea you're so talented. What else have you done?"

Chase sat still while she examined each of the ten canvases. He couldn't help chuckling. She was so excited, she was almost wiggling.

"We'll start you out at Frank's gallery. From there, we can hit all the big cities—Detroit, Philadelphia, New York, Boston. Then we'll head south and west. Is there an art gallery in Fort Wayne? Never mind, I'll find out. Is there such a thing as a traveling gallery? I'll find that out too. If not, we'll invent one. Of course, you'll probably sell out at the first showing and you'll have to paint more or we won't need the traveling gallery."

Chase couldn't hold back his laughter any longer. "Jasmine, you're making me dizzy!"

Jasmine grinned. "I get excited."

"No shit." He reached over and pushed her hair behind her shoulder. "I appreciate your confidence, but no one will want to buy my paintings."

"You're kidding, right? Do you honestly not know how wonderful these are? I'm going to call Frank right now and set up a meeting with you and him."

She was up off the floor and out the door before he could stop her. Shaking his head, Chase followed her into the living room. She was scrolling down the numbers on her cell phone. "Jasmine—"

"Don't tell me not to call. I'm calling." She pressed a button, then held the phone up to her ear. "I'll take that Coke now. Lots of ice. And a straw if you have one."

Chase had to rummage through the silverware drawer, but he found a wrapped straw from a fast-food place. He returned to the living room and set the glass on the coffee table before joining her on the couch.

"Frank, I promise you, he's incredible. The best I've ever seen . . . Do you remember that landscape I bought from you last year? The one for five . . . That's the one. Chase is better than Goen. The paintings I've seen so far will easily bring in five, maybe more . . . Fort Wayne . . . That won't be a problem . . . What time Tuesday? . . . Perfect. We'll be there."

Jasmine closed her cell phone with a snap. "Done. We have a meeting with Frank at his gallery Tuesday at eleven."

"You didn't bother to ask me if I have to work Tuesday."

She waved a hand as if that didn't matter. "Call in sick."

"That isn't an option with me, Jasmine. I don't call in sick just to take a day off."

"This isn't a day off, Chase. This is your *career*." She reached over and clasped both his hands. "Don't you see? This is *perfect*! You'll come back to Chicago with me today. We'll meet with Frank on Tuesday. He'll love your paintings and set up a showing for you, probably within four to six weeks."

Something in her speech stuck in his mind. "You want me to go back with you today? The meeting is on Tuesday. This is Sunday."

She nodded. "That gives me a day to show you my city."

"And where do you plan for me to stay?"

"With me, of course."

Her smile was positively smug. "You're sure I'll want to do that?"

"I'm very sure, because you love me."

He didn't remember saying those words. "I've never told you I love you."

The smugness faded from her expression. Love shown in her eyes as she touched his lips. "You didn't have to say the words. I knew as soon as I saw the painting of me."

Chase kissed the fingertips gliding over his lips. "I'm still not sure about our getting involved. It isn't fair to you."

Jasmine took both his hands in hers. "I want to tell you about a story I read on the Internet news this morning. A man and woman got married Friday. She had a massive heart attack and died at their wedding reception. She was only twenty-six."

Chase winced. "That's sad."

"Yes, it is. Do you think that bride had any idea that would happen to her? Do you think her husband never would've become involved with her if he'd known she'd die? No. They loved each other, for better or worse, and until death." She squeezed his hands. "You can't live in a vacuum, Chase. You have to take a chance, grab happiness when you can for as long as you have on Earth. I might live to be one hundred. I might die at forty. Whatever happens, I want you to be part of my life."

He turned his hands over and entwined her fingers with his. Some of the worry, the doubt, crumbled away from Chase's mind. "You make quite a convincing case. Maybe you should've been an attorney."

"I'd rather be your agent."

The idea of someone's liking his paintings enough to buy them was a pretty heady thought. "You really think I can sell my work?"

"Absolutely. I have no doubt."

"Five hundred dollars is a lot of money for a painting."

"Five hundred?" she asked, confusion in her voice.

"That's what you told Frank you paid for some painting you bought from him."

Jasmine chuckled. "Chase, I paid Frank five thousand for that painting."

"*Five thou*—" He couldn't even say the word. "For one painting?"

"That's nothing. He sells paintings up into the hundreds of thousands." She shrugged one shoulder. "It's an investment. I've bought several paintings from new artists who are now quite famous."

Chase decided there must be a lot of people in the world who had way too much money. "You don't honestly think I could ever sell one of my paintings for that."

"I have every confidence you'll be a smashing success. How can you help it with me by your side?"

She had that right. As long as he had Jasmine, he could accomplish anything. Leaning forward, he kissed her gently. "I guess I just hired an agent. What percentage do you charge?"

She scooted closer to him, her eyes twinkling with mischief. "I'm sure we can work out an arrangement you'll find satisfactory."

He went willingly when Jasmine pushed him to his back. Whatever payment arrangement she suggested, Chase was sure he'd gladly pay it . . . plus a bonus.

LYNN LaFLEUR was born and raised in a small town in Texas close to the Dallas/Fort Worth area. Writing has been in her blood since she was eight years old and wrote her first "story" for an English assiagnment.

As well as writing at every possible moment, Lynn enjoys reading, scrap-booking, photography, and learning new things on the computer. She's a software junky and loves to try out new programs, especially anything to do with graphics.

After living on the West Coast for twenty-one years, Lynn now lives seventeen miles from her hometown in Texas. She's a romantic at heart and can't imagine ever writing anything but romances. A full-time writer, she spends her days creating stories of people who find their happily-ever-after, sometimes with the help of an alien or psychic or vampire.

Learn more about Lynn at her website: *www.lynnlafleur.com.*